CALL OUT THE GHOSTS

Call Out the Ghosts

A Novel

Joan Wexler

International Psychoanalytic Books (IPBooks)
New York • http://www.IPBooks.net

Published by IPBooks, Queens, NY
Online at: www.IPBooks.net

The characters and events portrayed in this book are
fictitious. Any similarity to real persons, living or dead,
is coincidental and not intended by the author.

Book cover design by Kathy Kovacic of Blackthorn Studio
Typesetting by Noel S. Morado

ISBN: 978-1-969031-07-6

For Linda Gravenson
"From the attic to the basement and back again."

Author's Note

After the publication of <u>Make Me the Sky</u>, I often thought about the Horvath and Liebermann families. I wondered how they were doing. I missed them all, even the bad guys. They left their homes in Eastern Europe in the early years of the 20th century because they experienced poverty, humiliation, and violence, only to arrive in New York City, where they often faced more poverty and violence. Through the redemptive power of friendship, love, resilience, and luck, they came to do well in their new country. That is where I left them.

As time passed, I wondered about their ghosts, meaning the persistent and tormenting memories and painful losses they carried from their troubled pasts. For example, how did the untimely death of a beloved, an act of violence or a question of paternity continue to haunt them? Did the ghosts of the elders also haunt their growing children? Did the children have their own ghosts? I decided to revisit them to ask and listen to what they had to say. They answer in <u>Call Out the Ghosts.</u>

Joan Wexler
Hamden, CT

Cast of Central Characters

The book begins in the year 1925

The Horvath Family

Fannie Liebermann and Marek Horvath—Central couple, Ashkenazi Jews. Fannie was born around 1895. Marek is 6 or 7 years older. They both left Eastern Europe in the early 20th century when they were teenagers. Neither they nor their siblings have records of their actual birth dates. They married in 1914.

Horvath Children

Adela—Born 1910. Marek's daughter by his first wife who died in childbirth when Adela was two years old.

Daniel—Born 1912. Fannie's adopted son, born to Hannah Weitzner, Fannie's closest friend. Hannah died in Palestine in 1913. When Hannah knew she was dying; she sent baby Daniel to America to be raised by Fannie.

Simon and Miriam—Born 1917. Fannie and Marek's biological twins.

The Liebermann Family—Includes four of Fannie's siblings who arrived in America in 1919, and Rachel Kaminski.

Aber Liebermann—Born 1892. Fannie's eldest brother.

Rivka Lieberman—Born 1893. Fannie's eldest sister. Rivka is now married and lives with her husband and his children.

Kayla Liebermann—Born 1907. Fannie's youngest sister. She was twelve years old when she arrived in America in 1919.

Jacob Liebermann—Born 1909. Fannie's youngest brother. He was ten years old when he arrived in America in 1919.

Rachel Kaminski—Friend of the family. Rachel is single and works as a librarian. Kayla and Jacob have lived with Rachel since their arrival in America. Rachel with the help of Aber is raising Kayla and Jacob.

<u>Fannie's Siblings in Europe</u>

Yehuda Liebermann—Born 1894.

Lazer Liebermann—Born 1896.

Esther Liebermann—Fannie's twin who died in Europe in 1911.

<u>Important Family and Friends</u>

Mischa—Fannie's first beloved who moved to Palestine in 1911.

Itzak and Sadie—A couple. (Itzak is Fannie's cousin). Fannie, as a very young woman lived with Itzak and Sadie on the Lower East Side after escaping from a menacing uncle. Itzak died during the influenza epidemic in 1918.

Esther—Sadie and Itzak's daughter (not to be confused with Fannie's twin sister, also called Esther).

Contents

October 1925

Daniel and his friend Herman, both thirteen, are on their way home from school, P. S.189, on Amsterdam Avenue in New York City's Washington Heights neighborhood. They are headed to their apartment building on Fort Washington Avenue. They wear knickers and vest sweaters over cotton shirts and high-top leather shoes. Each carries a bundle of books strapped together with a leather belt. Using their free hand, they bounce a pink rubber ball back and forth as they zigzag along the sidewalk. When they turn right on 179th Street, Daniel freezes. He hears an eerie, shrill sound."

"Did you hear that, Herman?"

"Yeah, I heard it. It hurts my ears."

"It gives me the shivers."

"It's an animal. Maybe a cat."

"No, it's not a cat. It's different."

"It's a rat! Let's get out of here. I don't want to get bit."

"Wait!" says Daniel and grabs Herman's arm, "The sound is coming from that alley. I'm going to look."

"Dan don't go near that alley. If it's a big rat, we need to get out of here."

"It's okay Herman. It's okay."

Herman stands back. "If I get bit, my mother will kill me!"

Daniel looks in the alley through the gate. "All I see is garbage and a big paper bag. Come look."

Shuddering, his face pale, Herman edges closer and looks through the gate. "Yuck! It stinks in there, like piss." He backs off the sidewalk and stands in the gutter. "Where's that weird sound coming from?"

"Maybe from that paper bag." says Daniel.

Herman starts to run, "Dan please let's get out of here. If it's a wild animal, we'll get rabies."

"No, Herman. Wait, I'm going closer. I want to see."

"What if it's a big mean rat?"

Daniel pulls at the gate. It opens. He slowly approaches the bag and looks in. "Herman, it's a baby, a tiny baby!" He hands his books to Herman who stuffs the ball into the pocket of his knickers and takes Daniel's books. Daniel picks up the bag and brings it out of the alley. He bends over, reaches in and lifts out the baby. It is wrapped in a filthy blanket. Its shrill, mewing voice gets louder. Herman backs away again. His eyes wide,

"What should we do with it Dan?" he whispers.

"I'll bring this baby to Mama. She'll know what to do. Take the empty bag. I'll carry the baby."

Herman tucks both bundles of books under one arm and takes the bag. They walk slowly to their apartment building. In Daniel's arms, the baby's cry briefly sounds more human but soon peters out, and the eerie animal-like whine starts again. Daniel talks to the tiny bundle.

"Don't cry, little baby, we'll take care of you. Where's your mama?"

They reach the building where they both live and take the elevator to Daniel's 4th floor apartment and ring the bell. Daniel's mother, Fannie, opens the door. Stunned to see a baby in her son's arms, Fannie, cries out, "What's going on!"

"Mama, we heard this weird noise. We thought maybe it was an animal, maybe a cat, but then we found this baby in an alley left in a bag."

"In a shopping bag! *Oy, vey iz mir!* (Oh, woe is me!) Where? What street?"

"Near Amsterdam. What street was it, Herman?"

"179ᵗʰ."

Fannie reaches out to take the baby from Daniel and lays it gently on the table. Carefully she unwraps the filthy blanket, and sighs as she sees sores on the baby's skin. "It's a girl, a tiny girl, probably less than a month old. Danny, go to the dresser in *Tateh's* (Dad's) and my bedroom. In the dresser, in the bottom drawer, I have some of the twin's old baby undershirts and blankets. There are some diapers and pins there too. Also, bring me some wet rags. Wet them with warm water. We must clean and dress this tiny girl and find a way to give her some water and maybe milk, then get her to the hospital. She weighs no more than a skinny chicken. Danny, look in the pantry and see if we have any evaporated milk."

Daniel calls back. "There's one can Mama."

"Open it for me, please."

The other children in the apartment hear the commotion. Eight-year-old Simon and Miriam, twins, and Adela, age fifteen, the eldest, all rush in. Adela asks, "What's this about a baby?" The three come to the table where their mother is cleaning and dressing the baby.

"Oh, poor baby." coos Adela. "Mama, what are we going to do?"

Miriam pleads, "Oh Mama, can we keep her?"

"No, we can't Miriam. She's not our baby. We must try to find her mama or someone in her family."

Fannie mutters to herself, "Leaving a baby in a bag on the street! What a way to begin a life! What kind of person does that?"

Simon asks, "Why isn't she with her mama now'?

"We don't know Simon. We'll take her to the Medical Center up the street and hope they know where her mama is. She looks newborn.

Let's hope she was born at the hospital and maybe they can find who she belongs to."

Fannie sighs, puts her head in her hands, and thinks. *How can we get some water into this forsaken child?* "Adela, get me another clean rag and get it wet under the tap. Adela brings the wet rag. Fannie pulls and twists it, like a teat, and puts it into the baby's mouth. The baby sucks vigorously. They wet the rag several times. The baby can't get enough.

"Adela, take some of the evaporated milk and mix it with a lot of water." They give the diluted milk to the child the same way as the water. For the first time the baby opens her eyes. They are a cloudy blue and unfocused.

"Danny, get me my blue shawl. It's getting cold." Fannie finishes dressing the baby and wraps her first in a clean blanket and then in the knitted blue shawl. Fannie hands her to Adela, while she puts on her coat, then takes back the baby. Thet all start out the door.

"Oh wait! Adela, Tateh will come home and wonder where we are. Run to the tailor shop and tell him what happened and where we went. We'll be home right after. Danny, turn off the oven for me."

"Mama" calls Adela as she rushes out ahead of them, "I'll come to the Medical Center and meet you there right after I talk to Tateh."

"Okay, Dela, okay, we're ready. Get your coats on and let's go. Danny, take the shopping bag with that dirty blanket. Maybe it will be a clue to find the mother."

Fannie sees Herman has planted himself stiffly in a corner of the room. She says, "Herman, go to your apartment now. Your mama will wonder why you're so late coming home. Thank-you for helping Danny bring this baby to me."

As Herman leaves, Daniel calls after him, "I'll come by tomorrow morning so we can walk to school together. Bring the *Spaldeen* (Spalding rubber ball) with you."

Fannie carrying the baby, Daniel, Simon, and Miriam, walk up Fort Washington Avenue to the Medical Center. The baby's haunting, whining sounds persist. They talk to each other over her barely human bleating. Fannie says, "Let's hope this baby was born in this hospital and they have some way of finding the mother or some relative."

Miriam asks, "What if she wasn't born in the hospital?"

"They'll know what to do. This isn't the first child to be abandoned."

Simon emphatically says, "If they don't find a relative, she'll be an orphan and have to go to the orphanage."

It's late October and beginning to get chilly with a stiff wind coming off the Hudson River. Fannie holds the baby close to her chest and wraps her coat around them both. They reach the Medical Center and enter the building.

Adela arrives at the tailor shop. Her father, Marek, is in the back room cutting out a suit. She goes straight to the back and says "Tateh, I have to talk to you." At the same time, a customer walks in. Marek sticks his head out to greet his customer. "Good afternoon Mrs. Steinberg. I'll be with you in only a moment."

"It's ok Mr. Horvath. I'm not in a rush. I see your daughter just arrived."

"What is it my little love?" asks Marek, caressing Adela's cheek.

"Tateh, Danny was on his way home from school. He found a baby, a tiny baby girl left in an alley in a shopping bag. He heard a noise, crying or something, and went to look. He brought the baby home. Mama cleaned her and fed her. Right now, she's bringing her to the Medical Center. All the kids are with Mama, and I'm going there now to meet them. Mama wanted me to tell you so you won't worry if you came home before we get back."

"What! A baby left in a shopping bag! *Shande!* (shame!) What kind of person leaves a baby in a shopping bag! Ok Adela, go meet Mama. I'll be home at the usual time." Adela leaves.

Marek shakes his head. *The war is over. This is the sort of meshuga (crazy) thing that happened during the war in Europe. A baby left in an alley in a shopping bag in America! How long could that baby be on the street and still survive? The police should be called.*

Marek startles, remembering his customer. He hustles out to greet her. "Good to see you, Mrs. Steinberg. How's the family?"

Adela rushes to the Medical Center and asks where to find the Horvath family. She is shown into an examining room on the first floor. As she enters, she sees her mother with her brothers and sister standing beside an exam table. Adela goes to stand next to her mother. The others make room for her. Fannie tells Adela the doctor's name is Dr. Weiss.

On the other side of the table, Dr. Weiss, a tall older man, wears a starched long white coat; his gray hair is sharply parted on one side. He examines the tiny baby girl who lies listlessly on the table. Using his medical instruments, he checks her ears and mouth and looks carefully into each eye. Slowly he examines the sores on her skin, paying careful attention to her armpits and the skin between her fingers and toes. With his stethoscope, he listens to her belly and chest. He turns her over and presses his stethoscope on parts of her back. He lifts her onto the nearby baby scale, records her weight and then places her back onto the table, wrapping her in the clean blanket Fannie brought her in.

"Mrs. Horvath, if this poor infant can survive, it's because you and your son knew just what to do. She's very sick and profoundly malnourished. She looks like a newborn but is possibly as old as three or four months. and weighs barely more than five pounds. She should weigh twice that. She has a severe ear infection, and her lungs are congested.

I'm not yet sure what these sores on her skin are, but some are now infected. We'll take her into the hospital and do the best we can to nourish her and keep a watch on her. Also, we must notify the police. You found her in an alley?

"Yes Dr. Weiss, my son Daniel and his friend found her on their way home from school in an alley on 179th near Amsterdam Avenue." Fannie wrings her hands, "Oy! What a terrible way to start a life! What a terrible way to begin."

"Mrs. Horvath, we can only hope she will have a life. This little child is desperately ill."

"What a terrible way to come into the world! Will it be all right if we stop in from time to time to see how she's doing?"

"Of course, Mrs. Horvath. If she has a chance to survive it will be because of you and your son. But please understand, her chances are slim. Oh, and this is important Mrs. Horvath, we don't yet know if the lesions on the baby's skin are contagious. You and your son and anyone else who held this baby should wash carefully when you get home. If you find yourselves with any rash or sores at all, please come back to the Medical Center right away and ask for me."

"We will. Thank-you Dr. Weiss."

Dr. Weiss leans out of the door and calls a nurse who enters the room. "Please take this baby to pediatrics. We need to place her in isolation until her lesions are diagnosed and treated." He hands the baby to the nurse and turns back to Fannie and the children.

"Are these beautiful children all yours, Mrs. Horvath?"

"Yes"

"They all look so healthy and well cared for." Looking warmly at the children, Dr. Weiss turns to them, "Please tell me your names and how old you are and what grade you're in at school."

Daniel is very slender and small for his age, with bushy red hair and a light complexion. "I'm Daniel and I'm thirteen in 8th grade."

Adela is a well-developed adolescent girl with fine features and black hair she wears in a braid down her back. "I'm Adela and I'm fifteen. I'm a sophomore in high school."

Simon is a sturdy boy with brown hair and large brown eyes. "I'm Simon and I'm almost eight in 3rd grade."

Miriam is delicately built. She wears her brown hair in two braids. "I'm Miriam and I'm almost eight too and I'm in 3rd grade too." Pointing to Simon, "Me and him are twins."

"What a beautiful family you have, Mrs. Horvath. It's been my pleasure to meet all of you. You have all done a great *mitzvah* (*good deed*) today."

Hearing the word "mitzvah," Fanny asks, "Dr. Weiss, I hope you don't mind my asking, but I can hear you speak English with an accent something like my own. I'm from what was Galicia in Europe before the war. By any chance, are you from that part of the world too?"

"Yes Mrs. Horvath, I'm from Vienna. I came here after the War."

"Oh, I have two married brothers who moved to Vienna."

"What are their professions?"

"Lazer is a chef, and Yehuda is a bookkeeper."

"And you came to America. When did you come?"

"I came in 1910,"

"You must have been very young."

"I was somewhere between fifteen and sixteen."

"Did you come with any family?"

"No, alone."

"It was so hard for those who came alone, especially young women. I can see, just looking at you and your children, you've done well."

"Yes, Dr. Weiss, I am blessed."

"Horvath is a Hungarian name. Are you from Hungary?"

"My husband is from Budapest. I'm from what was Austria, now Poland, since the war. I'm from Bolekhiv, a *shtetl* (town) not far from Lviv."

"Bolekhiv, why does that sound familiar to me?"

"It is south of Lviv, not too far."

"Hmm. I'll have to think. I've heard of it somehow." Dr. Weiss looks at his watch. "Excuse me for now, Mrs. Horvath, I must see my next patient, but please feel free to get in touch with me again. Leave your address at the nurse's station and if I have news about the baby, or I remember who I might have known from Bolekhiv, I'll write to you to let you know. It's a pleasure to meet all of you."

They all thank Dr. Weiss. Fannie and the kids walk the few blocks home. Everyone is quiet on the way back. They reach the building and ride up the elevator. As Fannie opens the door to the apartment, Miriam asks,

"Mama, if the baby girl lives, maybe we can keep her?" Fannie is caught off guard.

"She isn't ours Mimi. Maybe they can find her mama, or *bubbe* (grandma), or one of her *tantes* (aunts). They would be the ones to take care of her."

Marek is home. Each child goes to him, and he hugs them. He is a broad-chested man with smooth black hair and brown eyes. The outer corners of his eyes droop slightly, giving him a serious and sometimes sad expression. When the children move on into other rooms, Marek opens his arms to Fannie, who lays her head against his chest and weeps quietly. Then quickly straightens up and pulls back from Marek, calling to another room, "Danny, remember, you and I and Adela too must wash well. We all held the baby."

Daniel calls back. "Ok Mama. I know." Adela echoes.

"Yeah Mama, we will."

After a delayed dinner, the children sit at the dining room table doing homework and soon all go to bed.

Fannie prepares tea for Marek and herself. She is a full-figured, although still slender, small woman with a long blond braid she wears over one shoulder. They sit together in the kitchen, an evening ritual for them. This is when they speak mostly Yiddish together. Yiddish is their intimate language. With the children, they go back and forth, speaking both Yiddish and English. Fannie is weeping.

"Here I go crying again. Marek, I'm so sad about this poor little foundling. She's so alone, so forgotten." Marek takes Fannie's hand in his.

"Fannie darling, your hands are so cold. I'll bring you your blue shawl. Where is it.?"

"It's on the back of my work chair in the alcove."

He brings it to her and drapes it over her shoulders and as he sits back in the kitchen chair, he says, "Fannie dearest, you're no stranger to being alone. You came alone on that ship from Europe."

"Yes, but I wasn't a helpless, sick baby. I was fifteen or sixteen on that awful ship. And I met my friend Hannah. We took care of each other from the moment we met. Oh Hannah! Oh, my poor dead Hannah, our Danny's first mother. All this is reminding me of how we got Danny." Fannie, sobbing, puts her face in her hands. Marek hurries over to the chair next to Fannie and pulls her to lean on him. She lays her head on his shoulder, and he gives her his handkerchief. She wipes her eyes and blows her nose. They sit this way for a few more moments and Marek says, "Here Fannie, our tea is getting cold. Have some of it." She takes a sip, then slams down the cup. Marek startles and pulls back. Fannie, her voice rising with anger, "What kind of mother does such a thing! Only a monster puts their own baby out on the street."

Trying to calm Fannie, "It's a shande Fannie, whoever did such a thing. But do we know it was the mother?"

"Oh! I thought it must be the mother. If it wasn't, that mother must be going crazy looking for her baby." Fannie pauses, turns away, then turns back to Marek. "Hannah," Fannie's throat catches, "May her memory be for a blessing, Hannah took wonderful care of Danny, even when that man of hers, that monster, that pimp, who got her pregnant, then told her to get rid of the baby or he'd put them both on the street. Hannah risked everything to protect Danny." Fannie's voice is now steady. "She loved Danny with her whole heart. She hid him. She found a woman to care for him until she could figure out how to keep him. And even then, she visited him every day, several times a day. She even nursed him. But there were rumors that she kept Danny. Brave Hannah, took him and escaped alone to Palestine, just to keep him with her and safe."

Fannie pauses here and sobs. She takes a moment to calm herself and keep talking. "I haven't thought about all this for so long. In Palestine, Hannah got cancer and knew she was dying. Yet still she took care of Danny. She had her sister bring him to me to raise as my son. I was devastated about Hannah and then blessed with our sweet Danny. I can't imagine our life without him."

Marek puts his arm around Fannie again saying, "No, I can't imagine our family without our Danny."

"Maybe this poor baby's mother is dead. Marek, if the hospital and police can't find someone to care for her, should we take her?"

Marek sighs and pauses. Fannie stares at him searchingly. He sighs again as he begins to speak. He doesn't want to speak. He cups Fannie's face with hands, "Fannie, no. We can't. We have four kids to take care of and hopefully educate. We have your youngest sister and brother, who we need to help. Hopefully, we can bring your two brothers and my family over from Europe. I often need your help in the store, and you're designing costumes for the Yiddish Theater. All our kids are now old enough that we can handle all of this. No sweet Fannie, we can't take on this sad, abandoned baby. If they can't find the mother or if, God forbid, the mother is dead, let's hope she has a relative who can care for her. We'll stay in touch with this doctor you told me about and hope for the best."

Fannie straightens up. "I know you're right, Marek. Something about this baby breaks my heart, beyond the obvious sadness of it all." Fannie pauses, she turns away from Marek, he rests his hand on her back, and again she sobs.

"Marek, who knows what might have happened after I was trapped in that brothel in Budapest? I think I was barely fifteen years old. If that kind boy, no older than me, hadn't rescued me, I could have gotten pregnant. How could I have taken care of a baby? That could have been me, frightened and desperate enough to leave a baby on the street."

"No Fannie. You would never put a baby on the street. And remember, we still don't know how this poor child got there. It could've been the mother, but my guess is it was someone else."

"What sort of beast would do that to somebody's child? Even Hannah's man said he would send the baby to the Foundling Home. That's bad but not like on the street in a paper bag! This baby, if she lives, could end up in the Foundling Home."

"Finding this baby gives you all these sad memories. Let's get some sleep. A night's rest will help."

Fannie and Marek get into their bed and pull up their quilt. Marek falls asleep right away, but tears rise and flow down Fannie's cheeks. Slowly she drifts to sleep.

I'm walking down a long street of apartment buildings in Vienna. I know it's Vienna even though I've never been there. At each apartment building, I enter through the front door and look at the names listed. I walk up every flight and ring every doorbell. I do this over and over, going from building to building. It's endless. No one answers.

After midnight, Fannie wakes to find Miriam patting her shoulder. "Mama, I'm afraid the little baby will die." Fannie gets up and brings Miriam back to her bed. She sits by her and sings *"Shlof Mayn Kind"* ("Sleep My Child") until Miriam is asleep. Fannie returns to bed.

I'm on an empty street somewhere. Heavy fog. Lost. Mama, Mama!

"Mama, Mama wake up." urges Adela, "Miriam and Simon are going to be late for school."

Daniel

A few days later, Daniel walks into the kitchen where Fannie is cooking supper and asks,

"Mama, how did I begin?"

"How did I begin?' what do you mean Danny?"

"I was thinking of that baby. When I brought her home, you said something like, 'What a way to begin!' So, I want to know how I began."

"You were born here in New York at Bellevue hospital, February 10, 1912."

"Really, here in New York?"

"Yes. You seem surprised."

"I thought I was born in Palestine. I once heard you and Tateh talk about Palestine, how people there sometimes shoot Jews or throw rocks at us. You were glad I was safe in New York. Why were we in Palestine Mama?"

"I've never been in Palestine, Danny, but I had friends who left New York to go to Palestine."

"But I was in Palestine?"

"Yes."

"How could I be in Palestine without you and Tateh?"

"Danny darling, give me some time so I can get this chicken ready for the oven, then we'll sit, have tea and honey cake and I'll try to explain what you heard."

Fannie thinks, *'How did I Begin?' He's already heard parts of it. He knows he was born in New York. He knows he came from another woman's body. Has he forgotten? Did it drop out of his mind? Where do I begin to explain all this again? He's thinking about finding that poor baby. He's still too young to hear the whole story about his birth. I can easily tell him Hannah loved him and caring for him was the most important thing in her life. That's true. How can I tell him why she had to go to Palestine? Oy! And Danny's father–how can I ever tell Danny about his father? Thank goodness I never knew him, only heard about him. Marek must help me with this.*

For the next hour, Fannie and Daniel will be home alone. Marek is at the shop. Rachel, Fannie's closest friend, a librarian whom the children call Aunt Rachel, took the twins for an afternoon of storytelling at the library. Adela just left for her violin lesson with her teacher, Mrs. Rutkowski, who lives in the building.

Daniel studies Fannie's face while she works at the sink. She looks serious, and he notices she sighs. Fannie briefly looks over at Daniel, and forces a smile, saying, "Just a few more minutes and we'll talk. Get out the honey cake and slice a piece for each of us and put the kettle on for our tea."

Daniel goes to the breadbox and takes out the loaf of honey cake, his favorite. He takes a knife from the drawer and cuts two even slices, sets them on small plates, and puts them on the kitchen table. He reaches for the sugar bowl from the cupboard and sets out two cups and the tea strainer, then sets the box of tea leaves next to the sugar bowl. Next Daniel pulls up a tall stool to the sink where Fannie is pulling out the innards of a plump chicken.

"Mama, tell me all the inside parts of the chicken."

"Danny, you know the names of the parts as well as I do. Every time I make a chicken; you ask me and then name them before I can."

"I know, Mama, but it's one of my favorite things we do."

"That's a good reason." Fannie pulls out the heart, liver, intestines, and gizzard, and Daniel quickly names each part.

"Open the gizzard, Mama. Let's see what this chicken ate for supper."

Fanny slices open the gizzard. They see a few kernels of corn and some small stones.

"Mama. You're bleeding! Your thumb is bleeding!"

"Oh! I guess I cut it opening the gizzard!" Fannie runs her thumb under the faucet. "Danny, there are Band-Aids in the bathroom cabinet. Get one for me." *What is the matter with me? I can't remember the last time I cut myself.*

Fannie dries her hands on a tea towel while Daniel opens a Band-Aid. "Here Mama, I'll put it on your thumb." He centers the gauze over her cut, wraps it, and neatly seals the sticky ends.

"Do you think you want to be a doctor, Danny, like that nice Dr. Weiss we met the other day?"

"I never thought about being a doctor. I want to be an actor. I like it when you take us kids with you to the dress rehearsals at the Yiddish Theater. You're there to check on the costumes, but I love watching the actors play their parts. And when the director stops them and tells them to do their lines or actions differently, that's very interesting to me."

"I didn't know you're thinking of being an actor."

"Mama, are you almost ready to tell me how I began?"

"Almost ready."

"While Fannie is still trying to get dinner started, Daniel, with urgency, says, "Adela likes to tease me. She told me you're not our mother. She was trying to fool me, right Mama?"

"When did she tell you that, Danny?"

"When you said we couldn't keep the baby because she was not ours. Adela said you kept us even though you're not our mother. She said we had other mothers before you."

He's heard all this already from Marek and me. Why is it news to him?

Fannie puts the chicken into the oven along with six potatoes and some onions. It is just the immediate family for dinner tonight. She slices carrots and puts them into a pot with water but does not yet set them to boil. Bringing the kettle of hot water with her, she sets it onto a tile on the table, pulls up her chair, and joins Daniel, who sits opposite her. She puts a teaspoon of tea leaves into the strainer and then pours hot water over them, first into her cup, letting them steep for a moment, and then pours the hot water over the tea leaves into Daniel's cup, making a weaker brew for him. Daniel takes two sugar cubes from the sugar bowl and drops them into his tea. Fannie takes one for herself.

Fannie reaches her hand across the table palm up and Daniel puts his hand palm down into hers. They squeeze each other's hand briefly, then let go. This is a familiar gesture for them, especially when something is serious.

"Danny darling, you are Tateh's and my son and will always be our son. Unlike Miriam and Simon, you were not born from my body but from another woman's body. There are different ways to have our own sons and daughters."

Fannie pauses here and studies Daniel's face. He's frowning, and Fannie realizes he is trying to take in this news, which isn't news. *He looks so confused. Is this the first time he's taken in what we've already said to him?*

She remembers his stunned little face when he woke up that first morning after his arrival in New York from Palestine. He was about a year and a half old.

Daniel, his voice rising, asks, "I didn't come from you? Adela says she came from Tateh, but not you. Did I come from Tateh?"

"You came from a different Tateh, Danny."

"Who was my Tateh?"

"I didn't know him. I knew your first mama very well. She was my dearest friend."

"Did you find me on the street?"

"Oh no. Your first mama, her name was Hannah, took wonderful care of you."

His voice sharp, "So why did she get rid of me?"

"She didn't get rid of you. Like Adela's first mama, your first mama also got sick and died. When she knew she was going to die, she had her sister, bring you to me from Palestine."

Daniel says angrily, fighting back a sob, "I want to come from you and Tateh, not from people I don't even know! Adela gets to come from Tateh. And she can remember her first mama."

Fannie tries to explain. "Danny, Hannah, the woman whose body you came from, loved you. She and I met on the ship coming to America and we always looked after each other. She trusted me to love and care for you."

"Adela says I came from Palestine. You say I was born in New York. Now you are saying I was brought from Palestine. Which is it?"

Fannie thinks, *This is even harder to explain than I thought!*

"You were born in New York, at Belview Hospital. Your first mama, Hannah, took you to Palestine when you were around six months old. You were there together for about a year before she got very sick and knew she would not live much longer."

"And how did I get back to New York?"

"She asked her sister to take the boat across the ocean and bring you to me here in New York. That's how you came back to New York and became Tateh's and my son. You will always be our son."

"Why did my mama Hannah take me to Palestine?"

How can I answer this truthfully?

Fannie takes a deep breath and says, "She thought you and she would have a better life in Palestine. We had a friend in Palestine who helped her get settled." *It's not a lie, just part of the truth. One day, he'll want to know more.*

Daniel is briefly quiet, then asks, "Who gave me my name, you and Tateh or my first mama?"

"Your first mama gave you the name Daniel. Tateh and I gave you your middle name, Moshe. Do you like your name?"

"It's okay. There's another Daniel in my Hebrew School class." A pause, "Did I speak Hebrew in Palestine?"

"You heard Hebrew spoken around you, but you were too little to speak. You were still a baby."

"At school in our chorus, the teacher was teaching us a Hebrew lullaby, *Numi Numi* (Sleep). I knew it but didn't know I knew it. I felt strange. Do you think my first mama sang it to me in Palestine?"

"She probably did. She liked to sing."

Daniel is quiet for a few moments. He struggles against crying but is overcome. He covers his face with his hands and sobs. Fannie pulls her chair around to be next to him.

I haven't heard him cry like this for a long time. That first day I brought him home, he cried so hard and for so long. I didn't know such a tiny person could cry so hard.

She rests her hand on his back. When she does this, he bolts upright, saying angrily. "Too many mothers die!" Then turns toward Fannie plaintively, "Promise me Mama, you won't die."

"I am well, Danny. I don't think I'll die for a very long time. Likely not until you're all grown up."

He yanks a handkerchief out of his pocket and wipes his face roughly, then jams the handkerchief back into his pocket. He sits a few moments, his head down, composing himself, then furrows his brow, thinking. "So, if I was born in New York, does that make me an American citizen?"

"I think so. Why?"

"In civics class, the teacher asked who in the class was born in America and who was born in other countries. She was talking about the ways people become citizens. I thought I was born in Palestine."

After a pause, Daniel asks, "You once showed me Simon and Miriam's birth certificate. Do I have a birth certificate?"

"I am sure you do, Danny."

"Where is it? I want to see it."

Fannie sighs, "Probably your mama Hannah had it. I don't have it. When you went with her to Palestine, we never expected she would die or that I would become your mother. She must have taken your birth certificate with her." Hearing this, Daniel puts his head in his hands, breathing out a sigh of frustration.

"Danny, would you like to hear more about your mama Hannah who gave birth to you? I knew her well."

"Not now Mama. Do I have some time before dinner?"

"Yes, a little time."

"I want to play stickball with Herman. We planned to do that today."

"Okay, play near the building. I'll send one of your sisters or your brother to get you when it's time to come in."

Later that evening, when Fannie and Marek are having their tea, she tells him about her conversation with Daniel.

"He can be so competent, so grown up beyond his years. And then I see he takes things hard and seems so much younger. It's strange because I've told him before how Hannah's sister brought him to me from Palestine and how, at first, he was willing to come to me only when I offered him a piece of apple. Sometimes he'd ask me to tell him again and always wanted a piece of apple to go along with the story. He seems to have forgotten all that."

"Has it been a long time?"

"Yes, maybe not since he was five or six."

"He cried. I could see he was trying not to. It had to do with Hannah's dying. Could he be living it all over again? Adela's mother died; Hannah died. This baby might die. And we don't know yet about the baby's mother."

Marek listens, then shaking his head, "Finding that baby keeps bringing up more and more questions, for Danny and Adela too. I wonder how it affects the twins."

Fannie asks, "Why do you think Danny didn't want to know more about Hannah?"

"I think he took in as much as he could for now. And you're probably right; being reminded that mothers and babies can die is what upset him. He'll want to know more someday, but not yet."

"I want to reassure him." says Fannie, "that his beginning is nothing like the beginning of that sad baby."

"I think, from what you told him, he knows that. And maybe for now it's all he needs to know."

"I hope so. Everything I told him is true but there's so much more to the story. I dread the day he realizes there must be more to why Hannah had to escape to Palestine." They clear the table of the teacups and go into their bedroom.

While lying next to each other, Fannie says, "Tateh, make me the sky."

Marek shifts onto his side and pushes himself up on his elbow. "What did you just say, Fannie?"

"Tateh, make me the sky! Do you remember that?"

"Of course I do. It was Adela's game with the blue tablecloth. She wanted me to throw it up in the air and let it fall over the two of us like the sky. After Miriam died, it was the only game Adela wanted to play. Later, she got Danny to play it with her. What makes you think of it?"

"It was the beginning of us."

"What do you mean?

"I had Danny with me because Hannah died. When Adela's mother died, you were alone with Adela. Adela needed a mother and Danny needed a father."

"Right."

"We asked the same matchmaker to find us a match, and she found you and me."

"Yes. But what does that have to do with Adela's game?"

"Don't you remember?"

"No, sorry, remind me."

"We got married first for our children, but then after a while, not a long while, I realized I loved you. And one day as Adela and Danny were playing 'Make me the sky.' with each other, I said to you, 'Marek darling, you make me the sky' and do you remember what you said?"

"Hmm, was it something about stars?"

Fannie turns toward Marek excitedly, "Yes, yes. You said 'Fannie, if I make you the sky, you make me the stars.' That was the moment darling, we knew our marriage had grown beyond having a mother and father for Adela and Danny. You and I also loved each other."

Marek puts his hand on the back of Fannie's head. He draws her toward him and tenderly kisses her. "Fannie, my love, you are wrong about one thing."

"What?'

"Yes, I first looked for a matchmaker because Adela needed a mother, but Fannie, I loved you the first time we met. It took you longer to love me."

They embrace, kiss, make love and both fall into a deep sleep.

Again, I walk street after street in Vienna. In building after building, I ring the doorbells on every floor. No one answers.

Letters

D r Weiss receives a report from the New York City Juvenile Court.

Dear Dr. Weiss,

Because you are the physician in charge of the medical care of Baby Girl X, our department is sending you a report of the findings of the investigation of this case of child abandonment. We thank you for your cooperation and for sending us your report.

Because the mother of the abandoned child is a minor, we give no names.

The mother of the baby is a girl of fifteen years. She gave us the following information. When she realized she was pregnant, she ran away from home. It appears a vagabond woman took her under her wing and brought her to her shelter under a bridge in Fort Tryon Park. When the girl was ready to deliver, the two moved into a vacant building where the woman helped with the birth of the baby. The girl was determined to keep the baby. The vagabond woman stayed with the girl for a couple of months, but when the infant became ill the woman abandoned the girl. Alone and frightened, the girl realized she could not care for her baby and brought the baby, wrapped in rags, to her own mother, leaving her outside the closed apartment door. She left a note asking her mother to take care of the infant. The girl says she tried to return to the vacant building, but a group of men had moved in, and so she went back to shelter under the bridge. She says she hoped to find the woman who took care of her before and remained there waiting for her. This is where the police found the girl.

We found the girl's mother, the infant's grandmother, to be living in the building next to the alley on 179th Street. The grandmother says she intended to care for the baby. However, the man she lives with and who supports her would not tolerate the baby being with them. One night, he took the baby away. The grandmother says she does not know where. She hoped it was to an orphanage. She has not seen him since that night.

We traced the grandmother's gentleman friend. With the grandmother's testimony, he was arrested on charges of endangering the life of a minor. He has a record of arrests for endangering minors, and he is also under suspicion of impregnating the baby's mother.

Dr. Weiss, we know from your report that the infant who remains under your care is gravely ill. Should the infant die, the accused will be further charged with murder.

Thank you again for your help with this investigation.

Cordially,
Myra O'Brian, Social Worker, New York City Juvenile Court

After receiving the letter, Dr. Weiss goes to check on Baby Girl X. She is in an incubator to keep her warm. He picks up her chart, noting despite regular feedings she has failed to gain weight. Her color is grayish. He suspects she had been so severely malnourished that her ability to absorb nutrients from her feedings has failed. She is on her back, arms and legs curled. She looks more like a minute shriveled old person than a baby. Dr. Weiss reaches into the incubator and lightly puts two fingers on the baby's chest. She stirs very briefly and quickly becomes still again. He picks up the chart again, opens it and writes, "Diagnoses: Severe malnutrition, failure to thrive" dates his note and signs it. He shakes his head, sighs, and starts to walk back to his office. Then he pauses, turns, and returns to the incubator. He opens the lid and gently lifts the child into his arms. She stretches and yawns. She opens her eyes. They are unfocused and cloudy. He is struck by her spontaneous response to being picked up.

He calls to her. "Baby girl, do you hear me?" He says this several times, making his voice louder each time. She does not react, except to yawn again, and move to shape her body to his. He paces the room with her in his arms, and she falls asleep. He places her back in the incubator and writes a new order in her chart. "Be sure to hold Baby Girl X for all her feedings and walk the corridors with her at least three times a day.

He adds to his note. "Possibly deaf"

Six weeks later, a letter comes to Fannie from Dr. Weiss.

Dear Mrs. Horvath,

I am writing to let you know what happened with the baby you and your son rescued. She is alive and now living with her grandmother and young mother. The baby's grandmother is now the legal guardian and agrees to raise the child. There is no question had this baby not been found and brought here when you did, she would not have survived. That is the good news.

The sad news is that starvation had already done its cruel work, and it is unlikely this infant will grow and develop as a normal child. We strongly suspect she is both blind and deaf. With the grandmother's care, she has the chance of doing much better than if placed in an institution.

The baby's mother is a girl of fifteen years. When she found herself to be pregnant, she ran away from home, finding shelter in public places. She soon recognized the baby was ill and knew she could not care for her infant. She left the child in front of the door of her mother's apartment. The grandmother took the child in but her live-in gentleman friend would not tolerate having the baby with them. He took the child, leaving her where your son found her. He was arrested and is now in prison on a charge of endangering the life of a minor.

We have reached out to the baby's mother, who herself is seriously undernourished. A social worker is assigned to the family to provide health and welfare support.

Mrs. Horvath, if ever I can be of assistance to you or anyone in your family, please contact me at the Medical Center.

Also, I remember how I had heard of Bolekhiv. When I was at medical school in Vienna, a fellow student was from Bolekhiv. His name is Piotr Nowak. I hope he survived the war. Do you recognize the name?

Yours truly,
Hans Weiss, MD

A week later, Fannie writes back.

Dear Dr. Weiss,

Thank you for your letter. What a sad beginning for this poor child. It pains me that she is likely blind and deaf. What a terrible life sentence! Thank goodness her grandmother will care for her.

Also, about your fellow medical student, I don't recognize the name, but please tell me what you can about him. If he knew my family in Bolekhiv, I might have heard about him later. When you knew him, I would have been very young.

Best Regards,
Fannie Horvath

Fannie brings her letter to the mailbox at the end of her street. She opens the chute and for a moment she holds the letter half-way into the opening. She pauses. Could this man possibly be...? I think it is alright to ask for more information. If it is him, do I want to know?

She pulls the letter out, starts to put it into her coat pocket, then jerkily opens the mail chute again and thrusts the letter into the slot. She walks home quickly.

Another letter from Dr. Weiss.

Dear Mrs. Horvath,

Piotr Nowak, I didn't know him well, but we all admired him. He stood out as an exuberant fellow with a big mop of red hair. He was not only an excellent medical student, but he was also witty and well-read, especially in philosophy and literature. Apparently, he was not formally educated but self-taught.

He came to Vienna alone and while a student worked as a carpenter for his room and board. I believe he had been a carpenter in Bolekhiv. He would be my age now, probably the age of your parents. I haven't seen him these many years. I heard he specialized first in orthopedics. I guess that makes sense for a former carpenter. But then I understand he heard a few lectures by Professor Sigmund Freud and became interested in psychoanalysis. He studied with Freud and changed his specialty to neurology and psychiatry. I would be interested if you possibly knew of him. You may not because he may have left Bolekhiv before you were born. I enjoyed remembering him again and thinking back on those days in Vienna. It was a good time until life got hard for all Jews.

I hope you and your lovely family are all doing well.

Yours,
Hans Weiss, M.D.

Over their evening tea, Fannie shows the letter to Marek.

"What do you make of it Fannie? Did you know of this Piotr Nowak?"

"I don't know. I told you so many terrible things about my past, but I don't remember if I told you this. After I left for America, my mother made a deathbed confession. She told my older sister Rivka, she had had a brief, secret love affair with a red-haired carpenter who came to the house to do some repairs. This man dreamed of going to Vienna or Budapest to study medicine. He soon left for Vienna, and Mama realized she was pregnant, with twins no less. She told Rivka that through the whole time, she didn't know if the father was her lover or my father. When she saw how Esther, my twin and I had fair coloring, and Esther was a redhead, she knew. Everyone else in the family has dark hair and eyes. According to Rivka, Mama said she never told Tateh, and if he suspected, he never brought it up. She thought Tateh might have favored us. I think that may be true. He was always extra loving toward Esther and me. I think more than to the other kids. He used to call me his *Abigail* (father's joy). I think he also called Esther, his Abigail."

"Are you saying you think this Piotr could be your real father?"

"It could be a coincidence, but the timing is right. He was a carpenter. He went to Vienna because he wanted to be a doctor. I'm not sure what to think. I always wondered if he was Jewish and my guess from his name, he isn't."

"Does that matter to you?" asks Marek.

"Not so much now. It might have mattered more when I was younger and was Orthodox because my family was Orthodox. You and I have changed a lot since coming to America. I still love our traditions and will always think of us as Jewish. I'm comfortable now at our reformed Temple Emanu-El. The other thing about Dr. Weiss's letter is that this man, Piotr, was scholarly. Esther and I were the bookish ones in the family, more than the other kids. Although Aber, my eldest brother has turned out to be quite the intellectual. I didn't realize that until we started exchanging letters during the war. If it's nothing more than a coincidence, there's still a lot that fits." Fannie becomes quiet for a long moment, staring down into her teacup.

"Fannie, what are you're thinking?"

Fannie looks up, tears filling her eyes. "I'm thinking of my dear tateh, may his memory be for a blessing. I can't imagine anyone one else being my tateh. Poor Mama going through that time, worrying her betrayal would be discovered. Then having not only one but two fair-haired babies. If Tateh suspected, he stayed silent. How could he not suffer suspecting his wife betrayed him? But if he acknowledged it, he would have to divorce Mama. He kept silent and loved us. How did he do that?"

"Fannie, remember, before we married, we told each other about all the things we had done that we were ashamed of. But we took each other as we were and have loved each other since."

"Yes, but Marek, while we were ashamed of what we did, we did those things before we married. It was shame, not betrayal. Mama betrayed Tateh. That's different."

"I see what you mean. But maybe he was ashamed that his wife took up with another man, that he wasn't enough for her."

"When I think of Mama's fear and silence and Tateh's silent suffering, it's painful to think how lonely it was for each of them. They didn't want to destroy the family with a divorce. It took a lot of strength. But their strength wouldn't make them suffer any less. I think that's why Mama had to confess it to Rivka, and she wanted Rivka to tell me. I only hope that gave Mama some peace at the end of her life."

"Are you going to do anything more about this letter from Dr. Weiss?"

"I don't know—not now. There's something about having his name and a few facts that settles me for now. Piotr sounds like a good man.

I had two good fathers. I wish Danny could know his first father was good." Fannie continues, "When I think of Danny, Adela and me; Adela was only two when your first wife Miriam died. She barely remembers her mother. I don't know the father whose body I came from, and Daniel has no memory of his mother Hannah, and knows nothing at all about his father. I can't bear the thought of ever telling Danny what I learned from Hannah about that man. His name was Mendl, but he called himself Jack. He was evil. How can I ever bring such news to our sweet boy? Thank goodness I never had to meet up with this Mendl."

"But Fannie, here we all are now. Look what we created together."

"Another thing Marek, the man's name is Piotr. In English, he would be Peter. My friend Rachel, who reads everything, told me I should read the New Testament. My father was Shimon. In his memory, we named our youngest boy Simon. In the Bible, Jesus changes the name of his disciple Simon to Peter. Isn't that strange?"

"Fannie, now I think you're looking for too many coincidences. A lot of Christian men are called Peter, and a lot of Jewish men are called Simon. No magic coincidences here, Fannie."

"Maybe, but it gives me the shivers."

Adela

December 1925

It's *Shabbos* (The Sabbath). The Horvath family has gathered for dinner. With them is Rachel, a close family friend and a librarian. And with Rachel are Fannie's teenage sister and brother, Kayla and Jacob. Kayla and Jacob have lived with Rachel since their immigration to America in 1919. Their apartment is in a neighboring building. Aber, Fannie's eldest brother, is also present.

The table is beautifully set with a white tablecloth and napkins, the good dishes, and wine glasses. It is the special Shabbos meal. At the center sits a vase of orange and red flowers.

On a sideboard are the Shabbos candles waiting for Fannie and Rachel to light them and recite the blessing. After, Fannie will bring in the platters of food. She will take her place at the end of the table closest to the kitchen, while Marek sits at the opposite end to lead the service.

Daniel grabs the seat next to Jacob. Jacob operates a ham radio and Daniel wants to hear about it. Simon takes the seat on the other side of Jacob. Miriam makes sure she gets the seat next to Kayla. A fragrant, warm *challah* (a braided bread) is at Marek's place.

Marek passes *yarmulkes* (skull caps) to all males, then goes to the kitchen to fill the cut glass carafe from the large bottle of sweet religious wine. It's prohibition, but wine remains legally available for religious ritual. After he pours it into the carafe, he is surprised to find the bottle almost empty. Hmm, *I must ask Fannie when we bought this bottle.*

He brings the carafe into the dining room and places it on a glass plate. There's a pitcher of grape juice for the children.

It's sundown; Shabbos can begin. But it can't. The seat next to Fannie is empty. Fifteen-year-old Adela is missing. She was due home an hour ago but hasn't shown up. Fannie's stomach clenches. She stands by Marek's chair. "Marek, Adela said she and Anna were going to stay after school to get some tutoring in algebra and then stop at Anna's house. She was due home an hour ago."

"Do I know Anna?" Marek asks, his tone unusually stern.

"Yes, she's the kosher butcher's daughter, you know, Mr. Kaplan. They live above the store."

"Anna should be at home now for her family's Shabbos, so Adela should be home soon. Maybe they lost track of time. She'll show up in a few minutes. Let's have the blessing and serve dinner. If she's not home soon, I'll go over there. We can't call. They won't pick up the phone. Go ahead light the candles."

Fannie strikes a match and lights the candles. She and Rachel together cover their eyes with their hands and recite the blessing. This is usually a moment of peace and reverie for Fannie when she brings together her thoughts of the home of her childhood and the home she and Marek created. For this moment, the years of hardship and loneliness between her immigration and her marriage dissolve in the light and warmth of the Friday evening ritual. Tonight, however, there is no peace. She recites the ancient prayer but is distracted and frightened by Adela's absence. *Where could she be? She's never this late.*

The service continues. Marek blesses the wine and the challah. He pours the wine and passes the challah. Each person tears off a bit of the bread, and comments on how delicious it tastes. Fannie brings in the platters of food and the meal is underway. Fannie can't eat. Marek is unusually silent.

The front door flies open. Adela, bursts in. She's dressed in a very short, dark pink flapper dress. Her stockings are rolled to her ankles, and she holds a pair of black, high-heel shoes. Her hair, her long black hair, is cut into a short bob. She can't stop giggling, a high-pitched, hysterical giggle.

"Adela," gasps Fannie, "Are you alright? What happened? Where were you? Your hair! What's this dress?" She runs to Adela, who still can't stop giggling.

Marek explodes out of his seat, his face bright red. He roars, "Adela, you're drunk! And God knows what else! Fannie, our daughter, is drunk! That dress is obscene." Adela stops giggling. She's dazed. Marek barks, "Get to your room and get to bed." Adela sputters something. Marek roars, "I don't want to hear anything from you. You've ruined Shabbos. Get out of my sight." Adela cries. Marek screams, "Did you hear me?"

Adela, now scowling, stomps to her room and slams the door. Miriam and Simon giggle nervously. Simon asks, "What did Adela do, Tateh?"

"We're not talking about Adela. Fannie, bring in the rest of dinner."

Fannie goes to the kitchen. She is weak and light-headed and leans against the counter.

What's going on? Thank God Adela is back. This isn't like her. I've never heard Marek so angry. I've never seen him like this. What happened to our Adela? Is she alright? Has she been with some man? Oy vey iz mir!

Fannie wants to check on Adela. She knows Marek wants her left alone. People at the table are eating silently. She gives into her impulse, opens the door a few inches calling into the room, "Adela, it's Mama. Are you alright?"

Adela is in bed, curled up. Her face is pressed into the pillow. When she hears Fannie's voice, she spins upright in bed and screams, "Get out. You're not my mother. My mother is dead. I don't have a mother!"

Fannie jolts backwards, as though she's been hit. Closing the door, shaken, she returns to the table. Somehow, they all get through the meal and prayers. People go home early. The usual hour of conversation doesn't happen tonight. Fannie tells Simon and Daniel to go to the room they share. "But it's too early to go to bed on a Friday night." complains Simon.

"Do something in your room until you're ready to sleep." Fannie turns to Miriam, who shares a room with Adela. "Miriam, you go with Simon and Danny into their room for now."

Miriam asks, "Where did Adela get those clothes? And her hair!"

"Never mind now. We'll talk another time."

"Can I sleep in Danny and Simon's room, Mama?"

"We'll see later."

Daniel asks, "Can I go to Aunt Rachel's house and stay over? Jacob has a ham radio set. He said he'll show it to me." Fannie says he can go.

Marek, still seated at the dinner table, is calmer but sits with his head in his hands and moans. Fannie takes the chair next to him and rests her hand on his back. After a moment, he straightens up. "Fannie, find out if she's dressed."

Tentatively, Fannie knocks on Adela's door. There's no answer. Opening the door, she sees Adela dressed in school clothes, asleep on top of her covers. She tells Marek, and he walks into her room without knocking. He shouts, "Adela!" She startles awake, sits up, is bleary-eyed but sober.

Marek is in control but stern. "Adela, where were you and who was with you?"

Adela sits upright, her legs over the side of the bed. She is sullen. "I don't have to tell you."

Marek, wounded, "What do you mean you don't have to tell me?"

"I'm old enough to do what I want. Mama was my age when she came alone to America. No one told her what to do."

Plaintively, "Adela, I don't understand. You've always been so sensible, so loving, so caring. I don't recognize you. Who are you? Where's my good girl?"

Adela, sharply, "I'm done being your good girl. I'm sick of this family. You and Mama are always so good, so kind. You never fight like my friends' parents. You're too good to be true! Are you real? No one is good all the time. You don't know how people my age feel. We want to be who we are, not who our parents want us to be. We want freedom and fun. And sometimes we want to be bad!"

Marek, trembling, enraged, bits of saliva fly from his mouth, "Is your idea of freedom to go missing, make us sick with worry! Freedom is getting drunk! Freedom is insulting your family for being kind! Is this my daughter, who I trusted? You come home drunk and look like a tramp. You betray me!"

"Tateh, you're accusing me of being a tramp and you don't even know what I did."

"You betray me!"

Adela now yelling, "I don't care Tateh. You don't own me. You were completely on your own when you were barely older than me. You came to America and made your own life. I want to make my life and that means deciding what I choose to do, what I wear, and who I choose for my friends."

She crosses her arms and turns her back to him. For a second, he lunges at her, then jerks himself back.

I want to slap her! I want to beat her! He thrusts himself out the door and slams it.

Fannie, in the kitchen, hears it all. She braces herself against the sink. Marek storms into the kitchen, clumsily wedges himself into a chair and slams his fist on the kitchen table. Fannie jumps. "Fannie, protect her from me! I'm violent. I'm afraid of what I could do. What if he raped her? She was drunk! She looked like a slut!" He puts his head onto the table, keening. "Help me, please help me."

I've never seen him like this! What's happening to him? Has he ever been violent? Then she remembers his confession before they married; he was sixteen when he came home to his family's apartment on the first floor and found a stranger raping his mother, his young sisters screaming. Grabbing a knife from the table, Marek drove it into the rapist's back, again and again. The man staggered outside, collapsed, and died. To escape the police, Marek left for America. As a Jew, if caught, he was doomed.

Marek's moaning gradually stops. Trying to sound calm, Fannie asks, "Marek, are you thinking about when you rescued your mother from that rapist?"

"Yes. I told you before we got married. I killed a man, Fannie, and it wasn't in a war! That makes it murder. I can be violent!"

"You rescued your mother and probably your sisters, too. What else could you do?"

"I should have pulled him off her and beat him up—not grabbed that knife. Anytime I pick up a knife to carve the meat or even pick up the big scissors to cut out a suit, I think of that moment every day. If someone hurt you or any of the kids, I could kill again. I'm sure I could." Marek stares past Fannie. "I can't bear Adela putting herself in danger." He weeps. "This was my little girl who clung to me for a year after my wife Miriam died. We were so close. What happened?" Marek covers his face with his hands. After a while, he sighs heavily and says, "Enough! Fannie, leave me alone now."

Fannie goes to Adela's doorway. Try to sleep Adela, we'll all be calmer in the morning." Then says, "Can I bring you something to eat, Adela?"

Adela's voice, muffled by the pillow over her face, mutters, "No."

Fannie leaves Adela's room and sees Marek standing at the door of the apartment wearing his hat and coat. "Fannie, I need to get out of here. I'll be back later."

"Do you want me to go with you, Marek?"

"No, I need to be alone." He leaves.

Fannie doesn't know what to do with herself. She goes to the window and can see Marek heading toward the river. She looks out onto the city night scene and a wave of fear and loneliness sweeps over her. *There's no way I can relax now.* She goes to her work area, an alcove off the dining room, takes her blue shawl, which is always kept draped over the back of her work chair, and with a deep breath, lays it over her shoulders. It's the shawl knitted by her twin sister Esther, who died soon after Fannie left for America. The shawl always brings Fannie some comfort. Once settled in her chair, she takes out a script for a play that just started rehearsal at the Yiddish Theater and takes up her sketchpad to sketch some ideas for the costumes. She thinks about the play now in performance, "The Dybbuk." *For Marek, this terrible memory is like a dybbuk, a tormenting spirit inside of him and he can't get rid of it.*

After an hour, she is tired and goes to bed. Soon Marek comes in and quietly gets ready for bed. He gets under the covers, turning away from her. Fannie says, "Good night." He says good night back. There's a pause. Without turning toward her, he says, "When did we buy that bottle of Shabbos wine?"

Fannie, puzzled at first, answers, "Maybe two weeks ago. Why?"

"Never mind. I want to sleep now."

Fannie is agitated. *Does he think Adela is stealing wine? Oy, this is too much.* Finally, she falls into an exhausted sleep.

Before dawn, Fannie wakes up to Adela, looking down at her. "Mama, I'm scared." Fannie puts her finger to her lips. She doesn't want to wake Marek. She gestures to Adela that they should leave the bedroom. They go into Adela's room. Miriam is sleeping in Simon's room. Fannie and Adela sit on Adela's bed. "Mama, I'm scared of Tateh. He hates me. I'm afraid it will never be the same with him."

"He doesn't hate you Adela, he's scared you were hurt or could have been hurt. But he is furious about your getting drunk and going out without our permission. We were terrified something bad happened to you."

"I'm sorry about what I said to you before. I know you're my mama."

"Yes, I'm your mama, but you're right, your first mama sadly died while having another baby."

"I never want to have a baby. Mothers die and babies die. Having a baby killed my mother and the baby too. I don't want that to happen to me."

Hearing this, a stab of pain pierces Fannie but she presses on, "Adela, what happened today?"

"I was bad Mama. I lied when I said I was going to stay late at school with Anna. I went with Anna's cousin for a ride in his car and we went dancing."

"Her cousin? This boy has a car?"

"He's not really a boy, he's twenty-one."

Fannie can't believe what she's hearing. "How does he come to have a car?"

"I don't know."

"You met him at Anna's?"

"Yes." Adela is suddenly lively, "He was telling us about the new dances everyone does now. They have funny names like The Charleston, The Texas Tommy, and The Shimmy. The music that goes with them is called jazz. And he told us how our generation, born in the land of the free, is finally becoming free of the old country and the old ways. We young people are breaking out of the rules the old people put on us. And in America, women are equal to men. We can vote like a man can." Her voice gets dreamy, "And we want to love whoever we want. We want to move our arms and legs, free our hair, and have fun. I won't ever wear long dark dresses with high necks like you and your friends and your customers. I will never, ever, wear a corset like all of you. I want to move, express myself, dance!" She freely waves her arms and looks toward the ceiling.

"Who's this man, Anna's cousin, who takes a fifteen-year-old girl in his car?"

"Sam, he likes me and kept asking me if he could take me for a ride and go dancing. I didn't say yes right away, but then I did. And Anna said she would cover for me."

"And the liquor?"

"At the dance, he had this metal container he kept in his hip pocket. It was full of what he called Gordon water. He kept wanting me to try some. He said it would help me relax and be freer. I tried it. I figured some kind of water wouldn't hurt. He kept after me to try more. I said it tasted like perfume. Then he admitted it was a liquor called gin. I felt strange and then I couldn't stop laughing, even though nothing was funny.

"You know liquor is illegal to buy."

"Yes, I know. Maybe he didn't buy it."

"Adela, I have to ask, did he touch you?"

"When we got back in his car, he pulled me over to him and he kissed me. It was okay at first, then he rammed his tongue in my mouth, and I wanted to throw up. I screamed at him to take me home. He was mad but drove me home. I couldn't stop laughing. I didn't want to laugh, but I couldn't stop."

"And where did you get this dress and the shoes?"

"The shoes belong to Anna's older sister, who let me borrow them. I made the dress."

"You made this dress!"

"Yes, I was excited at first that Sam wanted to take me dancing, but I couldn't go dancing in my skirt and sweater, so I made the dress. I got a remnant of the cloth from where you get cloth, Mama, downtown on Orchard Street. I have some money from baby-sitting for Mrs. Rutkowski."

Fanny takes the dress off the back of the chair where Adela threw it, and holds up the short, sleeveless, deep pink, silky dress with its straight vertical lines and horizontal lines of ruffles from the bodice all the way to the hem. She examines the seams. "This is beautiful, Adela, and beautiful sewing. How did you do it?"

"Anna made a dress too. She had a pattern, and I copied it onto newspaper. Her dress didn't have the ruffles, but I had the idea that when you dance in this dress the ruffles dance too. And they did!"

"If you're going to wear this dress again Adela, you'll need to make it longer. It's too short."

"Oh, Mama, I like it short."

"How about another big ruffle at the bottom?"

"I don't know?"

Fannie shrugs. "So, what about this, Sam?"

"I think he's disgusting. But Mama, I enjoy wearing this dress and dancing the new dances. And I like my hair; it's so much more comfortable than a long braid and so much easier to comb. I like how it feels swinging against my face."

Fannie touches Adela's hair, grieving for her long mane of shiny dark hair.

"Are you going to tell Tateh what I did?"

"He needs to know, and he needs to know you're alright and that you won't go drinking and riding in some man's car again."

"Will you tell him Mama? I'm afraid he'll just be mad and won't listen to me. I don't want him to hate me. As soon as I was scared, I got Sam to bring me home. I was bad for lying to you and getting drunk, but that's all I did, and I won't do it again."

"All right, I'll tell him. But this time you were lucky, not every man would bring you home when you want. Now, let's both get some more sleep." Fannie gets up to leave and turns back. "Adela, did you ever drink any kind of liquor before tonight?'

"No, Mama, never."

"Not even a little Shabbos wine?"

"Only when you give me a little sip. Why are you asking me?"

"I believe you. I just wanted to know if tonight was the first time you had liquor."

"Yes. You can tell Tateh, I won't drink again until I get married."

"I'll do that."

Fannie reaches Adela's door and again turns back. "Dela, will you lend me your pattern for your dress? I can imagine that some customers might want a dress like yours, only longer and maybe the Yiddish Theater will be interested too, for costumes. They may want to do a play about jazz and the new dances."

"Sure Mama, you can copy my pattern."

"You copied the pattern, but the color and cloth you chose and the ruffles you added really make it your creation."

"Thanks Mama."

Fannie sighs. *Dying babies, dying mothers, violence. Marek and I both know violence. My father was beaten at his job and never recovered. Mischa, my first love, his father was beaten in the streets of America. Hannah was forced into prostitution and so was I. I was rescued, but I've felt badness in me since. Hmmm, maybe I have a dybbuk too. Now our beloved Adela wants to be bad and wants to step into this violent world. My mother sent me alone into this dangerous world when I was no older than Adela. Fannie sighs again. Other than her mother dying, Adela hasn't known hardship or violence. She doesn't know it exists.*

At Adela's age, did I think about having fun? I wanted to dance touching a man even though it was forbidden. Mischa and I embraced and kissed. That would never be tolerated in Bolekhiv. I've broken many religious rules I was taught. And, oh yes, my mother had a love affair. We broke lots of rules. We did bad things. Hannah wanted to have fun. She had a wild streak. Maybe Adela has a wild streak. Was it Hannah's wild streak that got her in trouble? No, being poor and desperate is what did it. That beast Mendl, that pimp, said he'd take care of her and help her get her family out of Europe. Hannah had a hard life—then died too soon. Adela is full of life. I was that way at her age. Am I still full of life? She wants to dance and move. What happened to my urge to dance? Where has it gone?

Daniel and Jacob

Daniel arrives at Rachel's nearby building, a building like his own. He rides the elevator to the 5th floor and rings the bell. Rachel answers.

"Hello Daniel, did you come to see Jacob?"

"Yes, Aunt Rachel. Can I sleep here tonight? Miriam is sleeping in my room. I'd like to stay here."

"Of course you can. You know you can stay here anytime. Jacob is in his room."

Rachel shares the bigger bedroom with Kayla and Jacob has the second bedroom. Daniel knocks on Jacob's closed door calling, "Jake, it's Dan." Jacob opens the door with his finger to his lips. Daniel hears noises coming from Jacob's radio. He's receiving what sounds like a Morse code message from the radio set. Jacob sits and taps back. The exchange goes on for a while, and Daniel studies Jacob's profile. His thick, black curly hair makes his head look big, almost manly. A curl wraps around his ear and Daniel notices some dark fuzz on Jacob's upper lip. He's hunched over his code sender—tapping quickly, expertly, easily. He frowns as he sends his message and at one point laughs an abrupt laugh as a message comes in. Daniel wonders if he forgot about him. He may have. Daniel looks around the room. There is the long table made of rough wood for the radio set and a wooden bench where Jacob sits. Aber, Jacob's older brother, is a carpenter and helped Jacob make the table and bench. A small dresser, a bed and a wooden chair are the only other furnishings. The walls are bare and the only light in the room comes from an overhead light and the lights on the radio.

In the past, when Daniel stayed over, he shared the bed with Jacob, but recently, Jacob said it felt too crowded and wants Daniel to sleep on the sofa in the living room.

Jacob finishes transmitting with his radio buddy but then receives another signal. Into the microphone, Jacob says smartly, "Stand by." Daniel listens but is puzzled by the exchange.

"No, I didn't. Yeah, copy, copy, too bad, Yeah, too bad, a silent key, no ragchew now, someone's here, Roger, unkey." Jacob turns off the radio. Daniel asks,

"Was that Morse code you were using before?"

"No, my radio buddy and I started out using Morse, but then we've been making up our own code. If we have another war, we'll have a way to communicate without being understood. Do you want to see the radio?" Daniel pulls over the wooden chair and Jacob names the different dials and buttons and what they do. He speaks quickly, using technical language like feedline, crystal, duplexer, vacuum tubes, frequencies, and antenna. Daniel yawns but tries to pay attention.

"Where did you get the radio?"

"Aber got me the kit because I help him with carpentry on weekends. He and I put it together."

"Who do you talk to?"

"Men, I met on the ship. They taught me Morse code. You're not allowed to operate a ham radio unless you know Morse code. One guy lives in Brooklyn and one in New Jersey."

"Do you visit them?"

"No, we do our talking or coding on the radio."

"What do you talk about?"

"Not much. Maybe our radio sets. They talk about boxing and the other boxers. They're both amateurs and compete with other amateurs."

"Do you like boxing?"

"I don't know if I like it. They want me to come to their gym and try it. But I still don't weigh enough to box in their gym. When I get to welter weight, I may try it."

"What's welter weight?"

"Around 140. You fight with other men who are about the same weight."

Daniel imagines Jacob in a boxing ring, his chest muscled, shining with sweat. He's aware of smelling Jacob's sweat and something else. Mothballs? The rough wood of the table and bench? He breathes in deeply, more deeply. Warm and sleepy, Daniel yawns again. Jacob says, "I want to make another contact. Lie on the bed if you want. I'll wake you when I'm done, and you'll sleep on the sofa."

In the middle of the night, still on Jacob's bed, Daniel awakens to hear Jacob sobbing. He is curled up on the floor with a pillow pressed to his face.

"Jake, what's the matter? Are you sick or something?" Jacob doesn't answer. Daniel gets off the bed, onto the floor, and lies behind Jacob. Supporting himself on his elbow, Daniel pats Jacob's head, then is drawn to put his face close to his hair, again breathing in Jacob's scent. Daniel's heart beats quickly, and he feels the warm stirrings he has felt before, but only when he was alone. Why is Jake crying? Daniel rubs his forehead against the back of Jacob's head. Jacob stops crying but mutters. "Go to the sofa, Dan. I want to get into my bed."

Daniel is panicky. *What have I done? What have I done? I want to go home.* He goes to the sofa. *I'll leave as soon as it gets light.* He can't sleep. A scene he doesn't want to remember intrudes. No, this was not the first time.

It was this past summer, while riding the trolley. A man, maybe twenty years old, wearing white cotton trousers, sat next to him. During the ride, the man pressed his thigh against Daniel's thigh. At first Daniel wanted to pull away, but then he felt rising warm pleasure fill his lower body. He felt his penis move. Again, he wanted to pull away, but he couldn't. It was too exciting...what his body wanted...the heat, all of it. *I was in public! Could anyone see?* He heard the man's quick breath next to his. The trolley stopped. The man bolted out the rear door.

Am I that man on the trolley?

Daniel jumps up. He leaves the apartment quietly. He doesn't wait for the elevator, flies down the stairway and out the door into the gray morning. He runs home and races up the stairs to his apartment, lets himself in, and realizes Miriam is sleeping in his bed. Breathless and sobbing, he curls himself into a ball on the sofa, clamping his hand over his mouth to muffle his sobs.

He must have finally fallen asleep because as he opens his eyes, there is a moment before the scene of last night with Jacob comes flooding back. *Could Jake tell what I was feeling? Oh, I hope not. But maybe he could. We used to play wrestle. That was okay. This felt different. Was I like the man on the trolley? Why was Jacob crying? Did I make him cry?*

He pictures himself last night waking up in Jacob's bed, realizing *Jake was crying before I got onto the floor with him. Maybe he didn't know what I felt. Maybe he thought I was just trying to comfort him—which I was—but it wasn't the only thing. He was already crying; I didn't make him cry.*

Daniel is less worried. *Jake looks almost grown up. He has some mustache hairs. I don't have anything like that.* He remembers Fannie has a big mirror in her workspace and quietly gets up and walks over to it. He pulls off his shirt and looks at himself. He sees his narrow chest and shoulders, his skinny neck, and long thin arms. *I'm so puny! My hands and feet look so big compared to every-*

thing else. My red hair! It's so bushy. I can barely get a comb through it. And I have pimples. Yuck! I'm so ugly!

He hears someone coming and yanks his shirt on.

"Good morning, Danny," says Fannie, "I didn't know you were back already."

"Yeah, I came home, and everyone was asleep. Miriam is in my bed, so I slept on the sofa."

"Do you want breakfast?"

"No, not now. I want to sleep more."

"Oh Danny, I forgot to tell you yesterday; Rabbi Berliner called. On Sunday, he can meet with you to prepare for your bar mitzvah.

"Ok Mama."

Marek and Fannie

A half hour later, Marek is awake. He and Fannie sit across from each other over coffee. Fannie tells him about her talk with Adela last night. Marek is somber. Fannie asks him if he wants some toasted challah. He shakes his head'

"It's going to take time for me to get past this Fannie. I still feel betrayed by my daughter, who I so completely trusted."

"I know Marek. I think she knows she made a mistake. She's upset she hurt you."

"She should be."

"She's growing up in a world so different from ours. She hasn't seen evil, and violence up close the way we did."

"There's still plenty of evil in this world."

"We know that, but we've been able to keep our kids safe so far. Adela, and soon Daniel too, will go into the world as it is. We were forced into a mean world. Adela doesn't know about badness. She's excited and wants to be a part of all the excitement out there."

Almost growling, "I won't tolerate her going out with boys or men we don't know. Slamming his fist on the table, "And I'll never tolerate her getting drunk."

"If you were worried about Adela drinking the wine, I don't think she did. I asked her and I believe her when she said 'No'."

"You asked her!"

"Almost. I asked her if yesterday was the first time she drank liquor and she said it was. Then I asked if she ever drank Shabbos wine and she said, 'Only when you give me a little sip.' Maybe the bottle we bought was smaller."

Marek shrugs his shoulders. "I don't think so."

"Well, she's sorry about her escapade and very sorry to get you so upset."

"That's good." He nods righteously.

"Will you tolerate her wearing a flapper dress, longer than the one you saw, and go dancing to Jazz? That's what kids her age are doing now. Look at the new advertisements for clothes in the newspaper. They don't just show the clothes, they show the people wearing them having fun, playing sports, dancing."

"I can tolerate her dancing, if that's what she wants to do, but only if the dance is chaperoned and we bring her and pick her up after."

"When I first came to America and lived with my cousins Itzhak and Sadie, Sadie encouraged me to go dancing at the Settlement House. We did the Jewish dances and the American dances too, with a male partner."

"You did! Did your mother know?"

"She was in Europe. But no, I never told her."

"Hmm!"

"You should look at this dress she designed and made. She sews beautifully. She has the family talent."

"That dress is too short. It's lewd."

"I told her to lengthen it."

"I'll leave that to you, Fannie. I don't want to look at this dress. I want nothing to do with it."

"OK, I'll find out where there are chaperoned dances for kids her age."

"Do I have to get used to her short hair?"

"She likes it. She says it's easier than the braid."

"I hope you won't cut your hair."

"No, I like my hair. But I may get rid of my corset."

Marek struggles against wanting to smile. Then soberly, "You never needed it, anyway."

"And I may ask her to teach me the new dances."

Marek puts up his hands, palms toward Fannie to fend off the image. "Enough." Marek walks out of the kitchen into the living room, picks up the newspaper, opens it and disappears behind it.

Miriam appears in the kitchen wearing Adela's dress.

"Take that off now!" yells Fannie.

"But I want to show Tateh!" whimpers Adela.

"No!"

"Oh, Mama—why not? It makes me look pretty?" She stomps back to her room.

Days pass. Things are calm on the surface, but Fannie is preoccupied. *Are Marek and I too good to be true? I thought of him as safe, unshakable. Before we got married, we told each other all the bad things about ourselves. When Marek accepted me with all my badness, I finally felt safe, and I forgave myself for being bad. Now I see something I didn't know. Marek is a tortured soul. Can I feel safe and good with a tortured soul? Am I happy with Marek? I loved him. I think I still love him, but I'm loving a man who is not as strong or sure of himself as I thought he was. He helped me, but have I helped him?*

... too good to be true? What's not true about us? Are we afraid to be anything but careful and good with each other?

Suddenly, Fannie is startled to find herself thinking about Mischa.

Mischa was exciting. He was relentlessly intense about me and everything else, but I feared if he really knew me, he wouldn't want me. I didn't go to Palestine with him. Do I regret it? Do I miss him? Am I bad for thinking about Mischa? I kept the things he gave me, his mother's ring, and love notes. I can't think about this. I have a family to take care of. It is what it is.

Soon Fannie calls her friend Rachel to ask about chaperoned dances for teenagers. Rachel works at the library with kids Adela's age. Rachel says, "The YMHA on Nagle Avenue has chaperoned dances. I wish Kayla would go. She stays in the apartment except for school or to visit you. And Jacob only wants to play his ham radio. I'm worried about Jacob. I got a note from the high school saying he's skipping school. I'm meeting with his teacher next week. I'll ask Aber to come with me."

A Bespoke Suit

It's Sunday morning. Marek and Daniel walk into Marek's tailor shop. They will decide what kind of suit Marek will make for Daniel for his Bar Mitzvah in February. They'll choose the style from Marek's style book for boy's suits, and the fabric from Marek's cloth sample book.

Traditionally, bar mitzvah suits are black. Marek opens his cloth sample book to the black fabrics and says, "So Danny, as you can see, there is still a lot of variety you can have with black. You can have a thin stripe of white or a color. It won't show very much, but it gives the fabric some brightness. Or there can be a bit of color in the weave itself. You can choose the color, but I'm going to choose the fabric because I know what will cut and hang well."

Marek looks through the collection of black worsted material, touching each and rubbing it delicately between his fingers. "I think this weight might be right. It's sturdy material. It's also lightweight, so you can still wear it when the weather is warm. Touch it, Danny."

Daniel takes the fabric gently between his fingers, imitating the way he saw Marek do it. It's soft and pliant. He never thought about what fabric felt like before. These will be his first trousers. He has only worn knickers or shorts. He imagines with pleasure the soft cloth swinging against his bare legs.

"Yes, Tateh, it feels nice."

"Okay, we'll use this. Now look through the colors of black and see what you like." Marek hands him a magnifying glass, saying "Look closely and you'll see that each weave is a little different and will have some color in it that gives some life to the black."

"I see threads going up and down and threads going across. I always thought cloth was just smooth."

"Worsted is woven. That up and down and across is from the very fine threads of wool. It's what makes the cloth so strong, yet lightweight."

"Here is one with a little orange thread in it—sort of the color of my hair."

"Let's see Danny. Yes, I like that one. Is that what you want?"

"Yes Tateh."

"We'll order it. Let's look at the style book."

The style book for Daniel's size shows two suits; one with a belted jacket and the other is a typical suit that a grown man wears with cuffed trousers and a three-button jacket hanging straight with generous lapels.

"That one." Says Daniel, pointing to the grown-man suit. "Will my suit have a breast pocket, Tateh?"

"Yes, what is it about a breast pocket?"

"Because I see how you take your pen or wallet out of your breast pocket. It looks nice."

Marek smiles, "Since we're ordering the cloth, I think we should get enough to make you a vest and a pair of knickers as well as trousers."

"Can I have a cap too?"

Enthusiastically, "Yes, a cap too, for school with the knickers. While I'm at it, I'll also order some white percale cotton and make you a shirt. Then we'll go downtown and buy you a tie." Marek is smiling and speaking quickly, taking pleasure in the project and pleasure in Daniel's interest.

Marek goes on, "Your mother tells me her friend Sadie gave you her late husband, Itzhak's *tallit (prayer shawl)*. May his memory be for a blessing. This is good because Itzhak was a religious man and a cousin of your mother's, so it's handed down through the family. I have my grandfather's tallit, which of course I'll wear at your Bar Mitzvah.

Now we need to choose a lining and buttons. I think a dark gray lining will be good." Marek takes a bolt of silky material down from a shelf, then opens a drawer with many compartments filled with buttons of different colors and sizes. He takes out three black buttons of the same size for the jacket, three smaller buttons for the vest and three much smaller buttons for the trousers.

"So, let's measure you, Danny. Come, stand on this box in front of the mirror as straight and tall as you can." Daniel steps onto a wooden box so that he is the same height as Marek. Marek takes his tape measure from the large cutting table. Daniel is alert to Marek's quick, deft movements as he measures Daniel's shoulders, neck, chest, and arms, pausing after each measurement to write the number. He wraps the tape measure around Daniel's hips, then from waist to shoe. "Spread your legs." Marek measures the inside of Daniel's leg. Daniel takes a quick intake of breath. Then relief at Marek's swift, matter-of-fact action. He thinks, *He's like a doctor.*

"Oh yes! We need to measure your head for the cap."

"Okay," says Marek, "now I will make a pattern for you." From a big roll of paper, like the one at the butcher shop, Marek pulls out a sheet onto his cutting table. With a metal ruler and a pencil, he draws lines indicating Daniel's measurements. "See Danny, this will be the back of the jacket, and here will be the armhole." Daniel has no idea what he's looking at. All he can see are straight pencil lines in different directions. Marek goes on.

"And we leave extra room for the seam. You'll grow. So, for a boy's suit, we make the seams bigger to let it out as you grow. You should get a couple of years out of this suit and then we'll alter it to fit Simon." Marek rips off the paper and pulls out another sheet. He makes similar markings for the trousers. "Now I have your measurements, so I'll come back tonight and cut out the pattern."

"Tateh, have you made bar mitzvah suits for other boys?"

"Yes, of course. Why do you ask?"

"Are they all much bigger than me?"

"Some have been your size and some bigger. Why?"

"So, I'm small for my age?"

"You're on the short side and slim."

"Tateh, can you make the jacket, so it looks like I have bigger shoulders?"

"Why would you want that? If it doesn't fit well, the suit won't look good."

"I'm puny Tateh."

"What's puny Danny?"

"I'm skinny. I have no muscles. Jacob has muscles, even Herman has muscles, and he's younger than me. Jacob may try out boxing when he gains some more weight. It would take me forever to get big enough to try out boxing."

"Boxing! How do you know about boxing?"

"The kids at school talk about it and when I look at the *Forverts* (the Yiddish-American newspaper), they have stories about boxers. They even call it the Jewish sport."

"Yeah, I know about boxing. Does it interest you?"

"Would it give me muscles?"

"I don't know about the boxing, but the training would. Boxers must be strong and quick on their feet. *Hmmm, if he ever had to protect himself or someone else...*Let me think about this, Danny."

That night, while getting ready for bed, Marek brings it up with Fannie.

"I don't pay any attention to boxing, Marek. I think it's a shande for a Jewish boy to hit someone and try to knock him out. And our Danny is small. He'll be the first to get knocked out. He's a gentle boy and smart. He's not some street fighter. No, no boxing!"

"He's not going to start fighting right away, if ever. I don't think he cares about the fighting; he cares about building up his muscles. The training for boxing will make him strong and quick. He thinks he's puny."

"What's this 'puny'?"

"It's being weak and skinny, like you can't stand up for yourself if someone attacks you or if you want to protect someone from being attacked. If I had felt strong, I wouldn't have picked up that knife."

"Oh, so that's it. You want Danny to be a fighter because you didn't risk your life beating up your mother's attacker."

"You're not understanding me, Fannie! He may never want to fight. He only wants to be strong."

"How do you know he'll never want to fight when he sees the other kids fight?"

"Fannie, trust me on this. You know nothing about boxing. A boy hates being weak, and so does a man."

"Oh, so you're going to learn to fight too!"

"No, it's too late for me. I wish my father cared that I felt weak and skinny."

Fannie thinks, *He really can't let go of this dybbuk of his.* "Look, what if I say it's okay but only for what you call this 'training' and tell Daniel, from the start, it's fine for him to build up his body but no fighting, no knocking people out or getting knocked out." *I don't understand how he can still be so haunted. He did what he had to do with that knife.*

"Okay, I'll figure it out. Jacob may be interested in boxing, too."

"Marek, I can't think about that now!" *Oy! Is everyone going meshuga?*

Marek, now in bed, turns away. *I'll find some good training for Danny. He'll thank me for it and maybe Fannie will too someday. Danny will never have to use a weapon to protect himself or someone else—unless there's another war—please, God—No!*

Bar Mitzvah

It's an afternoon in early February 1926. Daniel is sitting alone at the dining room table studying for his Bar Mitzvah. The big day will be on February 20th. He must write a speech but pauses his studying and comes to Fannie, who is sewing in her work alcove. He pulls up a chair.

"Mama, I want to know more about my father. You said you didn't know him, but if the woman who gave birth to me was your closest friend, didn't she tell you about him?"

Fannie thinks, *Here comes the big question. Is he ready for the answer? Am I ready to tell him? I can't lie to him. It's not like I haven't rehearsed for this day.*

Fannie takes a deep breath, trying to steady herself and her voice. She starts off slowly. "Hannah, like me, when she came to this country, was very poor. She met a man who said he loved her and promised to take care of her."

"How was he going to take care of her?" asks Daniel.

"He paid for her rent and food. And he gave her money to send to her family in Europe. It was very important to her to help her family. She believed he loved her, but when she became pregnant with you, he told her she had to give you to the orphanage, or he would put you and her out on the street."

"He didn't want me."

"Hannah would never give you up. She loved you. For a while, she hid you with a woman who took care of you. Hannah visited you every day and even nursed you. She made this man believe she had taken you to the orphanage."

"Why didn't she run away from him when she knew he didn't want me?"

"Because then she'd have no money to live and care for you. Being so poor trapped her into staying with him."

"You mean she could have left me in a shopping bag like the baby I found?"

"Hannah could never do that. She was trying to find another way. If she kept you a secret from him, she knew you got good care, and she could be with you for a part of every day. But then a rumor started that she had kept you."

"Who told the rumor?"

"I think it was a relative of the woman who took care of you. The person may not have known it was a secret. But that's when Hannah took you and fled to Palestine to make sure you and she could be together and have a good life. We had a friend in Palestine, Mischa, who helped the two of you to get settled in a kibbutz. Hannah always wanted to be an actress. In Palestine, she created plays for the children of the kibbutz. Life was good there until she got so sick."

Daniel hears this and looks pensive. "So, Mama, my mother Hannah was a good woman, but my father was a bad man?"

"Yes, Danny."

There's a long pause. Daniel looks away pensively, then says, "Okay Mama. I need to study now." He leaves the kitchen and goes back to the dining room table.

Fannie takes a deep breath. *It's only a matter of time before he realizes the story isn't the whole truth. Should I have painted Mendl as bad? He was bad. If Danny ever finds out what he was, he'll know just how bad he was.*

It is the month of Adar, 5686. On this day, the Horvath family enters Temple Emanu-El, the reformed congregation where Marek brought Fannie soon after their marriage. Daniel already arrived an hour before his family. The rabbi offered to bring him, telling Marek and Fannie that this private time with the rabbi helped to quiet the jitters of the bar mitzvah boy before the ceremony.

Soon Fannie's brother Aber arrives. He is with Rachel, Kayla and Jacob. Next comes Fannie's friend Sadie with her daughter Esther. She is called "Little Esther" by Fannie because of Fannie's twin sister Esther.

Here comes Rivka, Fannie's eldest sister, with her husband Meyer. The sanctuary fills with friends and their families. The organ plays softly.

As people file in, Fannie and Marek greet them. Many hugs are exchanged between both men and women. Fannie and Marek, with their children, take their seats in the front row. The air smells of recently applied perfume and shaving soap. The organ is playing a melody Fannie recognizes from her childhood. She is transported to the great synagogue in Bolekhiv. A vision of Aber as a thirteen-year-old bar mitzvah is so vivid in her mind's eye, she gasps. In that old synagogue, with its tall windows, she remembers the Zodiac signs painted on the walls. All the men sit on the ground floor. She sits in the balcony reserved for women. With her are her mother, Rivka and her sister, Esther, dear Esther.

Daniel's friend Herman's family comes to congratulate Marek and Fannie, and Fannie is swept back to the present.

The organ plays louder, a cue for everyone to be seated. Fannie settles back and touches her blue shawl. The congregation continue to whisper among themselves.

Sitting on the *bimah* (platform) are the rabbi and Daniel. Daniel looks handsome in his suit with Itzhak's tallit draped around his shoulders. Several other members of the congregation also sit on the bimah. Again, Fannie is in the past remembering the day Hannah's sister brought Daniel to her from Palestine. *This was the first day of my new life. So many good things followed.*

Marek, seated next to her, reaches for her hand. They entwine their fingers. She looks up at him and sees he has tears in his eyes, and so does she. *We've traveled for greater distances than the miles between Europe and New York. Here we sit in a service not only next to each other, but we can touch hands and know here and now it is sanctified. The men who sit on the bimah with Rabbi Berliner and Danny are not all old with long beards. They're clean-shaven and only a few of the boys who are here today wear payes. (side curls). When I came to America, I had to work on Saturday. If I didn't change to American ways, I wouldn't have survived. This temple, with its polished dark wood, its stained-glass windows, and its well-dressed people, shows achievement and wealth. I came to America with nothing and here I am with my own family, with some of my brothers and sisters, and we're not poor.*

Marek takes out his handkerchief, wipes his eyes, and reflects, *I'm so blessed with my family here, but oh how I wish my mother and sisters could be here today. My father, may his memory be for a blessing, would kvell (be proud) to see his eldest grandson a Bar Mitzvah. They write saying they're all fine in Budapest. I hope that's so. They don't want to leave. My mother now lives with my sister. She could live with us.*

Look at our Daniel in his grown-up suit. It turned out very well, if I may say so. He's started to train at the boy's gym. If he gets the muscles he hopes for, that suit won't fit him for more than a year.

Marek is distracted from his thoughts when he sees Adela whispering to a boy in the pew behind her.

"Fannie, who's Adela talking to?"

"A boy from her confirmation class."

"At least it's someone her age. She looks good. Where did she get her dress?" Adela is wearing a turquoise velvet dress, cut in the flapper style, but not too short. Over it, she wears a short jacket of the same material.

"She made it Marek. She really is talented."

"Did she use a store pattern?"

"Yes. You know she really wants you to forgive her, and I suspect she may even want to work in the store with you after school."

"Hmm. I could teach her to make her own patterns. And she could help with the sewing after I do the cutting."

"Ask her."

"Maybe I will. Is she still interested in dancing?"

"Yes, I take her to a social dancing class at the Nagle Avenue Y. I've watched it. They do the traditional Jewish dances and the American dances. Same as when I went to the settlement house. But now it's jazz music instead of the waltz."

The rabbi rises and steps to the podium to welcome the congregation. He also announces that today, Daniel Horvath, the son of Marek and Fannie Horvath, brother of Adela, Simon and Miriam, and nephew of Rivka, Aber, Kayla and Jacob Liebermann, will be called to the Torah.

The Saturday morning service begins. When it is time to read the Torah portion for the day, Daniel steps to the podium. The rabbi stands beside him, blesses the Torah and points to the passage where Daniel is to start.

In a sweet mezzo-soprano voice, Daniel chants his Torah portion. He kept this secret from his family. He wanted to show he could not only read the Hebrew script but also chant it in the ancient way. Daniel concludes his chanting, and the rabbi calls Marek to the bimah to recite a prayer and bless his son. Marek comes up, recites a traditional prayer and in English says, "Daniel, I am so proud of you today, but not only today. You are a son who always makes your parents proud because of your good moral character and kind ways. On this special day, I thank the Lord for you and give you my deepest blessing." He cups Daniel's head in his hands and kisses him.

The rabbi calls up Aber. The next prayer will be given by Daniel's uncle, Aber Liebermann. Aber limps to the stage with his cane. He lost some toes to frostbite on the Russian front during the First World War. Aber is a tall man with a deep, resonant voice. He chants a traditional prayer in a melodious baritone.

Daniel takes a deep breath and is ready to begin his speech. Only the rabbi knows what he is about to say.

Daniel's voice is shaky at first and he clutches the pages of his speech. "Good morning and thank you for coming to my Bar Mitzvah ceremony. I want to thank Rabbi Berliner for helping me with my Torah portion and my speech. I want to thank my parents for loving me. Thank you to my little brother and sister Simon and Miriam for letting me boss them around. Thank you to my sister Adela for all the times she rolls her eyes at me and thinks I'm meshuga." *Laughter from the congregation.*

"I'll start." The laughter has put Daniel at ease and from here on his voice takes on a new resonance. He almost looks taller. "I asked the rabbi if the date of my bar mitzvah and Torah portion could fall during the month of Adar, the month when Moses was born. This meant delaying my Bar Mitzvah, but Rabbi Berliner said it was okay to do for a good reason. This portion of the Torah describes how Moses's mother, when she learned about Pharaoh's order that all newborn Jewish males be slaughtered, first hid her baby but soon, to save him from death, put him into a basket and set it to float down the Nile River. When Pharoh's daughter found Moses, she wanted to raise him as her son. She sent for a Hebrew woman to nurse him. Who should that woman turn out to be? It was Moses' very own mother.

I wanted the story of the baby Moses to be part of my Bar Mitzvah for a lot of reasons.

The first reason is my friend Herman and I found an abandoned baby on the street, a baby girl. Hi Herman! Daniel waves and Herman waves back. We brought the poor little baby to my mother, who cleaned and fed her. My mother and I, with my sisters and brother brought the child to the Medical Center where they cared for her. She had been kidnapped and then left on the street. We are happy to say she is with her grandmother now who will care for her.

This experience made me think about my own beginnings. My mother and father who raise me, who love me and who I love more than I can ever say, are not my first mother and father. I was born to a woman named Hannah. I will call her First Mother Hannah. My mother who raises me is Fannie and I will call her My Mother. My father, Marek, is my father who raises me. I don't know the name of the father who created me. I will call him Unknown."

Someone in the audience gasps.

"First Mother Hannah was my mother's best friend. They met on the ship that brought them to America from a part of Austria that is now Poland. They were only around fifteen years old and very poor. They each came alone, without their parents or brothers and sisters. Both hoped to work, send money to their families, and bring them to America. Being so young, they faced hard times, but they always helped each other and grew to love each other like sisters. Soon, First Mother Hannah put her trust in the man, Unknown. He claimed he loved her and promised to take care of her. But when he learned she was going to have a baby, me, he said she had to give me to an orphanage, or he would put both of us out on the street. First Mother Hannah was so poor that she depended on Unknown for her life and my life. Still, she refused to get rid of me. Instead, she hid me. But soon the secret was out. Quickly, she took me, and we fled to Palestine, to a kibbutz. Finally, we were together and safe.

But when I was about a year and a half old, she got very sick and knew she was going to die soon. She didn't want to die without being sure who would raise me, so she had her sister bring me to her best friend, Fannie, my new mother, where she knew I would be loved and cared for. And she was right.

My father, Marek, is everything I could ever wish for in a father. He loves me and all of us. He is kind and respected by everyone. I have the best family. People who know my family agree.

Going back to the story of Moses, my middle name is Moshe. First Mother Hannah did not give me that name. My parents, Marek and Fannie, added the name Moshe because, like Moses, I was first hidden and then given away as an act of love and protection. So why am I telling you this on this day of my Bar Mitzvah?

When the rabbi helped me prepare for today's Torah reading and for my speech, he said this would be a time to immerse myself in my Torah portion, to study carefully, and to note all the questions that come to mind. The right questions, Rabbi said, are more important than the right answers. So here are my questions as I studied the story of Moses.

Did Moses ever learn that Pharoh's daughter was not his first mother? And what about Moses' father? The only thing we learn about him is he was from the tribe of Levi. Half of Moses came from this man. Half of me came from Unknown. Who is Unknown? Perhaps, listening to this, you wonder why I should even ask the question. I'm being raised by a wonderful father. I don't need another father. You're right. I don't need a father. I have one. But I need to know about this missing part of me.

I'm glad my mother, Fannie, can tell me some things about First Mother Hannah. But there is more to know. But Unknown, I know nothing about him except that he was mean. Do I pass him on the street? Does he know who I am? Does he think about me? Did he have other children? They would be partly my brothers and sisters. Is he a good man now? Is he sorry for being so mean to my first mother, Hannah? I hope so. But even if he is still a bad man, I want to know who he is. This is a part of me that is missing. I'm grateful for the family I have, but I need to know who I came from.

I know I'm Daniel Moshe Horvath, beloved son of my parents Marek and Fannie. For most children, like my brother and sister Miriam and Simon, they can say that sentence about themselves and it's true from the moment they were born. They know who made them. I don't know the people who made me. My mother tells me when I came to her, I could walk and feed myself. I drank from a cup, and I had a few words, all Hebrew words. I said Ima for Mama. I learned recently when a Hebrew lullaby was taught at school; I seemed to know it and didn't know I knew it. What was it like for me to never see my first mother again? My sister Adela's first mother died too. Adela was two. She said she has some blurry memories. I have no memory of my mother, Hannah, even though she took good care of me.

Today, is my Bar Mitzvah. I join the adult Jewish community. My understanding of what it means to be a respectable and moral Jewish man is to never be afraid of the truth. In ancient times, the prophets taught us to seek the truth. It is a part of our heritage. I, too, will try to seek the truth through my life, but I must start with the truth of my beginnings. Even if I don't find the answers, I must still ask the questions.

Thank you for listening to my speech today."

There is a long silence in the congregation, followed by sounds of quiet murmurings.

The rabbi shakes Daniel's hand and begins to recite prayers that conclude the service.

Marek and Fannie turn toward each other. They both have tears running down their cheeks. Marek puts his arm around Fannie's shoulders.

Adela thinks, *Wow Danny, you're brave for a little brother. It makes me want to ask a lot more questions about what my first mother was like. But Tateh can answer those. Who can answer Danny's questions about someone unknown?*

Marek thinks, *I don't understand it. He has us. Let it be. Why does he think he has to know such a miserable story?*

Fannie reflects, *Oh Danny, Danny, Danny you will be so hurt. And yet I can understand. I felt something rest in me when Dr. Weiss told me about Piotr, if Piotr is who I suspect he is. If he is, he's a good man. I don't know why, but there is something about knowing a name. Hannah's man, say his name! Mendl, called Jack, is a devil. What do I need to tell Danny now? Can he bear the truth? Maybe knowing Mendl's name will be helpful. I don't think I ever heard his last name.*

Miriam leans toward Fannie, "Mama, can we visit the baby?"

A man in the congregation whispers to the woman next to him, "I'll bet somebody wrote that speech for him."

Herman thinks, *Why was I so scared to look in that bag? Danny is so smart and brave. Sometimes I wonder why he wants me as his friend.*

A woman in the congregation whispers to the man next to her, "I never heard anything so selfish! He's hurting his parents who have sacrificed for him and given him a perfect home. How ungrateful!"

Another woman whispers to the man next to her, "I'm not sure about these new personal bar mitzvah speeches the rabbi is encouraging. Shouldn't a speech be about helping the poor or healing the world?"

The man sitting with her answers, "He's asking questions and seeking truth. As he said, it's part of our heritage. First, he needs to seek the truth about himself."

Simon thinks *Danny could have gone to the orphanage, and I would never know him.*

Jacob thinks, *You little squirt! You have it so good, and you think you're so good. You want to go looking for trouble in your perfect life. I want to smash that baby face of yours!*

Aber thinks, *Oh Daniel, my boy, you are in for a rough ride. Maybe I can help. I'll talk to Fannie and Marek.*

Some congregants and many friends stop to congratulate Daniel and his parents. Slowly they file into a hall where there is a large challah and many bottles of wine. The rabbi blesses the bread and wine, and people take their seats at luncheon tables. Daniel and his family sit at an elevated table. The catered lunch is served. Conversation is lively and noisy. As the meal draws to a close, a klezmer band enters and starts to play. Many adults and children get up to dance. The smaller children run around while the music plays. A group of men approach Marek and Fannie. They already have Daniel in tow. They pull the threesome into the center of the room and sit them on three straight-back chairs. The klezmer band is playing the new tune from Palestine, The Hora. As soon as the three are seated, the crowd of men lift the three chairs and dance to the music, now played at breakneck speed. A crowd gathers around in an outer circle to clap or to grab the dancers' hands and join in. Soon Fannie and Marek are brought down and released. But Daniel is still aloft while the men vigorously pump his chair higher and higher. The music goes even faster. Daniel clings to his seat, both laughing and looking terrified. Next, a group of men do a bottle dance, the empty wine bottles balanced on their heads as they clasp hands in a line doing a graceful grapevine step.

Soon it's time for the band to play jazz tunes. All the teenagers and a few women join in to dance the Charleston. Fannie hesitates for a moment, but Adela grabs her hand, pulling her into the fray, shows her the steps and Fannie catches on. Adela breathlessly calls out over the din, "Jeepers Mama, you're really good. I never knew you could dance."

Daniel goes over to Esther, Sadie's daughter, who is the same age as he. Sadie has remained Orthodox. She and Esther are dressed conservatively in long, dark dresses with long sleeves. Sadie wears a *tichel* (headscarf) to cover her hair. Daniel asks Esther if she would like to dance. Esther starts to say "yes" but Sadie interrupts to say, "Esther may dance but only with other girls doing the Jewish dances." Daniel lingers for a while speaking with Esther. He looks around the hall to see if he can find Jacob. He doesn't see him, so he joins his friends.

The party ends. The tired, flushed crowd thins out. Gifts for Daniel sit on a table near the door. Rachel, smiling, walks up to Daniel, holding his gift. She hugs him and gives him the package, saying, "Danny, I want to be with you as you open this. I don't think anyone else will give you this. Open it now." Daniel tears off the wrapping paper. It's <u>Leaves of Grass</u> by Walt Whitman.

"Danny, when I chose this for you, I didn't realize how right the choice was until I heard your speech today. Whitman was a man who courageously pursued his need to know himself. Through his poems, he generously inspired others to do the same. I think this is what you did today." Daniel, holding the book, wraps his arms around Rachel and kisses her on the cheek.

At one of the tables, Aber is talking with Marek and Fannie. Soon, he comes up to Daniel and brings him to a corner of the room. Putting his arm around Daniel's shoulders, he says, "Dan, I'm proud to be your uncle. You are a deep thinker and have set for yourself an important and difficult quest. I will be honored to help you anyway I can."

"Thank you, Uncle Aber."

"I have a piece of advice for you now. Start your search where you already have some clues. You have almost no clues about the man you call Unknown, but you have some clues about your first mother. You know something about her good character from your mother Fannie, and you know you spent time with her in Palestine. I suggest you start by trying to learn more about your time with her there. Your mother has the friend in Palestine who helped. I think his name is Mischa. Maybe start with Mischa and what he may remember from that time. Looking for Unknown is going to be more difficult. Learning more about Hannah may lead to some clues about Unknown." Daniel is quiet. He nods as he listens to Aber.

Dear Uncle Mischa

Dear Mischa, I think I should call you Uncle Mischa, so, Dear Uncle Mischa,

I am Daniel Horvath. When you knew me, I was a baby, the son of Hannah Weitzner. Do you remember me? I was too young to remember you. When my mother Hannah died in Palestine, I was brought to America and given to my second mother, Fannie Liebermann Horvath. You were a good friend of both, so that is I why I should call you Uncle.

When I asked my mother, Fannie, if she knew anyone in Palestine who could tell me about my first mother, she gave me your address. She said she had not heard from you for a long time and was not sure if you were still living at Kibbutz Degania, so I hope you get this letter.

Two weeks ago, I had my Bar Mitzvah at Temple Emanu-El. My speech was about a question very important to me. While I love my mother Fannie, and my father, Marek, very much, I am curious about my first mother, Hannah, and my life in Palestine. You are the only person I know of who can tell me about that time. If you know anything about my first father, I hope you will also tell me about him.

Sincerely,
Daniel Moshe Horvath
P.S. I am including a copy of my speech.

Six weeks later, a letter arrives addressed to Daniel. It is not the usual thin blue paper letter that comes from Budapest or Vienna but is in a regular envelope and is surprisingly thick. It is from Mischa in Palestine. When Daniel opens it, photographs spill onto the table. One photograph is of a woman surrounded by children. The woman is wearing a plain short-sleeve shirt and pants and a scarf wrapped around her head. A long, thick braid hangs over one shoulder. She is smiling. Even in a black-and-white photo, she looks tan and strong. There is another photo of a baby holding two oranges and one of a woman holding a baby on her hip. Daniel immediately knows these are pictures of Hannah and himself, but it barely registers at first. He reads the letter.

Dear Daniel,

I am so happy to hear from you. From your letter, I get the sense that your family is doing well. Congratulations on your Bar Mitzvah. Your speech is very important and thoughtful.

Yes, I remember you and your mother, Hannah. May her memory be for a blessing. You and my daughter Shira were in the same nursery. Your mother and I picked you and Shira up at the same time after work. Often, on Saturdays, you and your mother visited my family. So, I have vivid memories of you. You were a cheerful baby until your mother fell ill. That was very difficult for you to understand at such a young age. Your mother's sister came to take care of both of you. I believe her name is Leah. She lived somewhere in Canada. After the sad passing of your mother, Leah brought you to live with your mother, Fannie. Well, Daniel, that was the sad part of your life here at our kibbutz. There was a joyful part before your mother fell ill.

Your mother, Hannah, was a talented actress and created a children's theater here at the kibbutz. They put on a lot of plays, sometimes written by the children and sometimes by members of the kibbutz.

The most memorable play your mother arranged was one in which each child told about their journey to Palestine. The children had come mostly from places in Europe, but there were also children from Africa and one from India. It was a wonderful production. By popular demand, it was repeated over the months several times.

I know your mother was a talented actress because she and some other grown-ups put on a production of Shakespeare's <u>The Tempest.</u> She had a leading part in that. Her character's name was Miranda. It was a good choice for the kibbutz. It's about a shipwreck, and the passengers land in a strange country. Everyone who comes here knows how it is to be a stranger in a strange land.

Every Tuesday and Thursday, the adults of the kibbutz gather to learn modern Hebrew. The adults are expected to teach the children. After your mother learned Hebrew, in her spare time, she helped others to practice.

Your mother also worked in the kitchen garden, where she tended the vegetables and herbs for our meals. When it was time to pick oranges—we have a large orange grove—your mother was a fast orange picker. In one photograph, you can see a picture of you. Maybe you were around a year old. You have a small orange in each hand. You must have been very pleased with yourself holding two oranges because, as you can see, you have a big smile.

When your mother picked you up at night, she lifted you up onto her hip and I don't think she let go of you until she brought you to the nursery again the following morning. When she came to supper, you sat on her lap the whole time and ate off her plate. You can see her holding you in one photo. I often heard her singing to you. You loved the Hebrew lullaby, Numi, Numi.

You were a curious and lively baby who smiled at everyone. But when your mother fell ill, you became more serious. You were especially upset because she could no longer get out of bed to play with you. You had just learned to walk, and you kept bringing her shoes to her. Still, from her bed, she sang to you. You usually tried to climb into bed with her. Whoever was helping would pick you up and tuck you in, and this soothed both of you.

Everyone in the kibbutz knew your mother, Hannah, and we all mourned her passing. We hoped you would stay, but we understood Hannah's powerful wish for her sister to bring you to your mother Fannie. Hannah and Fannie loved one another like sisters and always helped each other. Hannah's wish for you was right and was the wisest and best thing she could do. I supported her with that decision because I knew your mother, Fannie, would love you deeply and be a wonderful mother.

Before I came to Palestine, I knew your mother, Fannie, in New York. We met when we both worked at the Triangle Dress Factory. Please give her my warmest greetings. From what I remember about her, I am sure she would be glad for you to learn and know all you can about your mother, Hannah.

I know nothing about the man who was your first father. Almost everyone who came to Palestine at the time came because their lives had become very difficult. Usually, they were poor and had suffered. We welcomed everyone and never asked them about their previous life. If they talked about it, of course we listened. I know little about your mother, Hannah's, life in New York. However, she did sometimes talk about her life in Lviv before going to New York. She had a large family and could help many of them leave Europe and immigrate to Canada. I am sure your mother, Fannie, heard some of those stories from Hannah.

Life at the kibbutz has worked well for our family. Along with our daughter Shira, who is now twelve years old, we have two sons, Yoram, ten, and Omri, eight. My wife is a teacher for children ages six to eleven.

I am now an administrator of the kibbutz. As we keep creating this homeland for our wandering people, we know there is great meaning in our work. We believe in the power of a community with an important shared mission. It is not all work. We have a lot of music and dance here as a part of our life. Also, I love to go down to the Sea of Galilee at night and look at the stars. The night sky here is so bright and vivid. My children and I can name the constellations and often see shooting stars and comets.

Daniel, I wish you courage and luck in your quest to answer your questions about your beginnings. If you think I can give you more of the information you are searching for, please write again. Please know, if you ever come to Palestine, we welcome you to Kibbutz Degania.

Yours sincerely,
Uncle Mischa

Daniel tucks the letter back into its envelope. He brings the photographs to the window and in the afternoon light studies them carefully, looking as closely as he can at the image of the woman. He climbs into the picture and takes his place on her hip. His small legs wrap around her waist so tightly she does not really need to hold him for him to stay exactly where he is. But she holds him as snugly as he holds her. He can feel her arm around his back, supporting him like the back of a chair. Her hand against his hip is open, fingers apart and warm. If either she or he were to let go, he would still be safe in his seat. He rests his head against her shoulder. He looks peaceful but also curious at whoever takes the photo. Perhaps the photographer interrupted them. Who was the photographer? Was it Uncle Mischa?

Daniel takes the letter out of the envelope and reads it again. He's surprised to hear himself humming the lullaby, *Numi, Numi*. This woman, his first mother, looks so healthy in these photos. *I can't imagine her being sick. And I kept bringing her shoes to her!*

He rereads the letter and looks again at the photos. He arranges them, first Hannah with the group of children, then himself with the oranges and finally he and Hannah together. *Can I miss a mama I don't remember?*

Daniel puts the photos back in the envelope. He is tired, but not sleepy, just tired. He places the envelope under his pillow and lies down, facing the wall. His mind swirls with the images in the photos. They are now full of color, movement, and the fragrance of oranges.

Days pass. It is Friday morning when Fannie cleans for the Sabbath. She will change the sheets on five beds. She enters Simon and Daniel's room and pulls the sheets off their beds. She sees the envelope, picks it up to put it on the bedside table and gasps when she sees it's from Mischa. *So, he did write to Mischa. He didn't tell me. And Mischa answered.* Fannie reaches for the letter. *Leave it!* She scolds. She can't stop looking at it. *It's thick. It probably has photos.* Fannie allows herself to peer into the open side of the envelope and can see that indeed there are a few photos. *Leave it! He asked me if I knew Mischa's address. Of course, he knows I know he intended to write to him. I gave him the address. Why didn't he tell me? Could Mischa have written to him about our romance? Oh, I hope not.* She gathers the sheets and leaves the room. At two o'clock, she takes a break from the preparations for dinner. At the kitchen table with her tea, she tries to look at the newspaper, but her mind keeps drifting back to Daniel's envelope. *I won't read the letter. I'll only look at the pictures.*

Fannie goes back to Daniel's room and quickly takes only the photos out of the envelope. She goes to the window and looks first at the one of Hannah surrounded by children. *She looks so beautiful, so healthy. Oh, Hannah, I miss you.* Tears spring to Fannie's eyes. She looks at the photo of Daniel and the oranges. *Danny, Danny, there you are. That is the part of your babyhood I missed. I think you were about six months old when you and Hannah left for Palestine, and you were there for about a year. Look at you, smiling, so pleased with yourself.* Fannie pulls out the last photo of Hannah and Daniel. She looks at it and bursts into tears. She must sit down on the edge of Daniel's bed. *Why am I crying like this? Nothing surprises me about this picture. Hannah loved Danny with all her heart from the moment he was born, even before he was born. It's no surprise they look so loving together. What makes me cry so? I miss you, Hannah. I think of you every day. Who took this picture? Mischa? Could this have been my life? I still may have ended up with Daniel if I had gone with Mischa.* When calm again, Fannie takes the three photos and puts them back into the envelope. *Now where did Danny have this envelope? Oh yes, it was under his pillow.* She replaces it.

Two hours later Fannie hears Daniel screaming at Simon. "Simon, you idiot, how dare you look at my mail? That's my private mail. I could punch you! I should punch you!"

Simon, bewildered, "I don't know what you're talking about, Danny. I never looked at your stupid mail."

"Mama!" Daniel yells, "Simon took my mail, my private property." Fannie rushes in.

"No Danny, Fannie yells running into the room. Simon didn't look at your mail."

"See" says Simon, "I don't care about your dumb mail or any of your, oh so precious, stuff. You always blame me if something isn't exactly like you want it in this room. I can't wait for you to grow-up and move out."

"Okay Simon, enough. Danny knows now it wasn't you. Danny, come into the kitchen; I need to talk to you." Daniel picks up a sweater on Simon's bed and flings it across the room. "Okay Danny, enough!" scolds Fannie.

In the kitchen, Daniel is steaming. "Mama, I had a private letter under my pillow, and someone read it."

"How do you know?"

"There were photos in it, and I arranged them the way I wanted to look at them again and they were out of order."

"Danny, it was me who looked in the envelope. I saw it when I changed the sheets, and I saw it was from Palestine. I looked at the pictures, but I promise you I did not read the letter."

"Mama! That letter and the pictures are my private life. It's a part of my life you had nothing to do with. I was with my first mama then and I didn't even know you. That's mine and only mine, and you can't snoop into what isn't yours."

"Danny, I'm sorry. But your first mama as you know, was my dearest friend. When I saw the letter was thick and from Palestine, I hoped there would be photos of Hannah and you."

Daniel is shouting, "They were sent to me, not to you. She was my first mother, my first MOTHER! What's more important to a kid than a MOTHER! I don't care if she was your friend." He stomps out of the kitchen.

"Fannie is breathless. *What have I done? Oh Danny, what have I done?*

She hears Marek's key in the door. "I'm home! I brought flowers for Shabbos."

Within minutes, the doorbell rings. Rachel, Aber, Kayla and Jacob arrive.

The meal and prayers go on. Daniel scowls throughout dinner. Marek asks him what's wrong. Daniel says "Nothing, I'm just upset about something and I'm not going to talk about it."

Fannie thinks, *Is it all about my snooping or was there something in the letter that upset him? I don't get these teenage kids! Little kids I do fine with, but these teenagers, it's too hard! They are so different from me at their age, or anyone in my family. I can't talk to Marek about this, not about a letter from Mischa. Marek is a good man—but not as strong as I thought. Those pictures of*

Hannah. I could have gone to Palestine with Mischa. I'd have Daniel, but not the other three. But I'd have Mischa's kids. Hannah and I could have worked together in the theater there. I'd design the costumes. I could have helped when she was so sick.

Fannie comes out of her reverie. Marek is saying the closing prayers. Sensing something is going on in the family, Aber, Rachel, Kayla and Jacob leave early. Daniel tells Marek he's going to his friend Heman's apartment. Marek tells him to be back by nine.

Marek offers to help clean up. Adela and the twins are bringing in the plates. Fannie tells them all to relax. She'll deal with the cleaning up tonight. They seem surprised but don't insist. Fannie is glad to be alone in the kitchen. She turns on the water and starts soaping and scrubbing the pots. The running water, the suds and the warmth soothe.

Could Mischa and I have brought Aber, Rivka, Kayla and Jacob to Palestine? Mischa and I would never have had the money to do it. But maybe some Jewish organization would have helped them? What a different life I might have had! Would I have been happier with Mischa? Some part of me got lost when I came to America. STOP IT FANNIE! This is a waste of time. What IS is what IS. These teenagers turn my head upside down.

Hmm, there was no photo of Mischa. Maybe he took the pictures.

I was so lively with Mischa. I see that life now in Adela. Is it gone in me? I've gotten stodgy. Oh Mischa! Maybe Marek isn't the only one with a dybbuk. Mischa, are you my dybbuk? And Danny isn't the only one who hides things. I still have that rucksack hidden in the back of the closet, filled with the things Mischa gave me. Should I get rid of it? How would I ever explain to Marek why I kept it? Maybe I'll ask Rachel to keep it.

I hid myself from Mischa. I didn't tell him all the horrible things I did before we met. I couldn't. Before I loved Marek, I told him, and he loved me anyway. He said, "Trying to survive can be ugly." Marek seemed so strong then. Now he thinks Danny must learn to fight!

Rachel and Aber

Rachel leaves the library early. She has an appointment at Jacob's school, George Washington High School, where she and Aber will meet with the principal and Jacob's homeroom teacher. As she walks, Rachel hears the quick clicks of her short, stout one-inch heels. Her wildly curly brown hair is held in place by her cloche hat that is pulled down to the tops of her large brown eyes. Today, under her coat, she wears a calf-length pleated skirt and jacket, intending to look more sedate than in her usual drop-waist dresses that allow her to move easily with the children in the library. Aber is waiting for her outside the school's entrance. He is cold and his somewhat hollow-cheeked face looks even more pinched under his black wool knitted cap. He too comes from work and wears his customary work clothes, an un-ironed, buttoned shirt with a gray canvas vest and jacket, black woolen pants and scuffed short boots.

Rachel joins him. They don't speak but when their eyes meet, Rachel shrugs slightly, conveying, *I don't know what to expect here.* Aber understands and nods. As they enter, Aber pulls off his cap. The two are directed to the office of the principal, Miss Sinclair. The door to the office opens. Miss Sinclair is a tall, slim, fine-boned woman in her fifties. Her straight blond-gray hair is caught up in a low bun resting at the nape of her long neck. She wears a tailored tweed skirt and jacket.

"Mr. and Mrs. Liebermann, please come in. Miss Kelly will be along soon." Her manner of speech has the diction of a New Yorker whose relatives arrived many generations ago.

Miss Sinclair points to two wooden chairs and they all sit. Rachel immediately explains,

"Miss Sinclair, we aren't Jacob's parents, and we aren't a married couple." Gesturing to Aber, "Aber Liebermann, is Jacob's eldest brother, and I'm Rachel Kaminski, a close family friend. Jacob and his sister Kayla Liebermann, a junior here at the school, both live with me."

Miss Sinclair looks at Rachel and Aber. There is a pause as she takes in the information. She asks, "Are Jacob and Kayla's parents living?"

Aber answers, "No, Miss Sinclair, our parents both died in Europe some years before we came to America in 1919."

She answers, "I'm sorry I but don't understand."

Aber repeats what he said more slowly and apologizes for his heavy accent.

"So sorry." She says and makes a note on her pad.

Miss Kelly knocks and enters. She is a round and pleasant-looking woman in her forties with high color in her round cheeks. She is dressed in a brown wool skirt and a silky beige blouse that slightly strains over her ample bosom. Miss Sinclair explains who Aber and Rachel are and that Jacob was orphaned when he lived in Europe. Miss Kelly settles into her seat and Miss Sinclair suggests Miss Kelly begin.

"I'm so glad to be meeting with you. I've been worried about Jacob because there's been a gradual change in him since he entered high school. At the beginning of the year, I could see that, while he is a quiet boy, he was serious about his schoolwork and came to school regularly. But his performance in school has fallen off. He's been absent more often. I think he looks quite sad and tired too. I have reports from his teachers that he sometimes falls asleep in class. What have either of you noticed about him at home?" Aber speaks first. Miss Kelly has no trouble understanding him.

"I don't live with Jacob, but I see him on both days of every weekend. He helps me in my carpentry business. Sometimes he seems tired when I pick him up but soon, he perks up and seems to like the work. He's on his way to becoming a decent carpenter. I rely on him."

Rachel chimes in. "At home, Jacob spends a lot of time in his room on his ham radio. I'm so sorry to hear he's missing school. I leave early for work at the library; I wake Jacob and Kayla before I leave and get home after they do. The change I've noticed is that since the school year began, Jacob spends more and more time in his room."

Miss Kelly speaks, "I didn't realize, Kayla Liebermann is Jacob's older sister. She too is quiet, but she's an excellent student. In her freshman year, she was also in my homeroom. I hope she can go to Hunter College when she graduates."

"I hope so too." Says Rachel. "I graduated from Hunter. But how can we help Jacob?"

Miss Kelly continues decisively, but warmly. "I think first he should see a doctor to make sure he's healthy. He also seems troubled. I see his sad expression. It sounds as though he's at his best when working with you, Mr. Liebermann, so obviously that should continue. A lot of the boys have become fascinated by ham radio. I don't think it's a bad thing, but it sounds like it has taken over Jacob's time at home and maybe during school time as well. So, we'll have to see how to manage that. Miss Sinclair, do you want to add anything?"

"I'm glad to have this meeting so we can get a broader picture of Jacob than we had. We have a significant number of students here who were orphaned during the war, and goodness knows what else they endured. How old was Jacob when each parent died."

Aber answers. "Jacob was a baby when our father died. He must have been around three or four when our mother died, so he may have some memories of her. We're seven brothers and sisters. We were eight. One sister died."

"Oh, my goodness!" gasps Miss Kelly.

"Jacob is the youngest of us. When our mother died, my sister Rivka really stepped in to be the 'mother' of the family. She's married now and caring for her husband's children."

"And the other siblings?" asks Miss Sinclaire.

"Two brothers and I were in the army when Rivka, with the youngest kids, fled to Vienna to live with relatives. One sister, Fannie, had already come to America. She helped Rivka, Kayla, Jacob, and me to immigrate in 1919."

"Are any of your family still in Europe?"

"Yes, two brothers."

Miss Kelly asks, "How old were Jacob and Kayla when you arrived?"

Aber answers, "I think Jacob was around eight and Kayla must have been around ten."

Miss Kelly nods as she tries to absorb all the information then says, "Jacob has been through a lot. He's had a lot of loss and change in his young life." She turns to Rachel and asks, "And you Miss Kaminski, when did you come to America?"

"I came with my parents from Lithuania when I was seven. We had some relatives in New York who sponsored us."

"Is it working for you to have Jacob and Kayla living with you?"

"Oh yes, I love having them with me. I'm sorry about not knowing Jacob wasn't coming to school and will figure out some way to make sure he gets to school. Also, I know some of Jacob's relatives have received care at the Medical Center. I think they know a Dr. Weiss who works there. Are you familiar with him?"

Miss Sinclair answers, "Oh yes, Dr. Weiss takes care of many of our immigrant students. He has made it something of a specialty. He speaks several European languages. He would be a good person for Jacob. Follow up on that, and perhaps we can meet again in a few months and see how things are going for Jacob." Aber and Rachel stand, say goodbye and leave.

As they walk back to Rachel's apartment, Rachel sighs, saying, "I feel terrible. I didn't know he wasn't getting himself to school. I assumed they could do that at their age, fourteen and sixteen. At least Kala is getting there. They have a tight bond, so I guess she would never tell me. But I should have figured it out."

Aber responds, "I should've too. I see him every weekend and I could have asked more about school. But look Rachel, don't blame yourself. At the library, you're almost running a settlement house. People want to come in early to get warm. Kids come in because it's quiet and they can get their homework done." As they walk, he reaches his arm around her back and gives her shoulder a warm squeeze. "Don't worry, Rachel, we'll figure it out. I think Jacob will be okay." Rachel is surprised by the power his touch has on her. Even through her coat, his hand is warm and strong. Her eyes fill with tears.

They reach the entrance to Rachel's building and again, to her surprise, Aber says to her, "Can I come up for a while? I have something with me you should see, and we need to talk about."

Rachel stammers, "Yes, yes, of course. I'll make us some tea." They are silent in the elevator. Rachel glances at Aber's face. He's frowning and looks preoccupied. They reach the apartment, Rachel lets them in and says, "Here, give me your coat." He hands her his coat and cane, and they go to the kitchen. Suddenly, Rachel thinks that Jacob might be home. She calls his name, then checks his room. He's not there. She thinks, *I hope he's at school, but from what I heard today, probably not. So where is he?*

Aber sits at the table while Rachel makes the tea. She asks, "Do you want some *babka (sweet bread or cake)*?" and senses she wants to delay hearing what Aber wants to tell her.

"Yes" he says, "That would be nice."

"I can warm it in the oven."

"No need. Just as it is, is fine," Rachel cuts two slices. From the cupboard she gets two plates and puts the babka on the plates. She brings the cups of tea and then the plates to the table and sits facing Aber. Aber opens the rucksack he always carries and pulls out a book. He lays it on the table between them. The cover is dark blue with an eagle and a swastika in gold. The title is *Mein Kampf*. The author is Adolf Hitler.

"A friend of mine from the army, who now lives in Berlin sent this with a letter saying every Jew in the world must read this book and take it very seriously, not dismiss it as some nonsense written by a half-educated clown or a psychopath, but something that can really happen. Hitler is convinced Jews are becoming too powerful and dominant. He argues that Jews are racially inferior; they are a plague that threatens to infest and ultimately destroy Europe's racially superior Aryan race. He claims they've taken over too many businesses, done well economically and then marry non-Jews, polluting and destroying the purity of the Aryan. I've bookmarked some pages you should read."

Rachel is lightheaded, but she reaches for the book and opens it to the places Aber marked.

The stronger must dominate and not blend with the weaker, thus sacrificing his own greatness.

All the human culture, all the results of art, science, and technology that we see before us today, are almost exclusively the creative product of the Aryan. This very fact admits of the not unfounded inference that he alone was the founder of all higher humanity, therefore representing the prototype of all that we understand by the word 'man.' He is the Prometheus of mankind from whose bright forehead the divine spark of genius has sprung at all times, forever kindling anew that fire of knowledge which illumined the night of silent mysteries and thus caused man to climb the path to mastery over the other beings of this earth. Exclude him–and perhaps after a few thousand years darkness will again descend on the earth, human culture will pass, and the world turn to a desert.

The Jew is only united when a common danger forces him to be or a common booty entices him; if these two grounds are lacking, the qualities of the crassest egoism come into their own, and in the twinkling of an eye the united people turns into a horde of rats, fighting bloodily among themselves.

He is and remains the typical parasite, a sponger who like a noxious bacillus keeps spreading as soon as a favorable medium invites him. And the effect of his existence is also like that of spongers: wherever he appears the host people dies out after a shorter or longer period.

Here he stops at nothing, and in his vileness he becomes so gigantic that no one need be surprised if among our people the personification of the devil as the symbol of all evil assumes the living shape of the Jew.

With satanic joy in his face, the black-haired Jewish youth lurks in wait for the unsuspecting girl whom he defiles with his blood, thus stealing her from her people. With every means he tries to destroy the racial foundations of the people he has set out to subjugate. Just as he himself systematically ruins women and girls he does not shrink back from pulling down the blood barriers for others, even on large scale. It was and it is Jews who bring the Negroes into the Rhineland, always with the same secret thought and clear aim of ruining the hated white race by the necessarily resulting bastardization, throwing it down from its cultural and political height, and himself rising to be its master.

In the political field he refuses the state the means for its self preservation, destroys the foundations of all national self-maintenance and defense, destroys faith in the leadership, scoffs at its history and past, and drags everything that is truly great into the gutter.

Culturally he contaminates art, literature, the theater, makes a mockery of natural feeling, overthrows all concepts of beauty and sublimity, of the noble and the good, and instead drags men down into the sphere of his own base nature.

If we pass all the causes of the German collapse in review, the ultimate and most decisive remains the failure to recognize the racial problem and especially the Jewish menace.

As Rachel reads, Aber watches her expression. She looks puzzled at moments and needs to reread certain passages. At one point she gasps. Several times she shakes her head. She closes the book and puts it on the table. "This is hideous. It's insanity. When did he write this?"

"In 1923, he was in jail. You remember, he and a bunch of his fellow Nazis attempted a coup in Munich to take over the government, but they were stopped. He was convicted of high treason and sentenced to prison for five years."

"So, he's in prison still?"

"No, he was out in nine months. He got a lot of publicity, wrote this book, and has a huge following that is getting bigger by the minute."

"How can that be? He's an uneducated buffoon and probably crazy. How can he have so many followers? Germany is an educated, sophisticated country."

"Yes, but since losing the war, morale is very low. The German people want a powerful leader to bring them back to greatness. He electrifies large crowds. People first come to hear him out of curiosity and by the time he's finished one of his ear-piercing, screeching speeches, the crowd is united, convinced that with Hitler as their leader, the Jews, those polluting rats will be destroyed and Germany, as a pure Aryan god-like race, will be the most powerful nation in the world. This crazy clown can't be dismissed. The Austrians are intrigued by him. And throughout Europe, some people are paying attention to his message that anyone not Aryan, but especially the Jews, is the problem. Hitler intends to get rid of the problem. I have my two brothers in Vienna. Marek has family in Budapest. This wild man wants to take over Europe and probably not only Europe. He may be a barely literate jerk, but he has a following, and he's created a paramilitary that protects him at Nazi rallies called the *Sturmabteilung* or storm division. You may have heard of them as the Brown Shirts. They are thugs who right now are attacking Jews in the street for no reason except for being Jews. We can't ignore this, Rachel. Any Jew who can, should get out of Europe right now."

"Do you think he wants to kill all the Jews?"

"Yes. Or at least sterilize us? Take seriously anything you can imagine. This fiend just might do it."

"It's getting harder to leave." Says Rachel.

"I know. It took a long time for us to get the right papers even though I'd been in the army. After I read this, I sent a letter to my brother Yehuda who you know works as a bookkeeper. My brother Lazar, amazingly, has his own restaurant now. We must talk to Marek and get him to write to his family. Warn them, tell them to start the immigration process before it gets too late."

"This is terrifying."

"It is. The threat is very real. I'm glad, Rachel, you don't brush this off as some temporary craziness."

"It is not as though hatred of the Jews is something new. It's always simmering below the surface."

"That's right, but this is more than simmering, it's beginning to boil."

"Do you think another war is coming?"

"I fear it might."

"It was only yesterday that we ended a war!"

Aber looks at the wall clock. "Oh! I must go. I have a job to build some steps in Brooklyn."

Aber stands while Rachel brings his jacket and cane. He puts *Mein Kampf* back into his rucksack and says, "I'm showing this to every Jew I know."

At the doorway of the apartment, Aber steps into the hall then turns to face Rachel and again puts his hand on Rachel's shoulder. His touch, through only her thin sweater, is electric in its heat and tight grasp. "We'll get Jacob back on track, Rachel. We are his team. I think he'll be alright."

"I hope so. First thing, I'll talk to him about getting to school. Also, I'll get him to Dr. Weiss too. I'll talk to Fannie about it right away."

"Okay. I'll talk to Jacob on Saturday. Take care Rachel. Let's be in touch. You can always get a message to me at the men's Y on West 57th. The people at the front desk are pretty good at getting messages to us."

She watches as he walks to the elevator. She's tempted to wait until the elevator arrives but forces herself to close the door.

Rachel drops onto her sofa. She is faint and lies down. A sob, deep and intense, rises out of her, followed by another and another. She sits up so she can try to hold her wracking body together. More sobs follow one after another. She is gasping for breath. "What's happening to me? Is it war? It's too much, too much, too much. I'm terrified. What is it? What's the matter with me?"

Her sobs come, one after another until, exhausted, she stops. Then, without forethought, she hears her own voice call a name, "Roland!" Roland was her fiancé who died in the war. His image is right there in front of her. She cries out, "Roland, Roland, how can you be dead? It can't be. You promised you'd return. Not even your poor dead body came back. Nothing, nothing! They brought me a flag, a stupid flag! I want you! Come home! Please!"

When Rachel recovers control, she is left with dark, cold sadness. She thinks of all that happened in the last couple of hours. *Too much! Mr. and Mrs. Liebermann she called us."*

She remembers Aber's touch and cries again, this time less intensely but with sadness and to her surprise, longing. She remembers his deep resonating voice as he chanted the prayer at Daniel's Bar Mitzvah. She longs to lay her head against his strong chest. She wants his voice, his warmth, his body's vibration, his heartbeat.

She hears a key turn at the apartment door. Kayla and Jacob enter and hang their coats in the vestibule closet. Rachel tries to compose herself. They walk into the living room and are surprised to find Rachel at home. Kayla says, "Rachel, you're home early. Are you okay?"

"Yes Kayla." Then to Jacob. "Jacob, your brother and I met with your home room teacher and the principal. Come, I'll tell you about it."

Kayla repeats, "Rachel, are you sure you're, okay?"

"Yes Kayla, I promise, I'm okay."

Letter to Marek from His Sister Olga

*D*ear Marek,

I read your letter about "Mein Kampf". Yes, Jews are hated here. We were not aware of "Mein Kampf", but we realize antisemitism is increasing especially since the end of the war. Most Hungarian Jews live in Budapest, so it gets called "Judapest". The fact that we are well assimilated into Budapest life, make many contributions to the culture as well as fought in the war on behalf of the Hungarian motherland, seems to make no difference. We are not alone. communists, bolsheviks, and intellectuals are also hated.

Some of our friends, recognizing the situation, have converted to Christianity as a way of continuing life here. We can't bring ourselves to do it. While we are not religious anymore, we have a deep Jewish iden-tity. To try to give that up would be a surrender to those who hate us.

Thank you so much for offering to bring us to America. But I hope it will be comforting for you to know that my family and Mama already have a plan to go to England. Sandor, my husband, has relatives there, and they will help us get settled and work. Sandor, like you, is a skilled tailor and hopes to get work in London, maybe on Savile Row. It is very hard to make this move. So far, we have not been bothered, and we have made a good life here. We still live well, but we see the writing on the wall. Friends from the synagogue are talking about it more, and some, like us, are also planning to leave.

You will be glad to know your younger sister Gina and her family are also planning to leave. Her husband has relatives in France. He is a greengrocer. He may have to find other work in France. They are going to Lyon. Maybe he can find something to do with a restaurant or a store.

I don't think Gina has many memories of you. She was still very young when you left with our brother Avram. It was terrible for me to suddenly have both my big brothers gone, and then, so soon after you both left, Avram died. That was a scary time. I had nightmares for a long time, and so did Gina. Mama was amazingly brave and really helped us to get through that. And then Papa died. Thank goodness Uncle Lev was able to help us some. Mama is still her dear self, but she is getting old and frail. She is always happy to get your letters and wants me to read them to her many times until you send the next, and then she wants me to read the newest one again and again. I am relieved she is coming with us.

I can't believe it, Marek, that we have not seen you since you were a very young man. And you probably think of me as still a little girl. I love hearing about your beautiful family. Do you think we will ever see each other again? Will we ever know each other's families? I hope so.

So dear big brother, I will keep you informed about our plans. In the meantime, send our warmest wishes to your family.

Love,
Olga

Marek finishes reading the letter. He wants to show it to Fannie. He starts to get up, but his knees buckle, and he falls back into his seat. A great weight descends on him and an overwhelming need to sleep.

When he wakes, it is dark outside, and he hears Fannie calling for the family to come to dinner.

He rouses himself. For a moment he's confused about the time of day, then the letter, still in his hand startles him into wakefulness. *Their husbands make these decisions. If Gina and Olga were the men, they would make the decisions and of course they would come to us. I may never see Mama again. Saville Road! What a snob. Maybe Fannie and I could go to London sometime? But when could we do that? How could we do that? We have the store; we have the kids. We do well but we're far from rich.* Fannie calls again and he pushes himself up and out of the chair. He is shaky but goes to the table. *At least they're getting out of Hungary.*

Against the Wall

October 1926

It is fall again, and Daniel is fourteen and a half. He is in his second semester at George Washington High School. Reluctantly, he continues his boxing training, although he has not gained the bulk and muscle he wanted. He remains short and slim. Meanwhile, Jacob has achieved welterweight and now fights in tournaments.

Daniel is walking home slowly and dreamily. It has been several months since hearing from Mischa about his life with Hannah in Palestine. His urge to keep searching has slowed since then. He thinks someday he will go to Palestine, to Kibbutz Degania, to meet some people who knew him, especially Mischa, and see the land. More people are immigrating to Palestine these days.

He is startled out of his reverie when two boys from the junior class suddenly flank him. They push him back and forth, back and forth between them. They are a head taller than Daniel, with deep gruff voices. "Hey, it's Horvath, baby Jew face Horvath. On your way home to your mama, baby Jew face?" Then the other taunts, "Hey Horvath, how come you look nothing like your mommy and daddy? Hey baby face, how come, how come?" They both start yelling, "How come?" still pushing Daniel back and forth between them. Suddenly they drag him into an alley and push him against a wall. One pins him and the other grabs a handful of his hair and yanks it. "Hey baby Jew face, where'd you get your red pussy hair? Did your mama do it with the iceman, maybe the coalman, or the junkman?"

Daniel, stunned, can only weakly cry out, "Stop, stop!" He whimpers as the kid twists his cheeks hard.

"Now, baby face, you have pink cheeks, like a real baby. You're crying like a baby. Your mommy should never have had you. She should have taken it HERE!" He squeezes Daniel's lips into a vertical opening. "Not HERE!" He knees Daniel in his crotch. Daniel groans.

"Take care of those tiny Jew balls pussy face. No one else is ever gonna play with them except you, all by your little self. Go home, suck-up. It's time to suck your mommy's titties." He grabs Daniel's cardigan sweater and pulls it apart. All the buttons fly off. They let go of him. Daniel falls, curling up in pain. One kid yells, "Let's get outta here." The other stays and pees on Daniel, and hisses, "You're disgusting!" They both run away.

As his pain subsides, Daniel's groans become sobs. He lies on the stinking ground for a while, crying. People pass by on the sidewalk but don't look into the alley. If they hear him crying, they move on without looking. Eventually, he gets up and collects the buttons torn from his sweater. He puts them in his pocket. He takes off the sweater, rolls it into a ball and carries it home under his arm. He runs his hand through his hair, trying to get it into some order. His cheeks have stopped stinging. He hopes they look normal again. As he walks home, he thinks, *I'm never going to tell anyone what happened. I could do nothing. I couldn't even swing at them, and I couldn't run. That stupid boxing training. So stupid!*

When he arrives home, he immediately gets some clean clothes and goes into the bathroom before anyone sees him. He takes a shower and changes his clothes. Fannie is surprised to see him coming out of the bathroom. He tells her he feels sick, that he took a hot shower and is going to bed. To check for a fever, Fannie puts her lips on his forehead.

She's satisfied that whatever ails him, Daniel isn't very sick. She says she'll bring his dinner to him. When Fannie knocks at his door with dinner, Daniel lies in bed, pretending to be asleep. Later, Simon comes into the room to go to bed. Daniel continues to feign sleep. When he is sure everyone is in bed for the night, he gets up and goes to Fannie's sewing alcove to get a needle and thread. He goes to the window of the living room and, by the light of the streetlamps, sews the buttons onto his sweater. Then he goes into the bathroom to wash the sweater. He squeezes out the water and hangs it to dry in the back of the closet in his bedroom. Once back in bed, he lies face down on his pillow and cries until exhaustion and sleep overtake him.

Daniel wakes before the rest of the family. From his bedside table he takes out the book Rachel gave him, <u>Leaves of Grass</u>. He opens it and finds a poem he has read many times.

I DREAMED in a dream, I saw a city invincible to the attacks of the whole of the rest of the earth,

I dreamed that was the new City of Friends,

Nothing was greater there than the quality of robust love—it led the rest,

It was seen every hour in actions of the men of that city,

And in all their looks and words.

He closes the book and gets ready to go to school.

Letter from Vienna

From Lazar

Dear Aber and Fannie,

Yes, I am aware of Hitler and the groundswell of excitement about him. It is all about how the German and Austrian people are so humiliated by losing the war and they are grasping at any promises any fool will offer. This will pass. You shouldn't worry about us here. The Austrian and German people are much smarter than to go following some crazy buffoon. They will come to their senses very soon. I even know a few Nazis. I'm not convinced they really believe in Hitler's claims about the Jews. They are always very friendly to me and come into my restaurant all the time. I, of course, don't tell them I am Jewish, but how could they not know, given my name? Lazar Liebermann is not exactly a Christian name. But as you know, my wife, Margo, is Christian. She looks Aryan; tall, blond and blue-eyed. I am sure any suspicious Nazi will give me the benefit of his doubt. The fact that I served in the army on behalf of the fatherland protects me as well. I never forget that I was born a Jew, but assimilation is good for everyone, the Jews and Gentiles alike. I don't miss our old religious rituals. So, in every way, despite my name, I am seen, not as a Jew but as an Austrian citizen contributing to Austrian society.

Margo has been working as the restaurant's hostess. She is beautiful and gracious, warmly welcoming each customer as they come in. She remembers every regular customer's name and amazingly seems always able to give them the table they request. I am excited to tell you she will not be working much longer. She is expecting twins. As you know, we are a family that regularly produces twins. We are thrilled.

The restaurant is very successful. Jewish clientele flock here because it is kosher, and Christians come because it is vegetarian. I made it vegetarian because during the war, when I was in the army and it was hard to get anything but horsemeat, I became an expert vegetarian cook. Vegetables cost a lot less than meat. I hear some customers go home and try to imitate my recipes. I am making humble country vegetables into gourmet food. My overhead is less than restaurants serving meat, so my prices are reasonable, and this brings in even more customers. Also, and this is a bit of a sore point, there is a new enthusiasm for vegetarian dishes because Herr Hitler is a vegetarian.

One of the Nazis who has contact with Hitler says he might suggest Herr Hitler come in some day. I don't think that is going to happen, and I hope it doesn't, but it gives you a sense of how we are able to manage here. This is why I don't think any Nazi who comes into the restaurant is going to hurt me if they think my restaurant is even good enough for their Fuhrer.

Some of Hitler's ideas, if not Hitler himself, may even benefit this country so ravaged by the war. The antisemitism, I am confident, will pass. It is simply people grasping at some crazy reason for why they are suffering.

I should let you know about our brother Yehuda. He continues to work as a bookkeeper, but he is leaving his job and is coming to work for me He and his family will live with us too. I was able to find a bigger apartment even closer to the restaurant. I suspect he was overreacting, but he thinks one of his bosses was dropping hints about Jews taking jobs away from the Christians. Once he comes to work for me, his job is secure. He and his wife won't have to worry.

So dear Aber and Fannie, I hope I have reassured both of you.

Your loving brother,
Lazar

Lazar's letter was addressed to Fannie, and she soon shows it to Aber.

"That stupid, self-satisfied little fool!" yells Aber after reading it. "He's blind, dazzled in the brightness of his success! What a smug little burger he's turned out to be! I never would have guessed it about him."

"But Aber, do you think he's in danger?"

"Of course he's in danger. Being married to an Aryan is the last thing to protect him or her. It's exactly what Hitler hates about Jews. They're supposedly polluting the pure race with their mongrel children. Every one of them, including his unborn kids, is in big danger. I'll write him back right away—if it will do any good. He thinks he knows better than anyone—stupid little punk."

"Aber, do you know that Marek's family is getting out of Budapest? They're going to England and France."

"Why not come here?"

"It's where the husbands want to go. Something about where they can keep up their businesses and where they have relatives."

"It may be better than staying in Hungary, but I'm not so sure. Don't underestimate Hitler for a moment. He has his eye on everywhere."

"Here too?"

"Who knows? Not impossible; nothing is impossible."

City Hall

It is Spring 1927 Aber joined the family for dinner and is getting ready to leave when Daniel, who recently turned fifteen, comes up to him.

"Uncle Aber, do you remember you gave me some good advice. You said I should start my search for the people who gave birth to me by finding out about the time my mother, Hannah, and I were in Palestine."

"Yes, Dan, I remember."

"Well, I heard from Mischa. He wrote me a long letter, and I have a good picture now of my mother, Hannah, and me as a little baby. I want to do more now. Are you still willing to help me?

"Yes, of course."

"Mischa knows nothing about my father. Mama doesn't have a birth certificate for me. My friend Herman says there's an office downtown where they keep records of everyone born in New York. Will you go with me and see if we can find my birth certificate there? Maybe it has information about my father on it, like what he did for work or his address."

"Sure, Dan, when do you want to go?"

"I have an early dismissal from school next Tuesday. Can you go then?"

"Let me see if I have a job lined up then." Aber takes out a small spiral notebook and turns over a few pages. That day, I have a job way downtown on Houston Street. The City Hall is not far from there. Do you think you could take the subway after school and meet me? It's easy. The subway stop is called "City Hall."

"I can do that."

"Okay. Are you going to tell your parents we will go together?"

"I only want to tell them I am going to meet you downtown for the afternoon and I'll be back in time for supper."

"Why just that?"

"From the time I was born until I came from Palestine to be with Mama, belongs to my life and that part of my life has nothing to do with Mama and Tateh."

"Well, your mama knew you a little because your first mother was her best friend."

"I know. But a lot happened to me I can't remember, and Mama doesn't know about. Until I know more, I want to be private about it."

"Well okay. Just so she knows you're with me for the afternoon."

"Sure."

"By the way, Dan, your parents have been worried about you. Your mother says you are quieter than you used to be and spend a lot of time staying in and reading instead of going out to play with your friends. She says you and Herman used to play a lot of stickball, but you don't so much anymore."

"I enjoy reading, and I have a lot to think about now."

"Okay. You know I'm here for you if you ever want to talk, and so is Rachel."

"I know. Thanks, Uncle Aber, I'm okay.

The following Tuesday, Daniel meets Aber in front of City Hall, and they find the office where birth records are kept. There is a long line. They wait side by side. Slowly they come to the window covered with an iron grill. A thin, sallow, elderly man with nicotine-stained fingers and a green eyeshade looks at Daniel.

"What do you want, son?"

"I want my birth certificate."

"Do you have an adult with you?"

"I'm fifteen years old."

"I can hardly believe you're that old, but fifteen is still too young. Do you have an adult with you, or not?"

"Yes, my uncle is here."

"Step aside and let your uncle talk to me."

Testily, Daniel says, "I can give you the information you need."

Gruffly, "I said, step aside kid. I can't give out information to anyone under eighteen, so move!"

Aber steps up, saying to Daniel, "Dan, give me the information. I'll deal with it."

Daniel, obviously frustrated and annoyed, says, "Tell him my name and that I was born on February 12, 1912"

"His name is Daniel Horvath, and he was born on Feb...."

"No, no, no, I wasn't Horvath then. My first mother was Hannah Weitzner; I was Daniel Weitzner. Does he have a Daniel Weitzner there?"

Aber doesn't need to repeat this to the clerk; Daniel shouted it. The clerk fingers down his lists of births on February 12, 1912"

"Born at home?" the clerk asks.

"No, Belview Hospital."

The clerk looks up and stares at Aber and Daniel. "Oh, the hospital no less." He drags his yellow finger down the page. "There's no Daniel Weitzner here. And no Hannah Weitzner."

Daniel, almost in tears, "How can that be? I know I have the date right. My mother always told me that date."

Aber steps closer to the grill. "Maybe see if there were any Daniels born that day."

"This is taking too long, complains the clerk." But he looks. "The are four Daniels recorded that day."

"And what are the mother's names?"

"There's Theresa Epstein, Molly Bragg, Anna White and Carla Fulco."

They start to leave. The next person moves up, and Aber spins around.

"No, wait, wait." He pushes himself in front of the woman who has just stepped up to the window.

"Hannah Weitzner, Anna White—she changed her name. It's Anna White. I think it must be Anna White. Can you tell us the father's name on the certificate?"

With obvious annoyance, the clerk yells, "It says 'Unknown'. That's all I'm doing here today. If you want the birth certificate, the kid's legal guardian must sign for it. Now go!"

"Was it at Belview?"

"Yes! Go!

"Please just tell me the address Anna White gives."

"I said, go!"

"Just the address, please." begs Aber.

"Washington Square—no number. No wonder she could go to the hospital! Fancy, fancy, now get out of here!"

Daniel looks stunned, but Aber is jubilant. "We have it, Dan. She changed her name, and we even have the area where she lived, across from Washington Square Park."

Daniel, still confused, "Why would she change her name? And does that mean my name was Daniel White? I can't imagine having the name White—Weitzner, I can imagine."

"Dan, we don't know why she changed it."

"So, what does that tell us?"

"For some reason, she wanted to hide her identity. She lived in a nice part of the city."

"I was hoping to get my first father's name. I know nothing more than I knew before we came here."

"Maybe we'll take a trip to Washington Square sometime and look around. See what we can learn about this mystery."

"I'm sick of stupid mysteries! I want facts!"

Jacob and Dr. Weiss

ber and Jacob wait for Dr. Weiss to come out of his office. Soon the door opens.

"Good morning, I'm Dr. Weiss." He reaches his hand, first toward Aber; they shake vigorously, then to Jacob who offers his hand but looks down. Dr. Weiss gestures for them to enter. He beckons to two seats and pulls his chair out from behind his desk so the three of them sit in the free space of the office.

Dr. Weiss begins. "As you know, Jacob, your sister Fannie contacted me asking if I would see you because you've been tired and having trouble getting yourself to school. Is that how you understand the reason for our meeting today?"

Jacob, still looking down, nods and says a barely audible "Yes, sir."

"And Mr. Liebermann, I understand you are Jacob's eldest brother, is that right?"

"Yes. I am the eldest of the surviving seven of us. Jacob is the youngest."

"Yes, I understand one of your sisters died while you were both still in Europe."

"Esther, my sister Fannie's twin died. She had a weak heart."

"Did her heart trouble occur after an illness?"

"Not that I'm aware of. Very early on, the doctor told my parents that Esther had a weak heart."

Dr. Weiss turns to Jacob and says, "Jacob, I'd like to examine you so that maybe we can understand why you are so tired. And I'd also like to get to know you a bit. Does that sound alright with you?"

Jacob looks up for the first time and says directly to Dr. Weiss, "Yes, that's alright."

"And maybe after we have our time, I'll ask your brother to come in at the end so if I have any recommendations he can hear them. Jacob nods in agreement."

"Mr. Liebermann, you're welcome to wait for us here. Would like a magazine or newspaper?"

While Aber pulls a book out of his rucksack, he says, "Thank you no. I brought a book with me." Dr. Weiss and Jacob go into an adjoining exam room.

Dr. Weiss does a slow and careful physical exam. As he picks up each of his instruments, he shows it to Jacob, names it, and tells him its purpose. He spends a particularly long time with his stethoscope listening to Jacob's heart and lungs. When he finishes, he says to Jacob, "You're a healthy and strong young man. The only other thing I think I should do is prick your finger with a small pin to test your blood to make sure you don't need a tonic. I suspect you're fine and it won't be necessary, but let's check." He pricks Jacob's finger, noting that Jacob does not flinch.

"You can put your shirt back on, Jacob. Let's chat for a while, so I can get to know you a little."

There are two chairs nearby. Dr. Weiss sets them at an angle to each other, so Jacob has the choice of looking or not looking directly at Dr. Weiss. "You can start anywhere you like Jacob. What would you like to tell me about yourself?"

"I don't know. I don't know what to say."

"Should I ask you a question?"

"Yes."

"Are there things in your life that go well?"

"I like operating my ham radio."

"Yes, tell me about that."

Jacob begins to perk up telling Dr. Weiss about his ham radio friends, about learning Morse code and how he and another operator is inventing their own private code, which they hope to teach a small group of people.

"How interesting. How did you get the radio?"

"My brother got a kit, and he and I put it together."

"And you and another operator are creating your own code."

"Yes."

"Is there a reason for inventing your own special code, beside it being an interesting challenge?"

"If there's another war and one of us witnesses suspicious activities, we can communicate with each other and then let the authorities know. If the enemy breaks in and listens to the transmissions, they might know Morse, but they won't know our code."

"Are you worried about another war?"

"I guess."

"And I understand you were in Europe during the war."

"Yeah."

"Do you remember it?"

"I don't remember much. Well, maybe the noise. I think we were on a train. It kept stopping and starting. There were big blasts of noise, like kaboom, kaboom, a lot louder than thunder! I guess it was bombs and planes dropping bombs." Jacob falls silent.

After a while, Dr. Weiss says, "So, Jacob, you've experienced war. You know how terrible it is, and you want to do your part in possibly preventing it, so you and your ham radio buddy are working on a code to communicate any danger you might observe."

"Yeah." A pause "War is death."

"I agree. War is all about death."

Dr. Weiss waits for a few moments then says, "Can you tell me what you're thinking about Jacob?"

Jacob shrugs and says, "I don't have parents. I live with a nice woman, Rachel. She takes care of Kayla and me, but she's not our mother; she's not even a relative. Kids at school always think she's my mother, the teachers too, and they even think my brother is my father. I don't want to explain it all to them. I feel weird, different from the other kids at school. I don't even know what my parents looked like. I don't know where my parents are; I mean, where my dead parents are. I don't know where they have their graves."

"You wish you had the usual kind of family, with a living mother and father, and you wouldn't have to explain who they are."

"Yeah."

Another silence and, for the first time, Jacob spontaneously says, "Another weird thing about my family is I have a niece, Adela, and she's older than me. Nieces are supposed to be younger than uncles. She teases me about it."

"Tell me more about Adela."

"She's okay when she is not teasing or thinking she's the boss of everyone."

"What makes her okay?"

"She likes jazz, and sometimes when I am at her house, she plays jazz records on the Victrola."

"Do you like jazz?"

"Some of it. I don't like the jazz she likes. She's always trying to make me learn dances and dance with her. That's not for me. But I really like jazz drumming, especially Gene Krupa; he tears those drums apart. It's so powerful. You can't dance to Gene Krupa."

"What about the other kids in that family?"

"I don't spend much time with the twins. I know Dan pretty well. He's okay. His first mother died, and Fannie adopted him. But Dan has no idea how lucky he is. He lives in a normal family. He actually likes school. He's a little squirt with a big head."

"What do you mean?"

"Well, he's bookish. People are always interested in what he has to say. Grown-ups even ask him what he thinks about stuff. They never ask me. He can be a smart alec." He pauses. "And sometimes I want to punch him in the face or trip him. I won't do it, but I think about it."

"How do you know you won't do it?"

"I just know. It's wrong."

"Do you think he has a perfect life?"

"Yeah, and he doesn't know it."

Both are quiet for a while. Dr. Weiss says, "I heard from your sister Fannie you're helping Aber with his carpentry business on the weekends."

"Aber is teaching me carpentry. He says I'm good at it."

"Do you like doing carpentry every weekend?"

"Yeah, I like it when we're working together on a job."

"Do you think it's where you belong, working with your brother?"

"Yes."

"Are you tired when you're working with Aber?"

"Just when I first get up. But once we're at a job, I feel good. I can fall asleep easily after a day at work."

"Are you having difficulty sleeping the other days?"

"I fall asleep, but then I wake up. That's the worst thing, being awake when everyone else is asleep and everything is quiet. I hate that."

"But you can fall asleep. Hmmm. Why do you think you can fall asleep?"

With this question from Dr. Weiss, Jacob drops his head. There's a long pause.

"Does my question bother you?"

Jacob shrugs. He picks at the skin on his thumb. Dr. Weiss had noticed the red and scabby cuticle during his exam. Dr. Weiss waits. Barely audible, Jacob mutters, "Sometimes I drink some wine, and it helps me fall asleep."

"Wine can do that. There's a problem with drinking wine to sleep. It works for only a little while. Then you wake up, and it can feel bad."

"Yeah."

"Maybe you can tell me about school."

"I hate school."

"What do you hate about it."

"I told you, I don't fit in. I'm embarrassed."

"When you lived in Vienna, did you go to school?"

"Off and on."

"Why was that?"

"Sometimes on the way to school or after, kids would call us dirty Jews. They'd yell 'Go back to where you came from.' Sometimes they threw dirt at us. So, I just wouldn't go, and my sister Rivka didn't make me."

"Has that happened here, kids calling you 'dirty Jew'?"

"No, or maybe not yet."

"Did you make any friends in Vienna?"

"Yes, a boy who lived in the same building. He had a set of toy soldiers. I went to his apartment because we lived with another family, and it was too crowded. We didn't like to go outside."

"Did he stay in Vienna?"

"No. He and his parents left one night. I don't know where they went."

"Do you have friends here now?"

"Just on the ham radio. Sometimes Dan is a friend, maybe."

"Can you think of anything that could make school better for you?"

"I don't know. I'm no good at school."

"What if you could take mostly skill courses, like furniture making, electricity, construction? I bet you could almost teach that one."

"Yeah, that would be better."

"How about if after I talk to your brother about it, I'll call your school and recommend you have mostly shop courses?"

"Really, you'd do that?"

"Yes. I think you're required to take a course in English every year and at least one course in American History."

"Rachel can help me with those."

"Okay, that's our plan. Is there anything else you want to say before we stop?"

Jacob takes a deep breath and squeezes his eyes shut. "There's one thing. I don't want to say it, but I have to say it. I've been taking the wine from my sister Fannie's house. I'll stop."

"Good idea."

"Dr. Weiss extends his hand, and this time Jacob shakes it with strength."

"Jacob, I can be your doctor now for routine visits and any time you might get sick, but I'm also here if you want to talk again." Jacob nods.

"Let's meet your brother in my office so we can tell him about the school plan."

After Jacob and Aber leave, Dr. Weiss writes a note in the chart.

Jacob is a well-developed seventeen-year-old immigrant boy from Galicia, an orphan. His physical exam is entirely normal except for his right thumb, which has a lesion from constant nervous picking.

He experienced major losses and the trauma of having lived in a war zone. He looks sad but can be engaged. He speaks of feeling "weird" which is his term for thinking he is different from his schoolmates and that he doesn't belong with them. He also says he is "embarrassed" because his family is so different from other families.

He listens to his ham radio, has invented a secret code with a friend and likes jazz drumming. I suspect these are the ways he tries to gain some personal control over the chaos of his early life. His brother tells me he has joined the gym at the Jewish Y to get training in boxing. When he wakes at night, he finds silence difficult.

He struggles with envy, anger and burgeoning sexual feelings. He has a strong, positive relationship with his older brother.

Old Wounds and Ghosts

A week passed since Aber and Rachel visited Jacob's school. It's after midnight. Rachel, unable to sleep, gets out of bed, goes to the kitchen where she takes a pad of paper and a pen and sits at the kitchen table. Jacob and Kayla are asleep. She hesitates for a moment, the pen poised above the paper, then writes.

Dear Aber,

"We are a team." you said after our visit to Jacob's school. Yes, we are. Since you arrived in America and Jacob and Kayla came to live with me, we have shared caring for and raising them. To say I appreciate your help and support is an understatement. I don't think I could do it without you. Lately, it has become more challenging than ever. How do we prepare these teenage youngsters for the big world they will soon enter? Also, how will our lives change when they leave us?

I'm a coward for choosing to write to you now rather than speaking directly to you, a coward because I am so aware of how I hope and wish you will respond. I want you to have time to think about what I will say. And I don't want you to feel cornered, as I fear you might if I were to bring it up suddenly in person.

Here is what I want to say. I want you, me and the children to become a family. I want us to be a couple. If another war is coming, and from what we hear about Hitler, it very well might be. Won't it be better to be a family and be together? Out of my respect for you, out of the pleasurable and serious conversations we have had about literature, ideas, and the world, out of the conversations about our families and about ourselves, and out of some hard times we have gone through together I have grown to love you. There is no other way to say it. There is no one else in my life I would rather talk to than you. And now I realize there is no one in my life I would rather be with than you. Saying this to you goes far beyond wanting to raise the children together. I want to be with you.

Rachel puts down her pen. There it is. I said it! She is breathless. No, no, I didn't say it. I only wrote it. She reads what she wrote. No, I don't dare send this. If he refuses me, it will ruin what we have now. She grabs the paper, scrunches it, starts to tear it up, and stops. She gets up and paces the kitchen and the living room, back and forth. She sits down. Her thoughts race. She cries.

Too much, I want him too much. I'm a coward because I want him so much. He may not want me. Then how do we go on? How do I go on? It was easier with Roland. He loved me first, and I grew to love him. I was terrified when he went to war. I didn't think I could live if he died. But he died, and I've gone on. How? My work helps. Friends like Fannie help. Having Jacob and Kayla with me helps. Aber helps me to go on. But have I loved anyone since Roland? No? Yes? Yes, I love Aber. I didn't let myself know it. I put my heart in the icebox. Why? Why do I let myself know it only now?

Rachel goes back to the scrunched-up ball of the letter and smooths it out. She takes another sheet of paper and starts copying it.-She shakes her head, goes back to the smoothed-out but wrinkled paper and continues to write on it.

Aber, this letter is wrinkled because I started to throw it out, but I didn't tear it up. This told me to go on despite the risk. I fear if you refuse my proposal, we will lose what we now have. I think I can tolerate your refusal if we can go on as we are. What we have now is precious to me. Maybe I want too much. If so, you will let me know.

I will sign this the way I feel.

Love,
Rachel

She puts on her hat and coat. Despite the late hour, she must mail it now. Walking to the mailbox at the end of the block, she takes a deep breath of the crisp air and smells the river and a bit of diesel fuel. She is surprised to feel....what...excitement, scared? Yes, but more... what... alive? Yes, I'm alive.

Five days later, Aber calls Rachel at the library and says he'd like to meet. He suggests the cafeteria on Broadway near her apartment, at around 9:00 pm. "It will be almost empty then and we can find a quiet place to talk."

"Yes, Aber, I'll be there." Rachel is suddenly light-headed. She thinks, *Have I taken a breath in the last five days?* She marches through the rest of the workday. She catches herself holding her breath. A high school student asks for help researching his history paper on the Boxer Rebellion. She does a story hour for grades three to five. Miriam and Simon attend. She checks out books and shelves the pile of returns on her desk. Finally, it's 6:00 and she can leave. She stops at the grocery store to get food for dinner and freezes when the butcher asks what she wants. "Oh, oh, chops, lamb chops, three." The butcher asks if she wants shoulder or loin. "Yes, yes, shoulder." Her thoughts race. She tries to remember what she had said in the letter. *It's a blur. What did I say?* Somehow, dinner gets made. She sits with Jacob and Kayla at the table until 7:30. Jacob is quiet. Kayla talks about an upcoming project on Greek tragedy. She must read and discuss two plays. Rachel suggests she come to the library after school tomorrow. They can look through what the library has available.

Rachel tells them she's going out at around eight o'clock and will be back around eleven. To her relief, they don't ask where she is going or who she is meeting. It is raining, but the cafeteria is close by. She wants time to try to walk off her nervousness. She leaves the apartment, opens her umbrella and walks around the block over and over until she can walk to the cafeteria and get there at the right time...*or maybe a few minutes late? I don't want to sit there alone. I want to see him there when I walk in. I'll be afraid to see his face when he first sees me. Just in case I get there first, I have my book. If I get there first, I'll start reading and not look up until he gets to the table.*

Rachel arrives at the cafeteria, pushes through the revolving door and looks around. The inside air is steamy and smells of wet wool, newspapers and meatloaf. She checks every table and looks at her watch; it is five after nine. After her walk, she felt less tense, but now her body is back in a grip. She finds a table for two in a far corner and sits facing the door. Keeping her coat on, she takes a book out of her bag and tries to read. She can't. She keeps looking at the revolving door. She stands up, searching every table again. *Maybe he went to the men's room.* She waits, looks at her watch, and tries again to read. It's ten past nine. *Maybe the subway broke down. Maybe he was hurt on a job. If he were hurt, who would they contact? Maybe Fannie or Rivka. I could call Fannie from a phone booth. No, I don't want to explain anything. It's twenty past. I'll give him another ten minutes. This is stupid! I've wrecked everything with that letter. The least he could do is show up and tell me! That coward! That mouse!*

Her body grows hot. She jerks out of her coat, then jerks it back on and heads for the exit. She pushes through the revolving door. The rain stopped, but now it's windy. She walks as fast as she can back to her building. Her jaw clenches. Her hands make fists. In a doorway, she passes an embracing couple. She breaks into a run and turns the corner onto her block. She spies an empty liquor bottle in the gutter, picks it up and at the first brick wall she comes to, she heaves the bottle against it. It shatters on the pavement and leaves fragments still clinging to the wall. She's stunned for a second, then breaks into sobs while she pushes some of the scattered fragments on the pavement out of the walkway and back against the wall. Still sobbing, she starts back toward her apartment. *I must pull myself together; the kids will still be awake.*

"Rachel, Rachel!" It's Aber behind her. She turns. He lurches toward her walking as fast as he can with his cane. She wants to keep running but stops. He's out of breath. Gasping, "Rachel, I'm sorry. I'm so sorry!"

Rachel shouts, "For God's sake, what happened?"

"I don't know, I really don't know. Suddenly I saw the time. It was nine o'clock. I don't know what happened. Please believe me. Can we go back to the cafeteria? Are you willing to Rachel?"

Rachel, confused, says "I don't know...well, okay, I guess."

They head back to the cafeteria, enter, and Aber points to the same table Rachel just left. This time she takes the seat with her back to the door.

Aber helps her with her coat and rests it on the back of her chair. He wears no coat, only a woolen scarf around his neck, which he leaves on but stuffs his knitted cap into his pocket and hooks his cane over the back of the chair. "I'll get us something. Do you want coffee or tea?"

"Tea" she says.

"Anything else?" he asks.

"N-n-n no Aber. Nothing." Rachel watches him hobble to the counter without his cane. He returns with two teas, sets them down, takes his seat and sighs. There's a silence. He looks down, then looks up at her; their eyes meet. He tries to smile, but his eyes are sad. He again apologizes.

"I need a minute." He puts his head in his hands, then rubs his face. He looks up, shrugs and says, "I really don't know why I didn't look at the time until it was already nine. I'm an idiot!"

Rachel thinks, *Yes you are.* When she looks at him, she sees how distressed he is, how sad he looks and softens, saying "Take a moment. You're here now. Have some of your tea."

Aber takes a few sips. "Rachel" He repeats, "Rachel, I read your letter. I read your letter many times. It was a surprise to receive it and yet no surprise at all."

After a long pause, Rachel askes "What do you mean?" Aber has his head in his hands again.

"Where was I?"

"You said my letter was a surprise, and yet it wasn't. What do you mean?" Aber nods several times and takes a deep breath.

"We've been good friends since the day I arrived in this country. When you offered to have Jacob and Kayla live with you, it was as if we became family at once. It was a great relief for Rivka because finally she could begin her own life, and a relief for me so I could figure out how I was going to earn a living. Aber pauses. He takes a breath and starts again. "But let me get to what you wrote and what I want to say, not really what I want to say, it's what I must say to you." Aber sighs. His expression is deeply sad. Rachel's breath quickens. "I don't know, I don't know where to start Rachel. I'm a man who can't love. I can't love anyone. I once could, but no longer, never again." Aber's eyes are downcast. He crosses his arms over his chest; his hands squeezed under his armpits, and hunches over. It is as though his body is a cave he wants to back into. He furtively glances up at Rachel while his head stays bowed.

Despite the overheated room, Rachel is shivering. Out of her tightened throat she squeezes the words, "How do you know?"

"I know it."

"Never?"

"Yes, never."

"You said you could love in the past?"

Aber begins, but his voice is oddly mechanical, as though he has rehearsed what he's saying or reads it from a page. "After my father was beaten and robbed, he left our home and then died. Then my younger sister Esther, Fannie's twin, died. And then my mother also died. I was full of grief, but I was young. Okay, parents die and sometimes a sister dies, but I could go on and hope to make my own family. After the war started..."

There is a loud crash. They both stiffen. Someone dropped a tray. The clatter of broken dishes and silver reverberates across the marble floor. There is a volley of startled voices, and two people from behind the steam table rush out with a mop, broom and bucket. Rachel turns back to Aber. He is standing stiff as a statue. His eyes wide open, unblinking.

"Aber, Aber, what's happening?" He is somewhere else. Seconds pass. His fists clench. He digs his nails into his palms. He bites his hand. She can see teeth marks below his index finger. "Aber, Aber!" she cries out.

As though waking from a horrible dream or vision, Aber answers, "Oh, oh! I'm okay. I'm okay." He sits again. *Oh no. It just happened again. Breathe, breathe. Think of something ordinary. Think of work—the boards I cut and measured today. Two more tomorrow—Pine, an inch thick, 12" by 18". Breathe, breathe.*

"Aber, maybe we should wait. You're not well."

"It's okay. I'm okay now. He sits down again. This can't wait. I must explain this to you. I should have told you a long time ago. It's the war. His focus is intense, but somewhere else. Not at Rachel, not looking down but somewhere ahead.

Rachel's eyes fill with tears. She has the impulse to move her hand across the table toward his but pulls it back and drops her hand into her lap. She can hear Aber take deep breaths. He takes a few sips of tea. His voice no longer sounds mechanical but urgent and at moments halting. His gaze is still ahead.

"After I went to the front, I met a woman, a wonderful woman. She was an ambulance driver, and I went with her to help pick up wounded soldiers and civilians. We fell in love and made plans to marry. She was a terrific driver, knew all the back roads and handled the ambulance with skill. But one day she drove over a buried explosive of some sort." Aber straightens up rigidly, squeezing his eyes shut. "I watched the woman I love blow apart."

Aber's breath comes fast. His lips are dry and parted. He forces himself to breathe slowly and seems to reach some equilibrium though again he looks past Rachel as he tries to go on.

"At the Russian front. It was too much, too much. Men in my company, wounded, screaming, bodies torn open." Aber stops. He is silent. He looks down. More silence.

"Aber?" asks Rachel. "Aber, do you want to go on? We can wait for another time." It is as though he has fallen into sleep.

Aber startles. "Oh, oh, where was I?"

"You were taking about being at the front."

"Oh yes, the men. I loved some of those men. What gas and grenades and bombs and bullets can do to human flesh in seconds. Too much, too much—mud, rats, disease, violence. It's dangerous to love anyone. Every day more death, more and more death." Again, his voice is mechanical and staccato. "The ground frozen. Couldn't bury the bodies. Covered them with snow. It melted. Bodies, everywhere bodies. I broke. Stood up. Stiff, like a frozen corpse. Don't remember it. Told I stood. Wouldn't move. Wouldn't sit or lie, wouldn't duck from bullets."

Rachel pictures what he tells her. She struggles to look composed but hears herself gasp and gasp again. Aber falls silent again. But soon he raises his head and looks at Rachel. He is fully in contact with her, composed, almost too composed. Only the quick pace of his words betrays his urgency to get his story out to her.

"I was taken out of combat, sent to a psychiatric hospital. I was lucky to have a *mensch* (admirable person) for my captain. He sent me to a hospital in Posen, where people like me received humane treatment. I was told by the psychiatrist, a Dr. Simmel, I had what's called shell shock, sometimes called war neurosis. The treatments at most other hospitals could be cruel, like electric shocks to your brain or shaming for leaving combat.

Dr. Simmel treated me with rest and quiet and carpentry work on the hospital grounds. Then we talked. He was trained in what was called 'The Talking Cure'. A doctor in Vienna named Freud developed it. He said that putting terrible experiences into words was healing for a troubled mind. He asked me to keep a journal and write in it every day. He helped me to tell him about what happened, and he listened. He wanted to hear about my dreams. When we talked about my dreams, sometimes I remembered things I had forgotten. I think it helped. I got better, better in the sense that I could think, talk, and move again, but my conviction that I can never depend on or love anyone again didn't change. Thank God I can still risk friendship...but no dependency. I don't dare lean on anyone or need anyone. If they died, I'd become a frozen corpse again. You can see, I have these moments when the war scenes come barreling back as though they're happening all over again. Not like the first time, but something like it and brief, thankfully brief.

I knew I'd be sent back to the Russian front, but as soon as some of that paralyzing fear got better, I wanted to go back. I was ashamed to be out of combat while my brothers were in peril. Also, I had to help my brothers get through the war. When I got back, it was the coldest part of the winter, and my toes were so badly frostbitten, they had to be amputated. So, I was back in the hospital again, and then the war ended. Later I learned that earlier in the war, my captain had shell shock, and he was sent to that hospital in Posen. That's how he knew about Dr. Simmel." Aber pauses. "So, Rachel, this is what I needed to tell you. He looks up at her furtively for a second then puts his head in his hands.

"Oh Aber, I've been a fool, a selfish fool."

"No, Rachel, if being able to love someone is being a fool. I wish I could be a fool again. Long live fools!"

Rachel cries and laughs at the same time.

"Look, Rachel, nothing you wrote changes what we have. I'm not surprised. But I can't risk taking what you offer. Think of me as a very poor man who can't afford the high cost of loving. I can't risk the pain of a possible loss. I can't live with the uncertainty that my beloved could die before me or leave me. I'm a poor man. As a man, I'm poor. And I'm terrified of going mad again."

"We all have ghosts, Aber. We're haunted by tormenting spirits. The old rabbis called them dybbuks, and they called them out with prayers. Your doctor called them out with kindness and talk."

"Yes, but only some of them. He is quiet. He looks directly at her. Their eyes meet. "I've burdened you with this."

Rachel replies, "What you tell me makes me sad for both of us. But not burdened. Discovering I can love you calls out a ghost of my own. I didn't believe I could love again." She moves her chair closer to the table and leans toward him. She tells him about Roland, then asks, "Aber, can you understand that what we've told each other today makes me both relieved and very sad? I fooled myself into thinking Roland was in the past and loving was in the past. I was over it. Loving you tells me that part of myself isn't dead. I am glad for that. I'm sad you're convinced it's over for you; that you can't love me the way I wish you to. But Aber, you are loving, maybe in a different way. You help people, you're humane, you help Jacob, and you help me in more ways than you know."

Aber sighs, shrugging his shoulders he says, "I think it's the only thing that keeps me from being an empty husk, or maybe a frozen corpse. At least I'm partly human. But a part of my heart stayed frozen." Another long pause. "I think the last straw was once I passed through Bolekhiv and saw what happened to our home. It was completely destroyed. Nothing left but the stone fireplace and oven where my mother cooked. It was devastating to see. I could have re-built that house, but I had to move on."

"Do you like being a carpenter?"

"It was one of the things Dr. Simmel and I talked about. He wondered if when the war was over, I might go to university. He knew I was a reader. I realized in that conversation carpentry means repairing and building things for people to use and live with. It's the opposite of destroying things. It's right for me. If I lost an arm instead of my toes, if I couldn't do it, I'd have to move on to something else. My brother in Vienna was a carpenter and lost the use of his right arm. So, he became a bookkeeper.

Rachel looks directly at Aber and asks, "Are we still a team?"

"We're a team for Jacob. And I'll always be available to help you."

"Can we still have our conversations about what we read and think about us and about everything else?"

"Of course. Nothing changes."

"It has though. We know much more about each other."

"Do you think I'm insane?"

"No, but you worry about falling ill again."

"True, only my brothers know about my breakdown. You're the only other person I've told. But I think it's the only way I could explain myself to you."

"Thank you, Aber, dear Aber." She smiles at him.

They rise to leave. Aber helps Rachel with her coat. They face each other for a moment and then spontaneously both put their arms out and embrace. They walk to the exit, leave through the revolving door, and breathe in the fresh, cold air. They wish each other good night and walk in separate directions.

On her way back, Rachel stops at the place where she threw the bottle at the wall. She notices the tiny shards still clinging to the brick and the pile of bigger shards she had pushed out of the walkway. *Oh Aber, your wounds are so much more than your poor toes.*

When she enters the apartment, the lights are out except for the light under Jacob's closed door. She can hear him on his radio.

She opens the door to the bedroom she shares with Kayla and sees that Kayla is asleep. Quietly, Rachel gets undressed and slips under her quilt. She takes a deep breath. She is sad but calmer than she has been since the visit to Jacob's school. Yawning, she thinks, *I'm scarred by Roland's death, but no longer wounded. Aber can't love me, but he shows me I can love again. Aber says part of his heart is frozen, yet he has given me a precious gift. She yawns again. The library just received a copy of a new novel, "All Quiet on the Western Front" I should read it.*

What is that! knock KNOCK, knock KNOCK, knock KNOCK! It's at the door—someone is at the door. Rachel leaps out of bed, looks through the keyhole, and opens the door. "Aber, you're back!" He grabs her into his arms and kisses her fervently. They are ravenously hungry for each other. He scoops her up and carries her to bed. But it's not her bed. It's her parent's bed. Rachel snaps awake. Knock KNOCK, knock KNOCK, knock KNOCK, goes her heart. Gradually her normal breath returns. *It felt so real. It is how I imagined Roland returning.* Cold sadness falls over her again.

Aber takes the subway back to the midtown men's Y. He gets to his doorway, starts to enter but turns around and heads toward Central Park. He enters the park at Columbus Circle and walks with the certainty of a walk taken many times. He knows where he is going. Darkness is no impediment. When he comes to one of the park's heavy stone arches, he takes a deep breath and walks under it. He lowers himself to lie on the ground. The chill of the stone beneath him is just right. He turns onto his side and pulls all his limbs into a fetal position. He is safe. He weeps until sleep takes him.

Washington Square

Several weeks later, on a Friday afternoon, Daniel and Aber take the subway to 8th Street and walk the few blocks to Washington Square. They sit on benches facing the handsome Greek Revival buildings across from the park. These attached red-brown brick buildings are immaculate. Sculpted green hedges grace the front of each building. Glistening, black, iron gates lead to the basement apartments. Ten steps lead up to the main doors. Each door, framed by white marble pillars, is painted a different glossy color; deep red, cobalt blue, forest green, or burnt orange. The windows are floor-to-ceiling rectangles framing eighteen small square panes within each frame. Two more floors rise above with the same rectangular windows framing twelve square panes and above those, under the roof, are attic windows framing six panes. The buildings glow in the spring afternoon, radiating comfort and tranquility.

Aber and Daniel are quiet. Daniel absorbs the scene. A gentle breeze wafts from the park behind them. Daniel tries to imagine the woman in the photo sent by Mischa, coming out of the doorway and down the steps of one of those buildings. He can't.

A man walks up the steps to one building, and Aber quickly crosses the street. Daniel follows him. Aber asks the man if he can tell him about someone who lived here and left about fourteen or fifteen years ago. The man is gracious and listens but says he moved in about five years ago so he would know no one who left before that.

Aber and Daniel leave and return to the same bench on Saturday. This time they see two teenage girls leave one building. They don't approach them knowing that even if they lived there when Hannah did, they would have been far too young to remember her.

They return on Sunday. Aber and Daniel take their seats again facing the buildings. A middle-aged woman appears in one doorway. She is dressed in an elegant wool suit with a cloche felt hat. She has with her a small black poodle with a fancy cut. They see her come down the steps, cross the street and go into the park. A few minutes later, she emerges from the park and sits one bench over from Aber and Daniel. She lifts the little dog onto her lap and from a small leather shoulder purse takes out a cigarette holder and a cigarette, which she lights and inhales deeply.

Aber, who sits closest to her, turns to her. "Excuse me madam, may I ask you a question?" The woman looks up with surprise and begins patting the dog, who looks up at her, blinks and settles into her lap. "Excuse me, my name is Aber Liebermann, and this is my nephew, Daniel. Do you live here at Washington Square?"

"Yes, I do. Why do you ask?"

Daniel leans forward so he can better look at the woman. "Someone I knew, maybe fourteen or fifteen years ago, lived here. I wonder if by chance you knew her. Her name was Anna White."

"Hmm. I've lived here longer than that. Did you say Anna White?"

"Yes."

"Anna White, Anna White, could you mean Hannah White?"

"Yes, she sometimes called herself Anna. Maybe she thought it was more American."

"Oh yes, now I know who you're talking about. She was a foreign girl. She spoke some other language. I don't know what it was. When she talked English, she talked with an accent."

"Yes, probably like my own."

"Yes, yes, I didn't know her, but I knew who she was. She was a beautiful girl and always dressed well. She kept to herself. I think she had a husband. I'm not sure. I rarely saw her and probably wouldn't remember her. But what happened at the end makes it impossible to forget."

Daniel stands to hear better what the woman says. Aber, trying not to seem too eager, asks, "Would you tell us about that?"

The woman now pats her dog vigorously. The dog stands and licks the woman's face, then settles back onto her lap. The woman then launches into what she has to say with the relish of a good, gossipy story.

"One day, Hannah or Anna suddenly left and never returned. That night her husband, or whatever he was, comes banging at her door and yelling for her, Hannah, Hannah. He comes back night after night, banging at the door and yelling, and then he comes again and throws a big rock through her bay window. He's screaming and cursing and threatening her. No question, he's drunk as a skunk. My husband called the cops, who came and took him away in a paddy wagon. That was the end of him, and I never saw Hannah again. I think that's all I can tell you. She seemed like a nice girl. I hope she's okay. It's been a long time."

"Just one more thing, if you don't mind. Did you ever hear his name?"

"Hmm. Oh yes, right, they fought about it. I think he was rough. Once I heard her scream 'Mendl, Mendl' and then she screamed things in that strange language of hers. Then he would scream, but in English, 'Never call me that, I'm Jack. You better remember that Jack, Jack, Jack. It sounded like he was hitting her. He was a doozy. She was smart to get away from him. I better go in now. It's time for this little fellow's dinner." Nuzzling the dog's wet nose, she squeals, "It's din-din time, sweetie. You're such a good little boy." She removes the remaining cigarette from the holder and stamps it out, then puts the holder into her purse. Tucking the dog under her arm, she turns to Aber and Daniel, saying, "Some story for Washington Square, right! I think it's the only time I saw the police come to these buildings. Things happen across the street in the park, but never on my side of the street." She crosses the street and enters her building.

Daniel stands wide-eyed. Aber puts his hand on his back, then around his shoulders. They are silent as they walk toward the subway, heading for home.

Charles Street Police Station

A week later Aber, alone, goes to the Charles Street police station, the station closest to Washington Square. A policeman, about Aber's age sits on a stool behind the polished high wooden counter. He says to Aber, "What can I do for you, sir?"

"Thank you, officer. I'm trying to locate a man who I understand was arrested sometime around 1912 at Washington Square. Possibly he was arrested for disorderly conduct."

Hmmm, 1912, I didn't work here. That may be hard to find out. But wait, let me call the captain. He calls toward a room at the back of the station. "Mike! Mike, can you come here a minute? Maybe you can help this gentleman."

A portly, white-haired police officer with bright pink cheeks comes up to the counter. "Yes sir, what can I do for you?" Aber repeats his request.

"That may be difficult, but why do you want to find him?"

"My nephew, who is now fifteen, thinks this man may be his father. He's not sure, but we know he was cruel to the boy's mother. At one point, he was arrested."

"He sounds like bad news, why look for trouble? Do you know if the woman is okay?"

"She took the boy and fled the country. Then sadly died of an illness."

"Oh, sorry. Is the boy in good hands now?"

"Oh yes, he's in very good hands and is doing well. He wants to know the truth about his first set of parents?"

"And if he's the one who wants to know, why didn't you bring him with you?"

"I thought about that. I guess if the news is bad, I want to break it to him carefully."

"Hmmm. I see. What is your name, address and occupation, sir?" Aber gives the policeman his information, including the document of his recent American citizenship."

"Congratulations on becoming a citizen."

"Thank you."

The policeman lifts a heavy loose-leaf book onto the counter. "Okay, you say sometime around 1912 at Washington Square. We rarely get calls from there. Do you have the name of the person?"

"Only his first name, Mendl, but he called himself Jack."

"Sounds familiar." He flips through the heavy book. "Do you have any idea what the date might be?" Aber thinks, *If Dan was around 6 months, mmm... July or August.* "I think maybe in the summer." Here it is. August 20th, 1912. Oh yes, I was on duty. I remember Mendl called Jack. Mendl Levy, he was. That was his first arrest. That night we booked him for disorderly conduct and intoxication. But we knew about him before that arrest. He was a well-known bootlegger and involved in a prostitution ring. He was clever and managed to avoid arrest for a long time. He must have made plenty of dough, known as a snappy dresser. He was a clever crook. After that arrest, he went downhill and kept slipping up. We arrested him plenty of times, usually for disorderly conduct and a bunch of times for assault. He beat up some girls who worked for him. He ended up a wino on the Bowery and got into a few slugging fests there too." He flips through more pages of the loose-leaf book. "Hmmm, he's had no more arrests for the past five years. Maybe he left the state. Maybe he died. Those Bowery bums have short lives. Some call it the last mile. Yeah, I remember him. A skinny, curly, red-headed guy had an accent of some sort." The policeman pauses a moment. "Ah yes, it's coming back to me. He was a deserter from, I think, the Russian army, and he was a stowaway on a ship to the U.S. You've got to hand it to him. He was smart and knew how to survive. But after that Washington Square arrest, he was really finished. Well sir, I'm sorry your nephew has to hear such tough news. You were right to hear it first. I have a grandson that age. I'd never want him to hear stuff like this from a stranger, let alone about his father." Shaking his head. "A kid takes stuff like that hard." He sighs. "So good luck, sir." The policeman extends his hand to Aber, and Aber returns the handshake, thanks him and leaves. But as he starts to go out the door, he turns back to the policeman. "It's prohibition, how do winos get their liquor?"

"Oh, sir, there's more drinking now than ever. Levy was a bootlegger himself, and he knew how to get it. Probably sold it on the Bowery. Also, you could go into any pharmacy and get alcohol. Sometimes those guys were so desperate for a drink they drank wood alcohol! We picked up too many dead bodies from that poison." The policeman beckons Aber to come closer. "I have to say, in New York, the cops really don't go after the bootleggers unless they have committed some other crime like assault or murder. We got Levy on disorderly conduct that first time. Later we got him on assault and vagrancy."

Aber walks back to Midtown, to his room at the Men's Y. *What should I tell Dan about this? Mendl was a deserter. Jews were horribly treated in the Russian army. They were the first to get killed. I don't blame him for deserting. A stowaway, wow! He probably starved. How did he get through Ellis Island? The guy was a real survivor—for a while, anyway. It's Interesting that he went downhill only after that arrest. What does that say about him? I can't hold all this back from Dan, but what should I tell him? I don't want to tell him about* the prostitution. He would figure out his mother was involved. Everything else is just about Mendl–Mendl Levy. We have his name now. That cop told me a lot. Survival can be brutal, even violent, especially for men. Women trying to survive are often the victims. What will Dan make of this? At some point he may figure out the prostitution stuff. So many poor immigrant girls got caught in that, especially if they came alone. I wonder if that's one of Fannie's ghosts. We all have ghosts. I sure do. That war broke me. Oh, I'm doing well enough. We're all doing well now. We're not in a war. We're not starving. Fannie and Marek, my brothers in Europe, and Marek's family in Hungary, all of us, even me—we are more than surviving. But we have our ghosts. Pain comes now not from what happens to us but from the ghosts we carry. Was Mendl always bad? He was desperate. Wow, a stowaway on that trip! Dan has his ghosts too. That's why he's searching. Dan will know his father was a wanted criminal. He already knows he was violent to his mother, and he didn't want him. All that will be on Dan's mind. Is that better than a ghost?

Underworld

I am so mad at Uncle Aber for going to the police station without me. He had no right to do that. It's great he wants to help, but this is MY life. First Mama snoops in my stuff, then Uncle Aber. Yes, he got a lot of information, but I should have been there to ask the questions and to hear what the policeman said. I'm getting this secondhand. I won't let that happen again. I'll do my own searching from now on.

Uncle Mischa's letter is so important. I got to ask my questions, and Uncle Mischa wrote only to me. Mendl Levy, Mendl Levy, Daniel Levy, Hannah Levy. If things were normal, the three of us would have been the Levy family. A deserter! A rich gangster! A drunk! He was violent to my mother! What if that's in me? I'll never drink wine, not even Shabbos wine, and I'm telling Tateh, no boxing lessons, not even just to get strong. Mendl was a skinny redhead and so am I. Oh please, please, I don't want to be him. I'm going to switch to track or maybe gymnastics, then no one can get hurt except me.

I get so mad at Mama and Simon. I'm always mad at Adela, and now I'm mad at Uncle Aber. I can't be so mad. What if I get violent like Mendl Levy, MENDL LEVY, the man who made me? Tateh wonders why I want to go looking for trouble. Maybe he was right. I've found trouble.

Later, around three in the morning, Daniel bolts upright. He is out of breath. There's a terrible pain in his stomach. Gasping, "Mama, Mama come!" Fannie flies out of bed and races into Daniel's room. Simon wakes up. "Danny, what's the matter?"

"Mama, I have a terrible pain in my stomach. I can't breathe. Am I dying?" Fannie's heart is racing.

"Show me where Danny." He puts his hand just under his ribs. When Fannie touches the place, she can feel a knot of hardness.

"Oh Mama, leave your hand there. It helps." The knot softens under the warmth of her hand.

"Danny, I think you just have a tight muscle cramp there. I'm going to get you a hot water bottle." She brings him the warm rubber bottle, wrapped in a tea towel. Soon the pain is gone, and Daniel breathes normally.

"Danny, do you think you had a bad dream?"

"I don't know. I'm okay Mama. Sorry I woke you up."

"You woke me up too." complains Simon.

"Oh, go to sleep!" *I'm mean to Simon, and I pay no attention to Miriam. I'm mean. I must fight it. I have to work at being a good person. It's the Mendl in me!*

Fannie says, "We can all go back to sleep now." She turns off the light and returns to bed.

Did I have a bad dream? Yes! It was night. I was walking down a dark street, dark except for some light from a store. I see a skinny old man with bushy hair like mine. I yell, 'Mendl Levy,' and he comes at me with a big knife and stabs me in the stomach. Daniel's gut clutches again. He pulls the still-warm hot water bottle back onto his stomach.

I need to know more. Uncle Aber says Mendl wasn't arrested for the past five years. Why? Maybe he tried to become good. Maybe he was good before he came to America and then turned bad. Mama and Tateh and my mother, Hannah, all had hard times when they came. But they didn't turn bad. Why do some people turn bad? Was Mendl Levy always bad? I have to find out. It's my life before I came to this family. Someday I'll find out and I'll do it alone. I never want to hurt anyone.

Fall 1927

Daniel gets ready to go to school. He reaches the school building, gets in line, and waits for the bell and the doors to open. On an impulse, he bolts out of the line and heads to the subway, the BMT J line. It will take him to the Bowery. As the train is about to reach the Bowery, it rises from underground and continues on elevated tracks. Daniel looks into the windows of the passing buildings. Men and some women lean out their windows, staring at the passing train. *Is one of them Mendl?* Where no one leans out, the windows look black, or rags or old clothing hang or blow in the wind. The train reaches the Bowery. Daniel exits. He descends the iron stairs. Under the tracks, he enters a world of dusk. Where to start? Which way to walk?

"Boy, boy, come here." A crackly voice calls out behind Daniel. He turns to see an old woman with long, straggly gray hair. She beckons him to come closer. "Boy, come here!" She sits on the curb and wears a big man's coat. Next to her is a shopping bag filled with old, dirty clothes. The flesh hangs from her face. Her eyes are almost swollen shut. White matter runs down the wrinkles along her nose. "Boy, you look rich. Do you have money for me? I'm hungry." Daniel reaches into his pocket and gives her a nickel. "What are you doing here, boy?"

"I'm looking for someone."

"Who?"

"Mendl Levy, do you know him?"

"Never heard of him. Do you have any food?" Daniel made himself a cheese sandwich before leaving the house. He takes it out of his jacket pocket and gives the woman half of it. She points her finger at his pocket. "The other half !" He hands her the other half. She waves him away. He walks on.

Daniel walks the Bowery. A wind gusts through the streets, blowing cigarette butts, scraps of newspaper, and what looks like bits of toilet paper. Gray men wedge themselves in doorways, drinking from bottles in paper bags Some sleep, pressing their bodies against the sides of buildings. They cover themselves with newspapers or torn cartons. The stench of urine and filth is everywhere.

He walks up to what looks like a hotel and stands watching. He listens to a group of men standing over a fire in a garbage can. Some cook hot dogs over the flame. Most have a bottle they constantly put to their lips, taking gulps. One man asks, "Has anyone seen Max?"

Another answers, "I saw an ambulance pick him up yesterday. He was limp. His face was yellow. I don't think he's going to make it."

A new man walks up to the fire. He also drinks from a bottle. He stands for a moment and asks, "Do you know where I can get a meal?"

Another man with a knitted hat offers him his cooked hot dog and asks, "Are you new in town?"

The newcomer answers, "Yeah, I came looking for work. Nothing!"

"Nah, there isn't much work anymore."

"Do you know where I can find a bed for the night?"

Pointing to the building where they stand, "This here's a flophouse. If you don't mind fleas, you can get a bed for a quarter a night. Then out by 7:00. But if you can manage not to drink, you can go to the Bowery Mission off Rivington Street. They make you sit through the service and sing a few hymns, but you get a hot meal and a clean bed. They take your clothes to fumigate themto get rid of the lice. You can get a shower, and they even lend you a razor to shave. They give you back your clothes when you give them back the razor. It's a good deal except for no drinking, all the time you're there."

The newcomer listens. He takes another pull from his bottle. "Thanks, and thanks for the hot dog." He walks away.

The man with the knitted cap calls to him, "Hey, good luck, buddy!"

Daniel walks over to check out the entrance to the flophouse. There is a heavy glass door. He tries to peer inside. But all he can see is his own reflection looking back at him.

"Here I am, right here! Ugly, skinny, son of Mendl! bowery bum!"

He hears a high-pitched voice from behind. "Hey kid!"

Someone tugs at his jacket. A tiny person, no taller than Daniel's shoulder, squeals, "Hi, I'm Johnny. Who are you?" Daniel, stunned, stops in his tracks. The person grabs Daniel's buttocks. Daniel screams, "Get away from me!" The men around the garbage can laugh. Daniel races back toward the train, tears up the iron steps, and pitches himself into the almost closing door of the train. He gasps for breath. Sweat drenches his shirt. A strangled sob erupts from his throat. He presses his forehead against the train window. Sobs wrack his body.

"Are you okay son?" a woman in the seat behind him asks.

"Yeah, I'm ok." gulps Daniel.

The woman asks, "Can I ask you where you're going, son?"

"I'm going home."

"Is that a good place for you.?"

"Yes."

"Good. It sounds like it's the right place for you to go now."

Daniel is surprised to find himself comforted, comforted by a stranger he hasn't even looked at. He can hardly wait to get home.

The next day Fannie says, "Danny, I got a call from your homeroom teacher." Fannie looks puzzled. "She said you were not in any of your classes yesterday. Is that so?"

Daniel's mouth goes dry. "Uh, yes Mama, I missed school yesterday."

"Where did you go?"

"Umm, I needed a day off from school."

"Why?"

"I don't know. Maybe I needed time to think."

"Danny, I worry about you."

"I'm okay Mama, I promise. Sometimes I just need time to myself."

"Where were you?"

"Uh, I went to Washington Square Park to look at where my first mama lived."

Fannie, taken aback, "How do you know that's where she lived?"

"Yeah, that afternoon, when I went out with Aber, we went to City Hall to get my birth certificate."

"Oh, do you have it? Can I see it?"

"No, the man at the counter didn't give it to me. But he told us where she lived."

"You skipped school to visit Washington Square?"

"Yes."

"Was Aber with you?"

"He was the first time I went. Not this time."

"You spent the whole day there alone?"

"Uh, yeah. I walked around the neighborhood and sat in the park, then came home when school would have been out." The sweat streams down from under his arms. He can smell it.

"Danny, I understand finding out about your first parents is very important to you. But you can't miss school, and you still need, at the very least, to let Tateh or me know where you're going."

"I told you, Mama, this is a part of my life that is totally mine, some of it, before I even knew you."

"No, I knew your first mama when she was pregnant with you, and I knew you from when you were first born until Hannah took you to Palestine."

"Did you know my first Mama wrote her name as Anna White on my birth certificate?"

"Really! No! I didn't know that."

"Aber figured that out when the man at City Hall said there was no Hannah Weitzner, but he went through the list of Daniels born that day and there was an Anna White."

"Aber is smart. Look, Danny, I must talk to Tateh about this. And I don't want you going off alone. If you go with Aber, it's okay. Maybe you won't want to tell us the details. But I want to know you're with Aber. Do you understand?"

"Yes, Mama"

"And you are NEVER to skip school."

"Yes, Mama."

"So, do we understand each other?"

"Yes."

Oy gavult! (shock or dismay) *God knows where he's going to end up when he goes looking for Mendl.*

Daniel goes into his room, throws himself on his bed and covers his face with his hands. Now I'm a liar! His heart is racing.

The next evening, Fannie talks to Marek, telling him what she heard from Daniel and that she is worried about him. "He seems so withdrawn. I've seen no joy in him for a long time."

"I'll keep an eye on him." says Marek.

Fannie must leave to go to the Yiddish theater to fit costumes. After homework is done, Daniel approaches Marek and asks if they can talk.

"Of course, Danny."

"Tateh, did Mama talk to you about my going with Aber when I am trying to find out who my first parents were?"

"Yes, she did. But I don't understand why you don't want to tell us where you're going, even with Aber."

"It's hard to explain, Tateh. This is a part of my life separate from you and Mama, and it's something I need to do in my own way."

Sternly, "And you promise never to skip school again."

"Yes."

"It's a sad thing about your first mama dying and you don't know about your first father. But remember, Danny, that man never raised you. You began with your first mother, Hannah, who only wanted the best for you and then with Mama, who is a wonderful mama."

"I know Tateh. You're the first father to take care of me, and I couldn't hope for a better one."

"Thank you, Danny. I can't say I understand why you're doing this and why you must have secrets from us. You and Adela both puzzle me these days. Maybe it's because your mama and I, when we were your age lived in such a different world. We were figuring out how to get by, how to deal with people who hated us Jews, and how not to starve. The last thing we thought about was our beginnings or who our parents were. Our parents were our parents!"

"I know Tateh."

"No, I don't think you do. It's a much easier life for you and Adela."

"Is it okay if I go to bed now, Tateh?"

Sighing, "Yes, Danny, go ahead."

Daniel starts to walk away and then turns back. "One more thing Tateh. I don't want to learn any more boxing."

Taken aback, "Why not?"

"I never want to hurt anyone."

Urgently, "But Danny, what about self-defense? What about protecting yourself or someone else? There are rough people out there. And I thought you wanted to get muscles! If you know how to fight, you can stop people from hurting you. You'd know how to stop them without killing them."

Surprised at Marek's intense reaction, Daniel says, "I can find other ways to get strong, maybe track, or gymnastics."

With contempt, "Gymnastics! Who does gymnastics? No, you'll never learn self-defense with gymnastics or track. Maybe track could teach you how to run away from some enemy; but what if you were cornered and couldn't run away? How would you protect yourself?"

Exasperated, "Tateh, why! Do you think I'm going to be in some fight?"

"Marek's voice rising, "You don't know what's out there. Gymnastics! Track! No." then pleading, "Please, Danny, give it some more time."

"Okay, okay, Tateh. I'll keep up the rope jumping and the footwork and the weights. But I think it's a waste. I'm as skinny as when I started. But I refuse to punch anyone!"

"You know Jacob started having matches, and no one is getting hurt. It's all well controlled."

His voice rising, "I'm not Jacob! I'll never be Jacob! Tateh, you think a street fight is controlled!! You think a street fight is a match!!" Daniel stomps out of the room.

Marek fumes. *What's the matter with him? Gymnastics and track! Ridiculous! Well, Fannie will be happy to hear he doesn't want to box. But what is he so afraid of? We must start Simon early on this, before he gets to be a teenager and has too many ideas of his own. A boy needs to know how to protect himself. A man needs to know how to protect someone else. I don't understand these kids. They have no idea how lucky they are. Fannie says he's withdrawn. Maybe he has been—but not with me! He's rebellious!*

Letter to Rachel from Fannie

Dear Rachel,

I'm honored you trust me enough to open your heart to me. Be reassured that what you tell me will never leave my lips. I only hope you feel some relief. I am sad to hear about Aber's response to you. I confess that from that first moment you and he met at our apartment, the day of his arrival in America, I hoped the two of you might one day marry. You are well suited for each other in so many ways. But Rachel, yes, the war changed Aber, strangely for both better and worse. I was still young when I left the family and he was my big brother, but I never thought of him as especially thoughtful until we exchanged letters during the war. He didn't tell me about some of the terrifying experiences he told you. He wrote about the futility of war and had many observations about our family. I did not know he was engaged. He never mentioned it. The horrible death of his fiancé, right before his eyes is unbearably tragic. How do you recover from that?

He always looked out for his younger brothers in the army, and then he and my sister Rivka protected very young Kala and Jacob during the war. It shows his devotion and sense of responsibility, all the while dealing with his own, what must be intolerable, suffering.

I wish I could advise you, Rachel. I think your broken heart is another casualty of war. And the war had already broken your heart when your beloved Roland was killed. The war ends but suffering keeps going on and on. The cruelty and dying on the battlefield are only one part of it.

Bear in mind, Rachel, you are my dearest friend. And I strongly believe that although you yearn for more, you are Aber's dearest and most trusted friend.

Love,
Fannie

Iago

It is February 1928. Daniel just turned sixteen. He is a few inches taller. Although still slender, his voice is deeper, and his face less round, more sculpted. No longer a child, he has become a youth.

Rachel started a theater group for high school juniors and seniors at the library. Daniel joined it as soon as he entered his junior year. Until now, he had only small parts, or he worked on production. For the next play, the theater group voted to do Othello. Daniel requested the part of Iago. He auditioned for it and was thrilled when he got it. Rachel required anyone with a major part to prepare a backstory of their character to present to the group. They are not to read anything written about their characters but to dig deep into their own life experience to understand what may motivate their character to have become who they are. Because this was Daniel's first big part, Rachel suggested he think about what makes a person bad. She also reminded him that although we think of Iago as one of Shakespeare's meanest villains, there was a time when he loved Othello, but when Othello turned his love elsewhere, all Iago's love turned to hate and cruelty.

Immediately Daniel thought about Mendl's meanness, and he knew it was time to return to the Bowery and see if this time he could find out more. He thought about calling Aber to accompany him but decided not to. He knew he should tell his parents but feared if he did, they would try to stop him. He knew he must do this alone.

On Sunday, Daniel decided this was the day to go. He told his parents he was going to a friend's house and would be home by suppertime.

On the train downtown, he remembers overhearing the men talk about the Bowery Mission, where you could get a free meal and a clean bed, provided you attended the religious service and didn't drink all the time you were there. *Maybe Mendl went to the Bowery Mission, and maybe someone remembers him.*

The train rises out of the tunnel, now becoming "the elevated". Daniel shivers, remembering the end of the last trip. *What if that happens again?*

At the Bowery stop, he climbs down the now familiar iron stairway and once again is under the tracks where night is always falling. As he walks, he sees the same old woman he saw last time She is sitting in the same spot. He turns into a small coffee shop and buys a tuna sandwich, a cup of coffee, and a Danish pastry to go. He takes the brown paper bag and walks over to the woman. He offers her the bag of food along with some change from his pocket and asks if he can sit and talk to her. She looks about the same, but he thinks she now may be blind. She turns toward his voice, but her eyes are cloudy and unfocused.

"Do what you want, mister!" She cackles. "What's this?" she demands, holding up the bag.

"It's food. I thought you might be hungry."

She plunges her hand into the bag, feeling around, pulls out the container of coffee, and then the pastry. She feels her way to opening the coffee and unwrapping the Danish, then wolfs down the Danish and gulps down the coffee. She closes her unseeing eyes, sighs, rocks back and forth a few times and seems about to fall asleep.

Daniel says, "I guess you were hungry."

"Hmmm."

There's a sandwich in the bag, too."

"I know that! And it stinks! Got any wine?"

"Sorry, I don't."

She is about to sleep. Daniel asks, "Before you take your nap, can you tell me where to find the Bowery Mission?"

"Straight down the Bowery off Rivington." She points to the right side of the street. "You know you can't go there if you're blotto."

"Yes, I know." He gets up to leave and says, "Enjoy your nap."

Sounding annoyed, she snaps, "Go!"

The Bowery is more crowded than the last time. Daniel sees a long line of men, and when he walks by the beginning of the line, he sees it's a bread line. Two nuns with baskets on card tables pass out a chunk of bread and an apple to each person.

Before he reaches Rivington Street, he sees a parked police car flashing its lights. Two men, handcuffed, are roughly pushed into the back seat. A small crowd of onlookers disperses.

Between Rivington and Stanton streets, Daniel finds the Bowery Mission. It's a five-story brick building with a large red double door. On the second floor, Daniel can see a huge stained-glass window. Outside, men stand against the wall of the building. Some seem to sleep standing. No one here is drinking. There are men on crutches and one man without legs who sits on a low wheeled platform and pushes himself along with his gloved knuckles. When the red doors open, the men file upstairs to the second-floor chapel. Two men carry the man without legs, and another carries the platform. As they mount the stairs, most men who wear hats take them off. Daniel, noticing this, takes off his cap. He takes a seat at the back of the chapel. The odor of sweat, dirty clothes, and urine is overwhelming. Over the altar hangs a crucifix as tall as a man. Daniel looks around. Here he is, a Jew in a Christian chapel in his good clothes. A few of the men curiously peer over at him but don't seem especially interested. They turn back to look at the minister, who now speaks. He is an older man with a notable British accent.

"Welcome all to our service at the Bowery Mission, with an especially warm welcome to those who are here for the first time."

He explains that the mission dedicates itself to offering hope, forgiveness and repair. Gesturing toward the stained-glass window depicting the parable of the Prodigal Son, he reminds the congregation how the prodigal could begin a new life when his father welcomed him with forgiveness and love. He speaks of compassion and love for your neighbor and for your enemy and then mentions the Ten Commandments. Except for several times saying "Our Lord Jesus Christ," the sermon could have been almost any sermon at Temple Emanu-El. This surprises Daniel. He looks around and wonders how many others sitting here are Jewish. Did Mendl ever sit here? Daniel hopes he had. The service ends, and while the men file out, Daniel awkwardly moves to a corner at the back of the room. He nervously twists his cap but is determined to find out what he can about Mendl. The last man leaves. The minister sees Daniel and comes over to him. He extends his large hand and gives Daniel's hand a vigorous shake. "Greetings, young man. I'm John Greener Hallimond, and you are?"

"I'm Daniel Horvath, and I wonder if I can speak with you."

"Of course you can, Daniel. What is this about?"

"I am searching for any information about my father, who I never knew, Mendl Levy, sometimes called Jack Levy."

The minister blinks and pulls his head back a few inches. He focuses intensely on Daniel's face. He takes in a breath. "Yes, Daniel, let's talk. Follow me to my study." Daniel follows Hallimond up another flight. A woman stands at the door. She has been waiting for them and asks, "What can I bring the two of you?" Hallimond introduces Daniel to Mrs.

Haliimond who smiles warmly and asks Daniel, "Would you like coffee or would you prefer cocoa?" Daniel says he'd like the cocoa. Hallimond says, "And maybe some of those Easter Biscuits if there are any left." Turning to Daniel, "I send for them from England. They are delicious."

Hallimond and Daniel enter the study, which is small but comfortably furnished with a desk, filled bookshelves and two upholstered wingback chairs facing each other. The lights are low, and the room is quiet except for the sound of footsteps above. Hallimond explains that after the service, the men can get a hot meal in the dining room just above where they are sitting. He says, "Usually Mrs. Hallimond and I join the guests for meals upstairs, but after the Sunday service, I meet with visitors here in the study." He gestures to Daniel to take a seat, and the two face each other. Before the conversation begins, there is a knock on the door and Mrs. Hallimond stands in the hall with a tray. Hallimond takes the tray and places it on a small table between the chairs. Mrs. Hallimond smiles at Daniel and leaves.

"So, Daniel it's good to meet you. May I ask how old you are?"

"I'm sixteen."

"And you are in high school?"

"Yes, at George Washington High School."

"That's up near the bridge. Is that right?"

"Yes, in Washington Heights."

"Ah yes."

"You're wondering if I knew Mendl Levy?" Daniel nods.

"Yes, I knew Mendl." Daniel takes a big intake of breath and for a moment is not sure he wants to hear more. "And you think he may be your father?"

Daniel realizes he is still holding and twisting his cap. He stuffs it into his jacket pocket. "Yes, Mr. Hallimond."

"It sounds like there's a big story behind your search. Tell me what you know, Daniel, and I'll add to it if I have anything to add. I'd like you to start by telling me about your life now."

Daniel takes a moment and looks at Mr. Hallimond. He is a big, portly man who sits slightly bowed, resting his elbows on the chair arms, with his hands folded and supporting his chin. His fair complexion and ruddy cheeks contrast with his sad, gray eyes. Daniel fears he is about to dive into a bottomless body of dark water. He takes a breath and dives. He begins with a description of his family and tells Hallimond what he knows about Hannah and what he learned from his visit to Washington Square and Aber's meeting at the police station. When he reaches this point, it is as though he just ran a race and needs to catch his breath.

"Daniel, can you tell me why, when you have a good father and a good family, who obviously love you and care for you, why you need to pursue this ancient history?"

With his fists against his chest, the phrases spurting out, "I'm his son! He made me! Uh... is his badness in me? He did bad things to my first mother."

"Yes, but what does that have to do with you?"

His thoughts racing, *What does this have to do with me? Hallimond makes no sense! How could Mendl not have to do with me?*

He repeats, "I'm his SON!" Hallimond does not respond. *Silence.* Daniel is pressured by the passing quiet seconds. He looks away, then back at Hallimond. "Not knowing my father makes me like...uh...uh... like a book with a bunch of missing chapters." *More silence.* "Uh... mmm...I guess...I guess I want to know if he ever became good. Uh... so if his badness is in me, I can also uh, uh... be good" The word good comes out like a bark. "But either way, I need to know. I need to know about the man who was my first father. Yes, uh, that's it. I need to know who he was."

"Sounds like you fear you're fated to be bad because Mendl did some bad things."

"Fated? What do you mean?"

"As though it's your destiny. As though you have no choice over what you do, as though all the care and learning you've received doesn't influence who you are. You have your own moral compass."

Daniel looks down and away. He needs time to take in what Hallimond said. *Mendl...destiny...my choice...*he takes a breath, and still looking down says, "Hmm. I never thought of that."

"Look, Daniel, I believe you are Mendl's son. You look a lot like him. Mendl was a complicated man. After he hit bottom and ended up on the Bowery, from time to time he came to this office and confided in me. I got to know him as well as anyone could know a man like him. Did you know he was barely older than you when he was in the Russian army?

"Yeah, my uncle heard about that."

"He told me how a group of soldiers picked him up off the street and he was suddenly at the front lines during the worst part of the war. The Russians conscripted as many Jews as they could because they put them into the worst battles at the front lines, hoping to protect the others behind them. Mendl was a survivor. As bad as life was for him, he wanted to live, so he deserted the army. But I'm leaving out an important part. Another reason the army picked him up was because he was a starving kid who looked younger than his age. Mendl was an orphan, with no family. Everyone in his family was killed in a pogrom."

"Wow, I didn't know that."

"They were yanked from their house, trampled by Cossack horses, and the house set afire. Mendl had gone into the forest with a friend to play and when he came home, he saw the mutilated bodies of his parents, brothers, and sisters and the ashes of his house.

After he deserted, he stowed away on a ship to New York. On the first day at sea, when passengers on the upper decks were at meals, he sneaked into their staterooms, where he stole clothes and money and used one of their bathrooms to clean up. Once dressed as an upper-deck passenger, it was easy to be part of the crowd. He pretended to befriend other boys on the ship and told them he was traveling alone to join his family on New York's Upper West Side. Families invited him to meals. He ate well. He was very smart and somehow finessed the language issues. He stole a considerable amount of money on that trip. The only hard part was at night, when he had to figure out where to sleep. He mostly slept in the lifeboats and was often cold and wet. But he survived. When the ship anchored, he didn't go through Ellis Island because he got off the boat with upper-deck passengers.

When he got to New York, he faced more trouble. He took up with an older woman who got him drunk and stole all his money. I'm not sure how he got in with a gang, but he was put in charge of a prostitution ring."

Daniel gasps and covers his mouth with his hand.

"Yes, Daniel, some of this is going to be painful for you to hear." Hallimond waits before he says more. Daniel seems to take it in slowly. After a while, Daniel looks straight at Hallimond; his eyes are moist.

"Was my mother Hannah a, a, a prostitute?"

"That's a complicated story Daniel and if you want, I'll get right to that."

"Yes, yes, tell me." Daniel is pale and shaky.

"Mendl told me Hannah was the only woman he ever wanted for himself. He felt possessive of her and jealous. At first, he just picked her out as a beautiful girl who wanted to be an actress. But then he became obsessed with her. He told her he had a business. He didn't tell her what kind. He said he would take care of her and see that she had money to get her family out of Europe. His boss threatened that if he didn't get Hannah started as a prostitute, Mendl would have to throw her out or the boss would expose him to the police. Clever Mendl figured out something else. As I understand it, the Jewish religion sanctions the pleasures of sex between a husband and wife so they will have many children. But very religious Jews raise their children so that boys and girls have little to do with each other and suddenly, on the night of the wedding, they're supposed to enjoy being sexual. Mendl told me, in Europe in the villages, there was often a woman who helped young men, who were engaged to be married, learn how to please a woman. There would be no penetration, but she taught them about women's bodies and their pleasure. This is the work Mendl wanted Hannah to do, and she would still be his alone. I guess the money to get her family out of Europe is what kept Hannah from running away. An older woman trained her. The bridegrooms' families paid well for this work.

But Mendl was so obsessed with Hannah and jealous of the men she worked with, he'd blow up and hit her. She still didn't run away. And then she became pregnant with you, and he couldn't stand the idea of a baby. I never understood what it was about a baby, and Mendl couldn't explain it. As you know, he threatened to throw both of you in the street if she kept you. I take it you know what happened with you and Hannah after."

Daniel nods and says, "Yes, we fled to Palestine."

"Oh Palestine! So that is where you went. And that is when Mendl, who had always cleverly avoided arrest, really fell apart, sometimes going berserk with assaults and heavy drinking. He ended up on the Bowery or in jail, back and forth. What you don't know is that after a while, all the fight in him seemed to burn out. He befriended another man here in the Bowery. They came to the mission often and eventually worked here. They cleaned and cooked for the guests. Mendl and Frank were more than friends. They were partners, and I believe they loved each other. Then Frank fell ill. He didn't want to go to a hospital because he feared they'd be separated. With the little money they earned here, they took a room somewhere, and Mendl nursed Frank, who became sicker and sicker. Mendl would sometimes stop by for a visit, and we would give him food to take back to his room with Frank. Mendl continued to do some odd jobs here. Pretty soon Frank became so ill that Mendl had to bring him to the hospital. It turned out Frank had TB and soon died. Well, Daniel, maybe you can guess what happened next."

"Mendl got TB?"

"Yes. He was in the hospital for a while. But I think after Frank's death, he had no more will to live. Mendl died on January 4, 1925. He was cremated, and his ashes scattered in the ocean." Hallimond pauses, then says, "I think that's the story, Daniel. At least the story I know."

Daniel sighs deeply. Then a long moan escapes from some place deep in his body. Then wracking sobs overtake him. Hallimond sits quietly for a while, then stands beside him, putting one large hand on Daniel's thin shoulder. Daniel's loud sobs slowly cease. He curls himself into a tight ball. After a long series of quiet whimpers, he tries to take a breath, but a few reflexive sobs keep coming. Looking up at Hallimond, he says, still gasping for breath, "Thank you."

"You are welcome, Daniel. Do you have more questions?"

"D-do you know if Mendl had...oth, other children?"

"I don't know. He may have but never mentioned them. Something about children seemed to frighten him. For a while, we had a woman guest here who had a young son. I noticed that if she and her son entered a room where Mendl was, he immediately left. It was strange." There is a pause. "Anything else, Daniel?"

"I don't think so."

"I hope what I could tell you can help and that your pain subsides."

"I think the pain has been in me my whole life. Today, some of it came out." They shake hands. Daniel climbs down the stairs and out the red door. Now he takes a deep breath and looks up to see the patterns of pale moted light coming through the open spaces of the elevated train tracks.

As he walks to the train, he stops and turns to enter the coffee shop again and buys another Danish and coffee, which he brings to the old woman. This time she says to Daniel, "God bless you, sir."

He climbs the iron staircase and stands on the platform waiting for the train. It is almost dinnertime. He imagines himself joining his parents when they have their evening tea. *Will I ever tell them what happened today? Maybe someday.*

The next morning, as Daniel awakens, he recovers his memory of the talk with Mr. Hallimond. He still has some time before he must get ready for school and then with a surge of energy and interest, remembers there is a rehearsal for "Othello" today. He gets up and goes to his desk to write the backstory for his character, Iago.

Iago was born in the city of Naples. He never knew the exact date of his birth because, as a very young baby, one night, he was found, naked and crying, on a heap of garbage. Whoever found him brought him to the city orphanage, where they named him Iago. As Iago grew, other boys often picked on him. They teased him about his bushy red hair and his puny small body. Sometimes they called him by girls' names. The grown-ups who worked at the orphanage paid no attention. Iago stayed at the orphanage until he was around six years old and then ran away. He tagged along with a band of Gypsy children who lived on the street. Soon he attached himself to an older boy who called himself "Capo". Capo liked Iago. He protected him, made sure Iago had his share of the stolen food and at night let Iago curl up next to him, which kept them both warm. This went on for a couple of years. They begged together, stole together, ran away from the police together, and kept each other company. However, as Capo grew, he would say to Iago that he found some girls on the street beautiful. Then one day Capo told Iago he was on his own now and wanted nothing more to do with him. He met a girl called Olivia, and they were going to be together from now on.

Iago was devastated. He wanted his Capo, and if he couldn't have Capo, he wanted to die. He tried to drown himself in the sea. He stood in front of galloping horses, hoping they would run over him and crush him to death. If he owned a dagger, he would plunge it into his heart. But he lived on and found he could survive alone. His grief turned into anger. He was going to get his gang to work for him. If the other kids wouldn't steal for him, he threatened he'd beat them bloody, or he'd kill their sister. But at night, when Iago tried to sleep, he was persecuted by dreams of being chased or stabbed. When he awakened every morning, he reached for Capo and found his hand touched nothing but air. In these dreams Capo never returned, but he left, over and over again. Iago became crueler and more ruthless each day, but every night, his terrified and tormented soul roamed the dark and viscous streets of his dreams. In the mornings his arms embraced only air.

One day, after emerging from a house with some stolen coins and a necklace, two soldiers kidnapped him. They stole the coins and the necklace, then forced him into the military. They threatened him with the police if he resisted. Eventually, Iago settled into the army, where he grew to admire and then to love his general, Othello. Othello befriended Iago and confided in him. But when Othello promoted Cassio over Iago, Iago felt betrayed. And finally, and worst of all, when Othello gave all his love to Desdemona, all of Iago's love for Othello turned to brutal hatred. Iago set out to destroy him.

Othello

It is spring, 1928. The play is cast. Rehearsals are underway. Othello is played by a boy in Daniel's class, Luc Auguste. Luc is a tall, athletic boy with bushy black hair and a café au lait complexion. His family emigrated from Haiti two years ago. His parents are artists and came to America when his father was offered the job of scene designer for the Metropolitan Opera. Luc, whose first languages are Creole and French, did not speak English fluently until last year. He and Daniel bonded in friendship when rehearsals began. After rehearsals, they like to go to a local coffee shop and talk.

They enter the steamy, overheated coffee shop, smelling of cigarettes, coffee and frying foods. They each order a soda and share a donut. Luc says to Daniel, "I really liked your backstory for Iago. That guy is as mean as a snake, but your story of his life makes us understand him better and be a little sorry for him. Why did you want that part? Everyone in the play either ends up hating Iago or dead. Then, Iago is tortured and killed.

"Yeah, I know." *Should I tell Luc the story of Mendl? I want Luc to like me. He could think it's too creepy.* "When I was a sophomore, I had a horrible experience when a couple of mean bullies attacked me on my way home. They dragged me into an alley, pinned me against the wall and beat me up. It took a long time to get over that. When we read the play and Iago was such a bully, I thought if I played him, maybe I could find out what makes someone so evil. What about you? Why did you want to play Othello?"

"I didn't want to play Othello. My English isn't great. I can speak better than I can read, and reading Shakespeare is torture. I haven't gotten used to school in America. I do fine in math and chem, but reading books and plays and history is hard, even though those were my best subjects in Haiti. But Miss Kaminski really worked on me to take the part. At first, I thought it was only because I'm Creole. But then she said Othello always feels like an outsider in Venice, and she thought I might understand what that's like. I think Miss Kaminski was understanding something about me that until she said it, I didn't think about. But it's true. I do feel like an outsider. She thought being a part of the drama group would help."

"Has it?"

"I'm sitting here with you, talking. That didn't happen with anyone else before I came to the drama group."

Daniel knows he is blushing. *Maybe he really wants to be friends.* "Have you written your back-story for Othello?"

"Not yet. I'm afraid it will have too many mistakes in it."

"If you want, I could look it over before you hand it in."

"Yeah, that would help."

They each leave fifteen cents on the table and walk toward their apartment buildings. They are silent as they walk. Daniel is aware that their strides match. The heels of their high-top leather shoes click on the pavement in unison. Daniel wonders if Luc notices. He longs to close his eyes and rest in the rhythm. When they reach Daniel's building, he wishes their walk could go on. But he looks forward to Luc's handshake, a French custom, at greetings and partings. When Luc reaches his hand toward Daniel, Daniel notices Luc's warm, fleshy palm is a little moist. And then, which he never did before, Luc leans forward and lightly kisses Daniel on each cheek, saying, "This is the way French grown-ups say hello and goodbye."

A blush rises from Daniel's throat into his cheeks. *I must be bright red!* He can't move, frozen in place yet on fire. Luc, however, is poised and says,

"Goodbye Daniel. See you tomorrow in chem and later at rehearsal. I'll bring my back-story with all its mistakes."

"Yes, yes, yes—uh, see you tomorrow." Daniel goes into his building but then turns back to the street. He doesn't want to break the spell of the last moments. He sets out to walk around the block and is surprised to find himself giggling. He wants to run, to skip; it has been so long since he has felt such lightness. *I think Luc really wants to be my friend.* His insides flutter.

The nineteen hours until he sees Luc again at chem class seem like forever. *And then another hour until rehearsal. And then finally getting back to the coffee shop.* He keeps circling the block. *I want to be a great actor. I want Luc to be impressed. I want to show how tortured Iago is about losing Othello's love for him. At the beginning of the play, Iago keeps saying, I hate Othello. He hates him so much because he once loved him and thought Othello loved him back, but he didn't, or he once did and now loves Desdemona. Hmmm, what can I do to show Iago isn't only mean? He's also tortured by love. Hmmm, I've been saying "I hate Iago" as though every word is equally important. I think it will come across better if I emphasize HATE!*

That night, in front of the bathroom mirror, Daniel says his line. On the word "hate" he bares his teeth, makes two fists, contracts his torso, jolts himself into a short squat, and screams "HATE", then bursts into laughter.

Later that night Daniel enters his bedroom quietly. Simon is asleep. He gets ready for bed and slips under his quilt. He remembers the moments of that beautiful walk with Luc, step matching step, the clicks of their heels thrumming in unison, then the handshake and the kisses, the kisses... what grown-ups do. Warmth rises from his thighs into his groin, his stomach, his chest, his throat, he gasps into the pillow and soon he sleeps. He wakes. It is around five-thirty. His quilt is all twisted around his legs. *What happened?* He gets up, straightens the quilt and crawls back under it and turns on his side. When he lays his head back on his pillow, he remembers his dream. *I am entwining my legs and arms with someone's legs and arms. It's wonderful, smooth, strong, warm. Who was it? Oh! Jacob! I don't want it to be Jacob! What's wrong with me? I don't want to be that man on the bus! I'm so weird, so puny, so ugly, so white with red pussy hair!* He grabs handfuls of his hair. *I wish I could pull it out. It's crazy Mendl hair. Mendl, who Hallimond said loved another man. Why did Rachel give me that Walt Whitman book? Does she know something about me? On top of everything else, Mendl was a pervert.... Hallimond didn't seem to think it was bad. That was when Mendl became good, taking care of Frank even though he probably knew he would get sick too.*

It is getting light out, still too early to get up for school, but Daniel gets up anyway and takes <u>Leaves of Grass</u> from his bookshelf and a flashlight and gets back under his quilt. He turns to a page where he placed a bookmark.

WE two boys together clinging,
One the other never leaving,
Up and down the roads going—North and South excursions making,
Power enjoying—elbows stretching—fingers clutching,
Armed and fearless—eating, drinking, sleeping, loving,
No law less than ourselves owning—sailing, soldiering, thieving, threat-
ening,
Misers, menials, priests, alarming—air breathing, water drinking, on the
turf of the sea-beach dancing,

With birds singing–With fishes swimming–With trees branching and leafing, Cities wrenching, ease scorning, statutes mocking, feebleness chasing.
Fulfilling our foray.

That afternoon at rehearsal, Daniel tries his new interpretation of Iago and again breaks up laughing. Rachel tells him to try again. He repeats it, and this time he becomes Iago's tormented soul.

"Good Daniel! That seems just right." Says Rachel.

Renaissance

A few days later, Daniel finds a note in his locker from Luc. He had slipped it into the narrow space under the locker door. Daniel thought it was going to be a rewrite of Luc's backstory of Othello. Instead, it is a personal note from Luc.

Greetings Daniel,

This coming Saturday, my parents and I are going to join some artists, musicians and actors who have arranged with a restaurant in Harlem for a late-night showing of films from Europe. Would you like to come? We will be out late. My parents say you are welcome to stay overnight.

Our apartment is close to the restaurant on 155th and Amsterdam Ave. I hope you will come.

Ton bon ami, (Your good friend)
Othello (aka Luc Auguste)

Marek and Fannie are relieved to see Daniel behaving like his old lively self again. Since he began working with Rachel on the play, he seems happier, not so moody. He must be a good actor for her to give him such an important part. He has mentioned his new friend Luc from Haiti several times. Even though they have not yet met Luc or his parents, they readily gave their permission to Daniel to join Luc and his family for a night of films.

At 6 o'clock on Saturday, Daniel rings the doorbell of Luc's apartment. Mrs. Auguste answers. She is tall and slender, dressed in an elegant, medium blue, long silk dress with a single strand of pearls and shiny black shoes with pointed toes. Her black hair is pulled into a chignon. She smiles warmly at Daniel and extends her hand, which Daniel takes He notices her long, cool fingers. "Daniel, I am so happy to meet you. Luc speaks about you often and says you are a wonderful actor and a good friend." He hears her accented English, although it is a different accent from the one he hears at home.

"Hello Mrs. Auguste, I am glad to meet you too."

"Daniel, please call me Jenine. Everyone does, and so does Luc." Daniel is taken aback. He has never called an adult by his or her first name. Even Rachel is always 'Aunt Rachel', although he has been trying to call her Miss Kaminski in the theater group. But he barely has time to think about all this because Luc and his father come in to greet Daniel.

"Good evening, Daniel, I'm Luc's father, Bertrand. He is also tall with broad shoulders and a large roomy chest. His voice is deep. He is dressed in a red silk shirt, black trousers and a pink vest. He has an accent as well, but it's different from Jenine's. Luc and Daniel are dressed in their usual knickers, but tonight instead of vest sweaters over shirts, they each are wearing jackets, shirts and ties.

When Daniel looks around the apartment, he sees the most colorful room he has ever entered. The walls are covered with vibrant paintings of figures and landscapes in reds, oranges and greens, but somehow these very familiar colors look different from colors he has ever seen. Some paintings have palm trees and huge flowers. Luc notices Daniel looking at the paintings and says, "Bertrand did most of these and some are by friends of Bertrand and Jenine." Again, Daniel is startled when he realizes Luc calls his parents by their first names.

Bertrand comes over to Daniel and asks what he thinks of the paintings. Daniel says that while he knows he sees red and yellow and green, they look different. Bertrand smiles and puts a hand on Daniel's shoulder. He is charmed by Daniel's interest and explains how he always mixes small amounts of another color into any color he uses. "For example, this green has a bit of blue in the mix. And this green has a very small bit of yellow, just enough so you will still call it green, but it's not the usual green. I love color. My country screams with color."

Daniel's eyes leave the paintings and shift to Bertrand's very large, dark hands and fingers that constantly move as he speaks.

Jenine invites everyone to have a seat. There is a table and three chairs. A beige sofa is covered with vivid printed shawls and pillows. Bookshelves are crammed full, and still more books lie on the table and piled onto the floor. There are lush potted plants everywhere. In one corner there is a baby grand piano. Jenine, Daniel learns, is a pianist and a jazz composer.

Bertrand brings in a carafe of red wine and pours four glasses, then passes them around, and says, "I propose a toast to our two actors, Luc and Daniel. May they each break a leg and enjoy doing it!" They raise their glasses to their lips.

Other than a tiny sip of his mother's sweet Shabbos wine, Daniel has never had his own glass of wine. But the family are all sipping, and so Daniel does the same. He is surprised to find it not at all sweet, even bitter, but he likes the way it is so warm going down. He senses a fluttering in his middle, which may be the wine but also may be the thrill of entering this new exotic world.

Jenine says they will soon set out for the restaurant rented for the evening by a group of fellow artists. "We'll have dinner, then music and dancing, and the films will begin around eleven."

When it is time to leave, they put on their coats and walk the few blocks to the restaurant. On entering, Daniel breathes in the warm, spicy fragrances that fill the dining room, different from any cooking aromas Daniel can recall.

Jenine and Bertrand are exuberantly greeted with many hugs and kisses by many friends. They greet Luc the same way and each time Luc introduces Daniel as "My good friend and fellow actor." Everyone welcomes Daniel, and they join four other people at a table, two men and two women, all as elegantly dressed as Bertrand and Jenine. One woman wears an emerald-green dress. Her hair is brushed out fully framing her face. The other woman wears a man's tuxedo and a shiny, multicolored turban. Jenine gives their names, professions and where they are from.

"Marie-Claire is from Martinique, and Annette is from Morrocco. The three of us often speak French together. They are both poets. And these gentlemen are William and Henry. William is from Alabama, and Henry is from New Orleans. I cannot tell you their professions right now because I understand they will have a surprise for us." Daniel shakes hands with each person. Sounds of a jazz trio warming up come from a corner of the room.

A dish of appetizers arrives at the table and is passed around. Daniel sees what looks like crispy bits in assorted shapes but recognizes nothing familiar. When the dish comes to Luc, he chooses two long things that he puts on Daniel's plate and chooses two for himself.

"Dan, you should try these because I suspect you have tasted nothing like them before."

Under the crispy covering, Daniel can see a bit of green. Gingerly, he puts it into his mouth. He bites into it and tastes a combination of spicy and bitter and then something gooey.

"That's okra, Dan. My dad grew up eating a lot of okra in Haiti. Do you like it?"

"I like the crispy stuff. The green part, not so much."

"Okay, try the other one now."

Daniel picks up the other morsel. He can see a bit of orange under the crispy part. He bites into it. Beneath the spicy crispness, he tastes something deliciously sweet and soft. After his first bite he finishes what is left on his plate. "Mmmm, I like this a lot."

"That's yam. That's another typical Haitian food." The platter of appetizers makes another round, and Luc picks out three more pieces of yam and puts them on Daniel's plate. He takes more okra for himself. "I like the okra, but maybe that's because I grew up eating it."

Before the meal is served, the saxophonist from the trio comes over and asks Jenine if she is willing to play a song or two with them. He has an accent like Jenine's. Jenine answers, "Bien sur." When she approaches the piano and slides onto the piano bench, the crowd bursts into cheers and applause, then silence. Jenine turns to the crowd and speaks.

"The Girl I Love" The crowd cheers.

Jenine, in her husky, accented voice, draws out each phrase of the lyrics and barely touches the piano keys. She comes to the end of the song. Daniel sees that Marie-Claire and Annette are kissing, not just a brush of the lips but a long kiss and an embrace. Daniel catches himself staring and quickly averts his eyes, pretending to be interested in the silverware. *Oh! Women too!*

Jenine and the saxophonist now play something upbeat and syncopated. The two men at the table as well as couples all over the room, men with men, women and men and pairs of women seem to spring out of their seats and fly into a jitterbug. Those who don't dance, clap. The musicians take a break while the main course is served.

Three large platters come to the table. Daniel recognizes chicken with what looks like red and black spice over it, then there is a crispy fish and then some meat that looks unfamiliar. There is also a platter of greens that looks something like spinach, but not quite. Luc says. "The chicken is called jerk chicken, a Caribbean dish. The fish is snapper. The meat is goat. I love it, but you might not. And the green stuff is a vegetable called collard greens."

Daniel says, "I'll try the fish." He puts a very small piece on his plate. He bites into the crispy and moist, delicate flesh. "Mmm, that's really good." And adds another piece to his plate.

"Do you want to try the goat?"

"Yes, just a little."

"I'll give you a bit of mine." Luc cuts a small piece and holds his fork to Daniel's mouth as Daniel takes it in. "It has a very strong taste."

"Do you like it?"

"I don't know." Daniel thinks, *I don't like it. I want to like it.* "I'll try another small piece." he says, and Luc cuts another piece from his plate and again offers it to Daniel from his fork. "I like it better than I did the first time." They do it again.

When the platter of fish comes around again, Daniel takes more. After he sees Luc pile the greens onto his plate, he takes some of them as well and tries a forkful. It has a taste somewhat like spinach but also different and salty.

"What makes this taste different?" He asks Luc.

"It's cooked with some ham for flavor."

"Ham!" *Oh my God, I'm eating traif* (non-kosher food)!

Seeing Daniel's look of surprise, Luc asks, "Is it okay?"

"Uh, yes, sure. It's fine." Sweat gathers on Daniel's forehead.

Daniel pushes the collards to the side of his plate and eats the fish. But he goes back to the collards and finds he likes the smoky taste. *It's a little like lox.*

The dessert is something that looks like a pie crust filled with a shiny, brown filling. Luc says it is called pecan pie. "It's my favorite."

Daniel takes his first mouthful of the buttery, brown sugar custard and the crunchy nuts and says, "This is the best thing I've ever tasted."

The jazz trio plays again; this time the music is slower. The room fills with couples dancing. Jenine and Bertrand now get up to dance. The two move as one body. The other dancers stop to watch them, then applaud as the dance finishes with Bertrand bending Jenine deeply backward, then whipping her up and into a spin. The two return to the table glowing. The other dancers continue, and Luc asks Daniel, "Would you like to dance?" For the first time this evening, Daniel is shy, even stiff, and nods "No". Luc nods and does not press him. *Oh! I hope Luc isn't disappointed in me.*

When William and Henry, both dressed in form-fitting tuxedos with bow ties, get up to do the fast dances, the floor clears. These men are performers. Their dances are obviously choreographed and rehearsed, full of complicated footwork, fast turns and acrobatic tricks.

After this grand finale, the guests are asked to retire to a lounge while the room is set up for showing the films. A movie projector is brought out, as well as a stack of flat, round metal containers. The tables are pushed up against the wall, and chairs are set out in rows facing a blank white wall where the movies will be projected. The guests return and take their seats.

Bertrand speaks to the crowd from the front of the room. "The first of the two films we will show tonight is Russian, written and directed by Serge Eisenstein. The title in English is "The Strike".

As they watch "The Strike", Daniel recognizes its theme is familiar to him. It is about the oppressive treatment of factory workers before the Bolshevik Revolution. Daniel has heard many conversations at the dinner table about the rights of factory workers, usually led by Aber. He also heard a lot about the oppressive and bad working conditions that caused the fire at the Triangle Shirtwaist Factory in New York, where his mother worked and thankfully survived the fire.

There is a short intermission as the reels are changed. The second film, a German film, "Different from the Others" is ready to start.

Bertrand comes to the front again to introduce it. It is written by Richard Oswald and Magnus Hirschfeld. "Hirschfeld", Bertrand explains, "was a famous German sexologist who championed same-sex love as part of the normal and fluid continuum of sexual desire. This film was shown in Berlin in 1919 and then was banned in 1920. I will not disclose how I came to own this copy." The audience laughs, and there is brief murmuring amongst them.

Daniel's head pounds. His heart races. *Did I hear what I think I heard? Normal!*

The film opens at a ball where men are dancing with men, *just like they were doing here!* Daniel exclaims to himself.

The story unfolds about two men, a violinist, Koerner, and his student, who fall in love. The violinist is exposed by an extortionist. Because homosexuality was against the law, it goes to court. The judge is sympathetic to Koerner, but when the case becomes public, Koerner's career is ruined, and he is driven to suicide. At this point, a sob rises in Daniel's throat. Luc turns toward Daniel and slips his hand into his. Daniel continues to sob softly.

"It's okay, Dan. Let it out. I'm sure you're not the only one in this audience who is crying now." Daniel leans against Luc's shoulder and Luc puts his arm around Daniel. Soon the lights come on.

The audience clap long and loudly and many yell, "Bravo Bertrand!" As the crowd disperses. Jenine comes over to the boys and hands Luc the key to the apartment, saying she and Bertrand will be stopping at some friends for a nightcap and will be home later. "We can all sleep in tomorrow as late as we wish."

Daniel and Luc get their coats and go out to the now empty streets. The refreshing night air tastes like a long cool drink of water. Daniel inhales deeply. Luc asks, "How are you doing Dan?" Daniel bursts into tears again and through his tears he also starts to laugh yelling,

"I've never been so happy in all my life!"

Luc clasps his arms around Daniel and starts singing, "Someday he'll come along, the man I love." Luc's smooth tenor voice is like another embrace. Luc invites Daniel to dance. Awkward at first, Daniel soon lets Luc take over and finds himself following the rhythm and footwork easily, so easily he joins in the song. Suddenly they hear a man's voice and stop short. Across the street, clinging to a lamppost with one hand and a bottle in the other, and lifting the bottle in a toast, they hear a gravelly voice call out, "Dance, dance all night, boys! Keep dancing!"

They get back to the Auguste's apartment and go into Luc's room with its twin beds. Luc kisses Daniel on the lips, and Daniel presses his lips onto Luc's. They say, "Good night" and each get into a separate bed.

On Monday, Daniel copies a poem on a piece of notebook paper, "We Two Boys Together Clinging" by Walt Whitman, the poem he has read many times that has comforted him. He slips it into Luc's locker. Later, he finds a folded piece of paper in his locker. It is "Tableau" by Countee Cullen. Daniel reads it.

TABLEAU

Locked arm in arm they cross the way,
The black boy and the white,
The golden splendor of the day,
The sable pride of night.
From lowered blinds the dark folks stare,
Indignant that these two should dare
In unison to walk.

Oblivious to look and word
They pass, and see no wonder
That lightening brilliant as a sword
Should blaze the path of thunder.

Daniel reads the poem once, twice, three times and kisses the paper, folds it and puts it into the left breast pocket of his shirt. *But why the sword and thunder? Maybe Luc will explain. Two hours until rehearsal. I can hardly wait.*

The rehearsal goes very well. Rachel is full of praise for the way the cast is pulling together. After, Luc and Daniel walk to the coffee shop. They say little to each other, and what they do say is stilted, almost formal. "How was your day?" "Miss Kaminski thought the rehearsal went well." so different from their usual non-stop bubbling over about the play, other kids, their tests, their teachers. They arrive and take their usual booth at the back of the shop. The waiter comes over. They each order hot chocolate. Luc leans forward, resting his arms on the table, looks Daniel in the eyes and urgently asks, "Are you okay?"

"Yes, Luc, I'm okay."

"Are you okay with me still?"

"Of course, I'm okay with you."

Luc sighs, his shoulders relax, and he says, "And the party and after?"

Daniel looks back at Luc, then closes his eyes tight and says, "I don't know how to say it." He looks away. Luc's stomach clenches. But then Daniel looks back at him, tearful yet smiling. "Luc, you made me feel like it's okay to be me, like I belong on this earth. I meant it when I said to you that night, I have never been so happy in my life, and you make me feel that."

Luc reaches across the table and grabs Daniel's shoulders. The waiter brings the hot chocolate. Luc pulls his hands back to his lap. The boys thank the waiter.

Staring into his cup, Luc says, "Oh Dan, I was afraid when you got home, it would all seem so weird to you, and you'd back away. My parents like you a lot. My dad loved talking to you about his paintings."

Luc and Daniel are both silent. They sip their drinks.

"What do you think your parents will think?" asks Luc.

"I don't know. I can imagine my mom being surprised. But if she sees that I'm happy, she'll be alright with it. My dad will have a harder time. He's always telling me the world is a tough place and that I must be tough and defend myself. I don't think he's ever forgiven me for dropping out of boxing. I hated it. He probably thinks I'm a sissy, so maybe he wouldn't be all that surprised. But I'm not going to say anything to either of them unless they ask me, and even if they do ask, I'm not sure."

His voice shaky, Luc asks, "What about my being black?"

"My mom will be fine with it. I'm not sure about my dad. What about my being Jewish?"

"I'm lucky that way with my parents. They will accept anyone as long as they're a good person. They've both experienced a lot of prejudice and hatred for who they are and who their friends are. Harlem welcomed them, and finally they knew they belong somewhere."

Daniel looks away thoughtfully, then turns back to Luc. "I always wondered why Aunt Rachel, you know, Miss Kaminski, gave me <u>Leaves of Grass.</u> I've been comforting myself with some of Whitman's poems, especially the one I gave to you. I wonder if Aunt Rachel somehow figured it out."

"Yeah, I can see that. Are you going to say something to her?"

"No, not now anyway. If I ever need help getting my parents to under-stand, maybe she could help. She's very close to my parents, especially my mother."

A girl approaches the table. It's Sally O'Neil who plays Desdemona. Enthusiastically she says, "Hi Luc." Then more subdued, "Oh, Daniel! Hi. Can I sit with you?"

"Sure." say both boys as each move closer to the wall, making room. She sits next to Luc.

"Luc, your collar is up in the back." She smooths it flat and chatters on about the rehearsal and the play, which will be performed a week from Saturday.

The Play

Folding chairs are set up in the main room of the library. Wings are created out of bookshelves. The actors in the first scene stand together behind them. There is no curtain, so the actors have rehearsed how they will quietly walk "on stage" and take their places at the beginning of each scene. Luc's father volunteered to paint the scenes, and we see a vivid painting of Piazza San Marco as the background. Families and friends of the players have gathered. Jenine and Bertrand sit in front on the right. Fannie, Marek, Aber, Jacob, Kayla, Adela, and the twins take up most of the seats in one of the middle rows. The sounds of greetings, conversation, and the rustle of the paper programs drift through the audience. Rachel steps out from behind one wing and takes center stage. Everyone is quiet.

"Good Evening everyone. We are excited to arrive at the day of our performance. Everyone involved in this production worked hard and committed themselves to this ambitious project of putting on *Othello* by William Shakespeare. Our cast and crew are juniors and seniors at George Washington High School and members of our library drama club. We are indebted to Luc Auguste's father, Bertrand Auguste, for creating our beautiful background scene of Venice and for a later scene, a Venetian interior. Thank you, Mr. Auguste." Everyone applauds vigorously.

Rachel continues, "Why *Othello*? The drama club wanted a play with an evil villain. They also wanted romance, and they wanted an immigrant in the play. We read several Shakespeare plays, and they chose *Othello*. I confess I was doubtful. I thought *Othello* was far too complex and ambitious for high school actors. I think you will see as the play unfolds, I was wrong. We have shortened the script some, but all the themes of love, envy, jealousy, treachery, being an outsider, and alas, murder and suicide are here. I underestimated how sixteen to eighteen-year-olds are capable of not only thinking about these powerful human feelings and actions but also struggling with them. All the major players wrote backstories about the personal history of their characters as a way of better understanding their motivations. We always left time in rehearsals to talk together about what it is like to play characters of such emotional intensity. So, enough from me. Let the play begin!" There is a burst of applause for Rachel. The actors, with quiet gravity, walk to their places.

When Iago does his "I hate Othello." speech, baring his teeth and clenching his fists, Fannie is startled. *Is that my gentle Danny? Oh, how I wish Hannah could see him now. He may become the actor she longed to be.*

As the play continues and Iago shows his violence and treachery, Marek thinks, *So, he does know how to be tough. Why can't he learn to protect himself? I've failed him with that. But he is convincing as the bad guy. An actor—why does he want to be an actor? How will he ever support a family?* He turns to Fannie and whispers, "Did you have anything to do with the costumes?"

"No, Adela helped using the kid's own clothes. She added things like headscarves and bits of fabric here and there." Marek nods.

After intermission, when the scene changes to the interior of a wealthy Venetian home, Bertrand's second backdrop is up. Before the actors come on stage, there is huge applause with people yelling Bertrand's name. Bertrand stands from his seat and takes a bow. Both Marek and Fannie realize this is Luc's father, who they still have not met.

Jenine whispers to Bertrand, "Luc shows such dignity and manliness on stage. Our little boy is growing up Bertrand." He looks at her. A tear drifts down her cheek. He takes his handkerchief out of his pocket and wipes it away.

Jacob thinks, *The little squirt is pretty good. I didn't know he had it in him.*

Miriam whispers to Kayla, "Othello is so handsome!"

The final scenes of treachery and unchecked rage play out and Iago is arrested and escorted out by the authorities.

Simon thinks, *Danny is scary. I'm glad he's going to jail.*

From the wings, Daniel watches Luc's final moments of the play.

Horrified, Othello realizes he was duped by Iago's treachery, and he has strangled to death the woman who loved him faithfully. Overcome with remorse, he plunges his dagger into his own heart and dies. Gasps come from the audience, then a few seconds of suspended silence.

When Daniel sees the dead body of Othello, a lump rises in his throat. The stage manager calls out, "The End". An explosion of applause and "Bravos!" follows.

Daniel is grateful the minor players have the first curtain call. They all come out in a line, blocking the view of the dead Desdemona and Othello on stage so the two can get up and disappear into the wings opposite Daniel's wing. When Desdemona, Othello, and Iago come out for their bows, the audience all rise, applaud long and loud with many yells of "Bravo!". Soon the players all come out and call in rhythm, Miss—Kam—in—ski, Miss Kam—in—ski. Rachel comes on stage, and the stage manager comes out with a huge bouquet of roses. The cast sends up loud cheers for Rachel. She faces them, yelling over the din, "You all did it, you really did it!!" She joins the line of the entire cast, and the applause continues. When it finally stops, Rachel speaks to the audience, thanking them for coming and especially thanking the parents for supporting their sons and daughters in achieving what they did tonight.

Slowly, the crowd leaves the library. Fannie and Marek go to where Jenine and Bertrand are standing and introduce themselves as Daniel's parents. There are greetings and handshakes all around, with many congratulatory comments on how wonderfully the boys played their parts.

Daniel and Luc together join the mingling audience. Many people stop to congratulate their performance when Daniel spies a chubby youth hanging back in the crowd dressed as a *Hassid* (sect of ultra-orthodox Judaism) with a long black coat and broad-brimmed hat. He has the scraggly beginnings of a beard and long side-curls. "Herman!" calls out Daniel. "I haven't seen you since you moved to Brooklyn." Daniel reaches out to shake Herman's hand and introduces Luc.

"Yeah, I heard you were in this play, here at the library, so I thought I'd come and maybe get to say hello."

"Great that you did Herman." Gesturing at Herman's attire, Daniel asks, "Are you at the Yeshiva now?"

"Yeah, I like it a lot. I always feel welcome. I'm going to keep studying after graduation. I want to be a Rabbi."

"Good for you, Herman."

"I think so. It gives my parents a lot of *naches*."

They all shake hands again and Herman disappears into the crowd. Luc asks, "What is naches?"

"It means happiness. He's bringing his parents a lot of happiness. I'm sure not bringing my father much naches. I don't want to box. I want to be an actor. I'm bringing my father *tsores*. It means misery." Luc pats Daniel on the back when they see the four parents all engaged in their lively conversation. They walk over and join them. The parents pause to hug their sons and congratulate them. Meanwhile, Fannie and Marek's other children come up to the group and each is introduced. Aber stands with Rachel on the other side of the library. Many people come up to talk to her. As the Horvath family gets ready to leave, Fannie invites Bertrand and Jenine to dinner the next night. Luc and Daniel exchange looks. Daniel takes a deep breath and thinks, *Oh, I hope this goes okay.*

Families

The three Augustes, the entire Horvath family and Rachel and Aber sit at the dinner table. The Augustes brought two bottles of wine. Marek decanted one into a crystal carafe. They have all toasted Luc and Daniel on their performances and talked together about the boy's wishes to become professional actors. Marek leaves the table, taking the only half-empty carafe of wine to refill in the kitchen. Miriam leans over to Fannie and whispers, "Mama, I think Luc is so handsome. Don't you?" Fannie nods. Miriam goes on, "Maybe Luc and Danny will become famous." Marek returns and refills all the adults' glasses.

When the adults aren't talking to the boys, Daniel and Luc, their heads close together, talk excitedly to each other.

When all finish enjoying Fannie's brisket with *tsimmis* (a cooked mix of root vegetables and fruit) and fragrant homemade challah Bertrand asks for the recipes. They are ready for dessert. Fannie goes to the kitchen and brings out the strudel she set to bake during dinner. It has perfumed the apartment with the homey scent of baking apples and cinnamon.

Luc and Daniel will not stay for dessert. They plan to attend a program of Charlie Chaplin movies now showing at the Odeon Theatre on 145th St. When they leave, Adela, who now attends Hunter College, says she must prepare for a test tomorrow. Simon and Miriam also have homework to do. Only the adults remain at the table. Marek pours tea for everyone. Everyone raves about Fannie's strudel. She offers seconds. Aber and Bertrand enthusiastically pass their plates to her.

Aber looks around and says, "Every one of us at the table has an accent speaking English. Well maybe not you so much Rachel."

Rachel responds, "That's because I was still a kid when I came. I learned English when I started school. I think some of my teachers were immigrants, but to teach in the public schools you had to work to not have an accent."

Aber turns back to the group, and making a circle with his arms, says, "We are a collection of immigrants."

Bertrand says, "And we live in a country of immigrants. It is what makes America strong. How many of us cried when we first saw the Statue of Liberty?" Murmurs of agreement circle the table.

"My Haiti is a country of immigrants as well."

Several people say, "Tell us about Haiti, Betrand." Jenine and Bertrand look at each other.

"You start, Bertrand," says Jenine, "I'll join you along the way." Bertrand begins.

"I was born in Haiti in 1890. Maybe you know this, but Haiti was colonized by Spain and France, and now, since 1915, it has been occupied by America. Africans were brought to Haiti as slaves, and then there are the Taino people, who were there before all the foreigners came. So, as you can well see Haiti, like America, is a country of people from different cultures. Its variety is one of the many reasons I love my country. Jenine and I left, but we will always return.

"Fannie asks, "Is Haiti beautiful?" Bertrand sighs and says,

"It is the most beautiful country I know. Would I have become a painter had I been born in a city? I wonder. You must wonder why we left."

Aber says, "Yes, Bertrand tell us."

"As a young man, I dreamed of going abroad to art school. I applied to art schools in Paris and in New York. I had offers from both cities. I went to Paris because I spoke French more easily than English. And in Paris I met Jenine."

Jenine adds, "I left Haiti to study music in Paris."

Aber asks both, "Had you met before in Haiti?"

"No," answers Jenine. "In Paris, a mutual friend introduced us. We were both so homesick that first year. When I heard Bertrand was from Haiti, I was powerfully drawn to him."

"And I to Jenine" adds Bertrand quickly.

Jenine continues, "We cooked for each other, spoke both Creole and French together. Creole is Bertrand's first language, and mine is French. I was born in France. My mother is French, and my father is Haitian. They returned to Haiti when I was around six."

Bertrand picks up the conversation. "Jenine and I married in Paris in 1911, and in 1912, Luc was born. We came back to Haiti to be near our families. I continued to paint. I had shows, but the Haiti art scene is not Paris. And Jenine performed and composed. But for music too, opportunities were limited. We heard from friends that Berlin was the place to be. It was cosmopolitan, full of artists from all over Europe and some from America. We went to Berlin. I guess that must have been 1925. It was everything our friends said it was, but I couldn't find work and there was something menacing as well. There was a growing fascination with Hitler. A friend gave us a copy of the book *Mein Kampf* when it first came out. Hitler wrote it when he was in prison. Have you heard of it?"

Aber and Rachel both sit up straight and together say, "Yes!" Rachel looks at Aber intensely while he speaks.

"Rachel and I read *Mein Kampf*. I'm begging my family to get out of Europe. Marek's family have at least gotten out of Hungary and gone to London and Lyon. But I have two married brothers who refuse to leave Vienna and dismiss what we see as a very real menace from Hitler." Aber becomes aware of Rachel's gaze and exchanges a glance with her then focuses back on Bertrand. Rachel too shifts her focus away from Aber but at moments quickly glances at him while others are speaking.

"Yes, yes," says Bertrand. "It is real and growing. Hitler would consider Jenine and me, with our mixed cultures and how we look, to be mongrels, polluters. They'd throw us out at best and probably much worse. We Creoles are everything Hitler despises and wants to destroy. We are French, Spanish, African, and Taino. We knew we had to leave Germany. So, we went back to Paris. The art scene was vibrant, but France felt too close to Germany. We were also hearing some sympathy for the Nazis while we were in France. So, where to go? We went back to American-occupied Haiti to figure things out. A friend who had been in New York suggested I see if I could get a job as a scene designer. He gave me the name of several American directors, producers, and playwrights. Nothing came of it. But then, through word of mouth, I received an offer from the Metropolitan Opera. I love the work. The Met hires many people who look like me, EXCEPT, and this is a big except, they had just put on a production about a jazz musician written by an Austrian composer, "Jonny Spielt Auf". Because there were romantic scenes with a white singer, the lead man was played by a white man in blackface. The Met feared they would be criticized if they showed a romance between a so called "mixed race" couple. It was cowardly and stupid. I must say I wondered whether the ugly tentacles of *Mein Kampf* were strangling the integrity of the great Met Opera. The very best part of coming to New York is being so warmly welcomed by the people of Harlem and the Harlem artists."

Jenine adds, "Harlem is the best place for us. New York is wonderful— the art, music, and theater—but there are places in New York too where we would not be welcome and certainly could not rent an apartment. But we have our Harlem Haven. We miss Haiti. There is a Haitian community here. It has worked out well for Bertrand and me, but I think all this moving has been hard on Luc. Bertrand and I, over the years learned English. But Luc never spoke English until we arrived here. School, which had always gone well for him, even with all the moves, was so difficult at first." She turns toward Rachel and says, "When you urged Luc not only to act but have one of the lead parts, he was terrified. But you really worked magic with him—not only to learn difficult lines in what was still a new language, but you gave him confidence to try."

Fannie turns to Rachel and says, "Rachel, you have a great talent. When I barely spoke English, you helped me read and understand some of Shakespeare's sonnets. Your talent is finding literature that has personal meaning for the student. And then the learning comes so much easier. I was able to translate my favorite sonnet into Yiddish and read it at Passover. I've read it every year at Passover since then. Let's toast our Rachel" Fannie raises her teacup, and they all call out, "Rachel, Rachel!!"

Aber, holding his teacup straight out towards her, his eyes shining and a wide smile, yells "Bravo!" Rachel blushes deeply, feeling the warmth go from her face down her neck, she says,

"Thank you. It's what I love to do." She pauses briefly then continues, "Luc did an amazing job as Othello. When I hear what you describe Bertrand and Jenine, it confirms what I sensed; that Luc, like Othello, felt like an outsider, struggling to understand how to be part of a strange culture."

Marek leans in, resting his forearms on the table. "I've been in America for many years, working as a tailor and raising a family. Teenagers these days, seem to be from a totally different culture than their own parents."

Rachel responds, "I think you're right, Marek. Teenagers seem to want something different from what their parents want for them. Perhaps immigrant teenagers are trying to be what they think is particularly American."

Fannie joins in, "We see that with our Adela. We hear her with her friends. They have these peculiar sayings that make no sense like, 'The cat's pajamas' or 'The bee's knees'."

Bertrand says, "Speaking of friends," He turns to Marek and Fannie and says, "Your Daniel has become the most important friend Luc has ever had. I haven't seen him so happy since we left Haiti."

Fannie responds, "Daniel was a sad boy for a long time. We were so worried about him. Since the play and meeting Luc, our happy Daniel is back. Thank you, my dear friend Rachel. And thank you, Bertrand and Jenine, for welcoming Daniel into you lives."

It is getting late. The guests get ready to leave. All promise one another to have more evenings together. Bertrand and Jenine, and Rachel and Aber, all leave at the same time. Once outside they warmly take one another's hands and comment on how good it was to be together. They part.

Aber, as usual, walks with Rachel back to her building before he will return to the Men's Y. He uses his cane with his hand closest to the street. From time to time as they walk, he bumps into Rachel's side. She wonders, *Is it only because his balance is unsteady?*

They reach the front of her building and Aber says, "The Augustes are good people and smart. When I heard they read *Mein Kampf,* I knew we could be friends."

"I had the same reaction." Rachel says.

Aber lingers. Touching her shoulder, he says, "Rachel, you did an outstanding job with those high school kids. It's incredible what you pulled out of them."

Rachel answers, distracted again by Aber's momentary touch, "Uh, I uh, I thought giving Daniel the character of Iago made sense because of his struggle with learning his first father was a criminal. He asked for the part. His backstory is excellent. Did you read it?" she asks.

"Yes, he showed it to me," says Aber. "I think he realized that for some people, being horribly treated by others can fill you with hatred and vengeance. Also, he has baby Iago found on a heap of garbage. That comes right out of his experience of finding that poor baby. But also, Rachel, Iago is a tyrant who seduces and manipulates people. Were you thinking of Hitler?"

Rachel is surprised. "I never thought about that. I was thinking of the kid's personal lives. You're right. Hmmm, Desdemona, married to an outsider, like a German married to a Jew. It all leads to a horrible ending. Wow!!

"Yeah," says Aber, suddenly changing the subject and stepping back

"Work for all of us, early tomorrow; Jacob and I have a big job in the Bronx. I'll pick him up in the morning." They give each other their usual parting, not too close, quick hug, and Aber leaves without looking back.

Rachel enters her apartment. Jacob and Kayla are both asleep. Rachel sits on the edge of her bed. *It's ridiculous for Aber, at ten o'clock at night, after a wonderful evening to think he must go back downtown to the Y. Does he realize how often he touches me? He loves me. Why can't he let himself know it?* She feels herself getting angry and hot. *What's the matter with him? He told me about his war problems but why the hell can't he get over it!* She leaves the bedroom and paces the living room and the kitchen. The anger drains out of her as she begins to cry. *We are so close in so many ways. We are raising these kids who are almost grown up. Jacob is better since he shifted to mostly shop classes. Kayla is at Hunter now. She and Adela have become close, and Adela has drawn her into a circle of friends. Soon, I could be living alone again. Are Aber and I, for the rest of our lives to give each other a quick parting hug and go our separate ways? I loved Roland. I thought I could never love anybody else. But I can. I love Aber! Do I have to pretend I don't love him and find someone else? Could I find anyone who is such a good companion as he is? Should I have a lover just to have a lover? I long for Aber. I think I would have to pretend my lover was Aber.* She sits in a kitchen chair, her hands over her face, and sobs. When her sobs slow, her body becomes heavy and exhausted. She returns to bed and falls into a leaden sleep.

Luc and Daniel are getting out of the Odeon Theater. They are still laughing as they recall the scenes of the little tramp. Luc walks ahead of Daniel, imitating the Charie Chaplin walk. Not to be outdone, Daniel does his own version of the walk. They both continue walking down the street like Chaplin. They are laughing so hard they can't continue. Daniel has hiccups. Luc bares his teeth and growls, thinking he is going to scare Daniel out of his hiccups. But Daniel only laughs harder. They arrive at the street where they must now go in different directions. People walk past them. Luc says in a very low voice, "I want to hug and kiss you Dan."

Daniel says, "Let's pretend we are wrestling."

"Good idea!" says Luc. He grabs Daniel by both shoulders as though he is trying to pull him off balance and force him to the ground. Daniel shifts his weight, and now Luc starts to buckle. A man walking by yells. "Cut it out, kids. It's time for you to be home in bed!" The boys stop, and as soon as the man is halfway down the block, they burst into laughter all over again.

"That felt great, Dan. A wrestle will be our public good night hug and kiss from now on."

"It's a deal," says Daniel.

Fannie and Marek cleaned up the kitchen and dining room. They sit together at the kitchen table. Fannie asks Marek if he wants some more tea. He shakes his head. They don't say it, but both are waiting up for Daniel. Fannie asks Marek if he enjoyed the evening.

"Well, mostly. But is Danny serious about being an actor? How is he going to make a living and support a family? I don't mind him doing it as a hobby, for now, but as a grown man! It makes no sense. Does he think we can support him for the rest of his life?"

"Hannah, you know, was an actress." responds Fannie. "Danny knows that about her."

"Hannah never became an actress." he says testily. "She just wanted to be one."

"Oh yes, she did." protests Fannie. "In Palestine, she acted in plays and also directed the children's theater."

"Oh, sure—on a kibbutz! She wasn't earning her livelihood doing it."

Fannie sighs saying, "Let's leave this for now. Danny just had a triumph. He's happy. We just spent a wonderful evening with Luc's parents. Didn't we?" Marek is glad to get off the topic of Daniel's future.

"Yes, they're good people. I wonder why they have only the one child."

"You heard, they've been going from country to country for years now. They are both very busy. They see it's been hard on Luc. That's probably why only one child."

"Yeah, I see what you're saying. In a way, they are not so different from us wandering Jews."

"And they are as worried about Hitler as we are. So, what do you think of Luc?'

"He seems like a nice boy. Are he and Danny the same age?"

"Both boys were born in 1912."

"He looks older, seems older."

"I think without sisters and brothers and traveling so much he probably spent a lot of time with adults." The door opens. Daniel is home.

"Hi Danny," they both call. Daniel comes into the kitchen and kisses his parents goodnight. He goes to his bedroom.

Fannie carries the teacups to the sink. Marek puts his hand on her wrist to stop her. In a voice hardly above a whisper, he asks, "What do you make of his friendship with Luc?"

Fannie pauses thoughtfully, then looking into Marek's eyes, says, "I think it's like the friendship in the Bible, the one between David and Jonathan."

Marek looks at Fannie quizzically, then says, "David and Jonathan were both married, weren't they?"

"I don't remember." Says Fannie. They get ready for bed.

Lenny

It is a Thursday afternoon in March 1931. Adela, now twenty, is alone in the tailor shop. Marek went to the Lower East Side to stock up on supplies. Since the depression, the store has survived because most of the work now is alteration and repair. People rarely can afford made-to-order clothes. However, Adela, who has become a skillful pattern maker, is designing patterns and selling them successfully. She has been trying to get Marek to sell dry goods so the cloth, sewing supplies and patterns can be sold together. Along with working in the store, Adela attends classes at Hunter College at night. She is an art history major.

She sits at the back of the store studying for an exam when she hears the bell on the door ring. She rushes out to greet a new customer. Standing at the counter is a young man who looks somewhat familiar to her, but she can't place how she knows him. He is short, and muscular, with an olive complexion and shining, large brown eyes. He is dressed like Aber dresses for work, in men's gray work clothes and wears a peaked cap. He carries a pair of heavy tweed pants. When he sees Adela, he stuffs his cap into his pocket, revealing his thick, brown, wavy hair. He looks at Adela for a moment before he puts the pants on the counter. Then asks, "Can these be fixed?" He shows her a big rip in one knee. Adela examines the rip. It is too ragged to be sewn together. She turns the pants inside out, checks the seams and the cuffs and finally the pockets where she sees the inner pocket is the same tweed material. She says, "This rip can't be sewn together; it is too frayed, but what I can do is use material from the pocket to make a patch and then remake the pocket with plain white cotton. Will that be alright?"

"Oh sure. You can do that?" he asks.

"Yes, I think I can." says Adela. "These pants are very well made."

The young man answers, "My mother made them. and she'd have a fit if she saw how I tore them. Yeah, what you can do is good. How much will it cost?"

"35 cents, is that okay?"

"Yeah, that's good. When can I pick them up?"

"Tomorrow?"

His whole face smiles, showing off his large, bright brown eyes and even, white teeth. "Great! You're saving my life!"

"Okay. Give me your name."

Adela takes a pad and pencil, and the young man gives his name, "Lenny Russo."

She looks up and says, "Do I know you from somewhere?"

"I was wondering that too" he says.

She tucks a bit of her straight black hair behind her ear. "Have you come in here before?"

"No, my friend told me you do repairs. This is my first time here."

"Hmm, did you go to high school at George Washington?"

"Yeah, I did. Did you?"

"Yes, I don't think I knew your name, but you look familiar. I'm Adela Horvath."

Lenny extends his hand. Adela takes his hand. She is aware of his moist and calloused palm. She also notices his broad shoulders and brown curly hair.

"Nice to see you, Adela." He doesn't immediately turn to go, but steps back, then forward, then back again, and says, "Uh, yeah, yeah, nice to see you, Adela." He gives her a long look, then makes a fast getaway.

Adela goes to the back room and closes her books. She can't concentrate on studying any longer. *Lenny Russo, Lenny Russo.* She picks up Lenny's pants and starts working on them, staying late to finish them, not because she couldn't finish them the next morning, but because she doesn't want to stop. *Those eyes! That smile!* As she uses the steam iron for the final touch, she takes a deep breath, enjoying the smell of damp wool. She hangs them up, is about to pull on the paper cover, pauses and rubs the slightly scratchy fabric against her cheek.

The next day, Lenny comes into the store. Marek is in the back working. Adela is at the counter. She takes the pants off the hanger to show Lenny the patch.

"That's beautiful, Adela. I can't even see the patch."

"Well, there was enough material from the pocket so I could match the weave exactly when I sewed in the patch." Adela's face is warm. She suspects she has turned bright pink. She wants him to linger, and asks, "So how did you get that hole in the knee?"

"Some guys were chasing me, and I tripped and fell on the pavement."

"Why were they chasing you?"

"I work on the docks. Some of us want to join a union. The big bosses, the guys who own the shipping company, are scared of a union. They're afraid they'll lose control of the workers. So, they want to get rid of us troublemakers. They send out their thugs to stop us."

"Phew! That's scary. What do you do on the docks.?"

"You know, loading and unloading ships. It's always been rough but rougher than ever now."

"Why?"

"Since '29, we don't have regular jobs. We show up in the morning and hope the supervisor picks us to work that day. My dad and I usually get picked because the dock supervisor knows us. He's a union guy too. But sometimes one of us, usually me, doesn't get picked."

"You load and unload the ships?"

"Yeah. We move these huge boxes and barrels off and on the ship." Lenny acts out, lifting a heavy barrel. "Guys are getting knocked down. It can get slippery." He rocks his body back and forth as though trying to keep his balance. "And it's always rush, rush, load and unload fast, the ships got to leave." He pretends to run, moving his arms as fast as he can. "We get yelled at all the time. Guys are always getting hurt. We're not allowed to stop and help if a buddy gets hurt. We're supposed to just move on. Can you imagine that? We're supposed to step over a fallen buddy!"

"That's horrible! Why do you work there?"

"That's what I know how to do. That's what my dad does. He's done it all his life. I need the work. We're lucky now to get what work we can. People all over the city are standing in breadlines. But we're still trying to get a union to make it a regular job, get better pay and make it safer."

"That sounds good."

"Yeah, but it can get rough. The owners are afraid they'll lose money if there's a union. And if you're union, they think you're anti-American. And if you're Italian or Jewish, they're sure you're a commie. They hire these gangsters to scare us off. One of those guys was chasing me, if you can believe it, on a Sunday. He saw me in front of the building where I live, and started chasing me. He probably wanted to beat me up. I was just going out on a Sunday afternoon. He must have followed me home one day, so he knew where I lived."

"Did you get away?"

"Yeah, but I tripped. That's how I got the hole."

Lenny is suddenly quiet. He shifts his weight awkwardly. Adela doesn't know what else to ask, so she asks, "When did you graduate from George Washington?"

"Nah, I didn't graduate. I left when I was sixteen. My family needed me to work. So, Adela, you work here every day?"

"Yes, it's my dad's store. I work here a part of every day."

"Your dad owns this!" He looks around. "This is a beautiful store. Everything is so neat, and a nice shiny cash register."

Adela goes on, "Before '29 we did a lot of made-to-order clothes for men, ladies, and kids. But no one can afford that now. Thank goodness we can do repairs and alterations. We've also started to make slipcovers for furniture. My mother works here too. And my brother does deliveries."

"What do you do when you don't work here?"

"I take courses at Hunter."

"What's Hunter?"

"It's a city college for women."

Lenny had been leaning on the counter. He straightens up. Suddenly clumsy, he bungles getting the change out of his pocket. He pulls out a nickel and two dimes then can't easily dig out the last dime. He finally gets it and adds it to the twenty-five cents on the counter. "Uh, so Adela, uh thanks. You saved my life with this patch. My mother would have killed me if she saw what I did to her pants."

"HER pants?"

"Yeah, I told you, she made them. They have to last. I have three younger brothers."

"Oh, now I get it." says Adela

Lenny backs up awkwardly. "Okay Adela, thanks." He opens the door, then turns back. "Okay Adela, bye."

She sees him break into a run.

Oooh, I shouldn't have said anything about Hunter! That was snobby. I'm an idiot. After I said that, he couldn't get out of here fast enough.

Twenty minutes later, Lenny is back in the store and gasping for breath. His words burst out one by one. "Adela—since we sort of recognize each other from high school—would you be willing, uh would you be willing to go out with me? Maybe we could go bowling or something and get ice cream."

Beaming, "Yeah, Lenny, we could do that. Ahhh…" She hesitates, then as though jumping off a cliff, she blurts out, "Maybe Sunday afternoon?"

"Yeah, yeah, no one will chase me if they see I'm with a nice lady."

Adela laughing, says, "And if they do and you fall again, Ill fix your pants again with the other pocket." Lenny laughs.

Lenny says, "Yeah, Sunday is good. You want to meet me somewhere? Or should I pick you up?"

Adela is caught off guard, not sure she wants her parents to meet Lenny, not yet anyway. Her thoughts race. *He's so different from the boys at the Temple Youth Club. They're so serious and boring.* She went out with some of them to chaperoned dances, sometimes to a movie or a birthday party. *If I sneak out with Lenny and get caught, Tateh will have a fit again. It was only after I started to work in the store that we got close again. I can't risk that.*

She mumbles, "Lenny, uh, are you, are you willing to pick me up where I live? My parents will be there."

Lenny's hands are sweating. He says, "Sure, sure, that'll be fine."

She tells him her address. He is smiling again. Lenny says, "Ok, see you Sunday, at say 2:00." Adela nods too many times.

Laughing, Lenny says, "I'll be wearing my like-new Sunday pants." He backs up toward the door, looking at Adela, then bumps into the door, laughs, and only then turns around to open the door and leaves.

Adela twirls, jumps up and hugs herself. *I'm all sparkles inside! He's so, so, so manly! And those eyes! That smile!*

Adela tells her parents she is going out for the afternoon with Lenny Russo, a boy she knew in high school, and he will pick her up at home.

Marek asks her what he does for a living. She tells him he works on the docks.

On Sunday afternoon, Fannie and Marek sit together on the sofa, nervously. When the doorbell rings, Adela rushes from the back of the apartment to the living room while Marek opens the door. Standing in the hallway, Lenny immediately extends his hand saying, "Hello Mr. Horvath. I'm Lenny Russo." He wears his tweed pants with a starched white shirt and an open navy-blue cardigan sweater.

"Come in Lenny. This is Adela's mother, Mrs. Horvath. Lenny does not extend his hand to Fannie, but Fannie extends hers and says, "Nice to meet you, Lenny. I understand you know Adela from high school."

"That's right, Mrs. Horvath."

"Have a seat, Lenny." Adela points Lenny to a chair.

There is silence. Adela looks around at the family living room—the overstuffed sofa with its collection of pillows, the upholstered wingback chairs she and Lenny are sitting on, the mahogany end tables with their marble tops and heavy table lamps, the velvet drapes—*Oh I hope this place doesn't look ritzy to him.*

Mercifully, Lenny breaks the silence. In too loud a voice he says, "Adela and I met again when I brought these pants in to be fixed. I tore the knee." Holding up his knee and moving it toward Marek and then toward Fannie, he says, "Look what a good job Adela did. You can't even tell it's a patch. It's perfect. They're like new." Marek looks over at where Lenny is pointing at his knee. He is suddenly animated and closely examines the patch.

"How did you do it?" Marek asks Adela. Lenny puts his knee down. Adela describes using the pants pocket and matching the weave. Marek asks Lenny to show him again. Lenny gives his knee back to Marek, who takes out his glasses from his vest pocket and looks closely at the work. "Very good work Adela. Look, Fannie, look at this fine work."

Fannie peers over at Lenny's knee. She says, "Yes, I can barely make out it is a patch."

There is another long silence and Fannie says, "So, what will the two of you do this afternoon?" Adela glances at Lenny, who doesn't pick up the cue.

"I guess we're going to take a walk." she says, looking at Lenny, who nods. "Or maybe we'll go bowling and get ice cream." Adela stands up. Lenny does too. Fannie and Marek get up. Lenny and Adela say good-bye and leave. Fannie and Marek exchange a look.

Marek, sighing, "I wish Adela would go out with someone whose family we know. Who is this dock worker Lenny Russo? He must be Italian. I never heard Adela mention him before."

"They haven't seen each other since high school until he came to the store." says Fannie. "Are you more upset that he's Italian or that he's a dock worker?"

"It's not about Italian. It's that he's not one of our people."

Fannie jumps in before Marek finishes his sentence. Angrily, pointing her finger, her voice loud, "Remember when she came home drunk? Remember! She sneaked off with a Jewish kid, not really a kid, but you could say 'one of our people'. Remember! He took her in a car and got her drunk. Fannie's voice gets even louder. Her words come faster. "This Lenny Russo comes to meet us. They tell us their plans, and there's no sneaking. Be grateful Marek. You get to meet Lenny Russo, who was perfectly polite and appreciates Adela's work. What more do you want? They're not going off to get married. They're going for ice cream on a Sunday afternoon! And who knows? Maybe he IS Jewish, 'one of our people' as you like to say. So, what!" Fannie is screaming. She jolts up off the couch and stands looking down at Marek. "Maybe I'm not one of YOUR so-called people. As you well know, I was born from a Polish Catholic man. For God's sake!" Her hands are fists, her face bright red. For a moment she stands with closed eyes then goes slack, her rage spent. She slumps back onto the couch, now sobbing. Marek reaches out to touch her shoulder, but she jerks away. She continues to cry, gets hold of herself, then beseechingly says, "Marek, please! Our beautiful, talented, competent girl is growing up. She's learned some important lessons. We can trust her. She's older than I was when I married you! My family didn't meet you. Let her grow up and be who she is. Lenny seems like a decent young man, probably from a poor family. We were each poor, and not so long ago."

Marek reaches out again to Fannie, and this time she lets herself fall against his chest. He folds his arms around her. After a while he says, "I need a nap." He goes to the bedroom. He takes off his shoes and groans as he lies on top of the bedspread in the darkened room. *I failed my kids. I haven't taught them right. Danny, so smart, is already accepted at City College. He could be a lawyer or a businessman, but he wants to be an actor. Ridiculous! And my Adela, also smart and in college. Already, she could make herself a decent living, and who does she choose for company? A dock worker! I bet he's a gold digger!*

Fannie is still sitting on the sofa. A heavy sadness blankets her. *This is the man who, when we first met, took me for who I was, with my bad history. He was so broad-minded, so accepting. What's happened to him? He's gotten so stiff and set in his ways. The only thing that livens him up is his work. Sometimes he just looks scared. Adela is a good kid. She works in the store and goes to college, and she brings home the boy to meet us.* She feels a wave of anger and sits up straight. *So what if he's Italian and maybe Catholic? Mama had her Piotr!* Her heavy sadness returns. *What's making him so sad, so frightened of life?* She looks at the clock. *Oy! I'll be late for dress rehearsal.* She looks in on Marek, who is still on their bed, lying on his back with an arm covering his eyes. "Marek dearest, I have a rehearsal. I'll be back at suppertime." Her eyes fill with tears.

Ice Cream

In Fort Tryon Park, Adela and Lenny recline on a cliff warmed by the spring sun and watch light play on the Hudson River below. The breeze ruffles the leaves. There is some traffic noise coming from a distance and occasionally the horn of a barge or a ferry on the river. They breathe in the scent of pine and warming soil. Adela sits up and says, "Lenny, I want to show you the places where I played as a little girl." They climb down from the rocks, and Adela leads Lenny to a nearby playground where she puts the purse she brought with her on the ground and sits on a swing.

"Do you want a push?" asks Lenny."

"Yes, but just to start me off," says Adella, "then I'll pump." As soon as Adela is swinging on her own, Lenny takes the swing next to her, steps several feet back and gives himself such a mighty push that almost immediately he is swinging as high as Adela. They look over at each other and start competing for who can swing higher. Lenny immediately wins and keeps going. Adela is frightened he is about to go over the top. "Stop, stop!" she yells and slows her swing down. Lenny, laughing, also slows down. They sit for a moment on the now still swings and Adela asks, "Did you come to the playground here as a kid?"

"No, not here. When we moved uptown, I was old enough to play on the street." says Lenny.

"My mother sometimes took us downtown to a playground." says Adela. "She had a friend with a little daughter who lived on the Lower

East Side. When we visited them, we'd meet at the playground at Washington Square Park."

"You're kidding!" blurts out Lenny. "I can't believe this! I played there too when I was a little kid. We lived on Judson Street."

"Wow!" says Adela. "You were at that park too!"

"Yeah," says Lenny. "That's amazing! We had to leave Judson when the building was condemned. We moved into a building with my aunt and uncle on East 125th. Do you know that neighborhood? It's called Italian Harlem."

"I think my brother does some deliveries there."

As they leave the playground and walk along the path, they approach the Heather Garden. Lenny stops and looks at Adela. With his big smile, he says, "I can't believe this. There we were, the two of us little kids together in Washington Square playground! Do you think we passed each other?"

"Yeah, I guess we could've." says Adela, aware of her insides sparkling again, imagining herself and Lenny on the playground and not knowing the other was there. "I would probably be on the swings." she says. "What did you like?"

"Oh, I was a daredevil." says Lenny, strutting. "I was probably hanging upside down on the highest monkey bars and falling on my head." Lenny gestures to the Heather Garden. "Doesn't that look beautiful! If it was allowed, I'd go right in there, Adela, and pick you a big bunch."

Adela pretends Lenny has just handed her the flowers and says, "Lenny, thank you; they smell wonderful."

Lenny flashes his big smile and says, "My aunt has a tiny yard in the back of her building. She is always trying to grow something. Usually, tomatoes and sometimes flowers too." He stares across the Heather Garden and into the distance. "Someday I'd like to get away from the docks and live in the country; maybe be a farmer, plant things and maybe have some chickens and a cow—live off the land." They continue along the path silently. Adela imagines Lenny in blue overalls with a farmer's hat.

They walk for so long; the sun is low in the sky. Lenny asks, "Do you still want to go bowling or should we go for ice cream?"

Adela says, "I need to get home by suppertime, so maybe bowling another day. Let's get some ice cream."

"Good," says Lenny, I'd like that too. I know an ice cream place near here on Broadway."

They walk past a couple of ice cream parlors, but Lenny says, "I have a favorite one I think you'll like."

They enter the ice cream parlor and find a small round white table with two twisted wire chairs. Each chair back is heart-shaped, and the seats are red. "So, Adela, do you like the furniture here?"

Adela giggles and says, "With this table and chair, I'll have to order strawberry ice cream. There's no other choice."

"Then I will too," says Lenny.

When the pink confections arrive in tall tulip glasses, with long spoons, they are both silent for moments as they take their first spoonful and utter, "Mmmm."

"Lenny, I know you have three younger brothers, who will all wear your tweed pants. Do you have any other brothers or sisters?"

"I have an older sister who is married and has a little girl. I'm crazy about my niece. She's two. The cutest kid I've ever seen. She's beginning to talk, and she calls me 'Renny.' I want her to call me Renny forever. It's so cute. Her name is Lydia. What about you Adela? I know about your brother who does deliveries, anyone else?" Adela tells him about the twins and goes on to tell him about her first mother who died having a baby and about Daniel's adoption."

Lenny says, "Wow, you have such an interesting family. My family just has babies the ordinary way and no twins." He pauses, and his expression becomes serious. "Some of the babies were born dead. My mother had a baby born dead, and so did my aunt."

Adela asks urgently, "Were your mother and aunt okay after?"

"Yeah, I think they were okay, just sad. The doctor said they worked too hard when they were expecting."

Adela feels a lump in her throat, "To think you look forward to your baby and then they're born dead, it's so sad it makes me want to cry." *And mothers can die along with their babies.* Adela breathes deeply trying to compose herself. *I don't want Lenny to think I'm some sad sack.* Struggling to get control, she asks, "What kind of hard work were your mother and aunt doing?"

"They were getting up early to clean people's houses and then coming home and cleaning their own places and taking care of all of us."

"Are they still cleaning people's houses?"

"My mom still cleans, but now in an office. The ladies she worked for could no longer pay a cleaner after '29."

"We better go," says Adela, looking at the clock on the wall. "My parents are expecting me home."

"Me too," says Lenny. "Uh, Adela, this was great. Uh, do you want to meet again next Sunday?"

"Sure," says Adela.

"Some friends of mine box, you know, prize fighting, and there are matches next Sunday. Do you like to watch boxing?"

"I don't know; I've never watched it. My uncle, he's my uncle, even though he's younger than me, he boxes but I've never watched."

"Adela, you have the most interesting family. I've never heard of an uncle being younger than a niece or nephew!"

"Yes. His name is Jacob Liebermann. He's been boxing for a couple of years now. Have you heard of him?"

"Jake! Of course, I know Jake! He's very good. He has a great coach who really believes in him. Wow! Jake is your uncle! We have so many coincidences, Adela. I think Jake is boxing that day. Do you want to go?"

"Sure Lenny. Do you want to pick me up at my place? My father is very interested in boxing. He got Jacob into it. He tried to get my brother Dan into it, but Dan hated it and quit."

They finish up the last of their ice cream. Lenny pays the bill, and they leave. As they walk back to Adela's building, Lenny notices Adela has switched her purse to the hand that is not next to his side. He takes her hand, and they swing their clasped hands all the way back to Fort Washington Avenue. When they reach Adela's building, they face each other. Lenny keeps his grasp on Adela's hand.

"Adela," he says.

"What Lenny?"

His voice breaking, "You're a swell girl."

Adela rises to her toes, totters for a moment, then quickly kisses Lenny on the cheek. She turns and runs into her building yelling over her shoulder, "See you next Sunday at the same time."

Lenny yells back, "Yeah!"

Too keyed up to wait for the elevator, Adela races up the stairway to the apartment. *I'm all sparkles inside from my toes to the ends of my hair!*

Love

On a warm spring day, Rachel and Fannie walk into Fort Tryon Park. They find a bench to sit and talk. They have both been busy, Rachel with the play and Fannie with the store and her costume work. It's been a long time since they have had the chance to be alone together. Rachel asks Fannie, "Catch me up on what's happening with you."

"Since your play, Rachel, Danny is sure he wants to be an actor. He now comes with me to the dress rehearsals at the Yiddish theater. He's fascinated by how the director coaches the actors. I have to say, it has improved his Yiddish. As soon as he graduates from high school, which is only a couple of months away, he wants to audition for a part. He's also been accepted at City College. I don't know if he can do both."

"Maybe he can go part time." says Rachel. "A lot of students who work take fewer classes each semester."

"I hope he can. He's smart. I want him to go to college. It's a great opportunity."

"Are he and Luc still good friends?" asks Rachel.

"They are the best of friends. I haven't seen Danny so happy since he was a little kid. He's grown up a lot, but I also see that little exuberant kid in him again. Do you know that Luc is as serious about acting as Danny?"

"No, I didn't. It's amazing, given how much difficulty he had at first with his English."

"He's going to start auditioning after high school too. His father knows some directors, and that may open things up for him. Luc's parents are good people. Bertrand offered to help Danny, too. He thinks they are so different from each other, they would not be competing. So, we'll see. Hannah would be thrilled to see how Danny has turned out. He's living her dream."

"And Marek, what does he think about Danny being an actor?"

"Marek loves Danny and all our kids, no question, but he doesn't understand Danny or Adela. He thinks both are ruining their lives and chances to do as well as we have. He can't see how Danny can raise a family as an actor. He's also disappointed Danny gave up boxing. He wanted him to learn how to protect himself. Danny tried it to please Marek, but then he quit. He was miserable every time he went. I hear Jacob is staying with it."

"It's true. Jacob seems to love it. Also, Jacob has become religious. He's been going to that schul on the Lower East Side."

"Really! The one on Eldridge Street?"

"Yes."

"That surprises me about Jacob. I never would have guessed it. Is he still doing his ham radio?"

"He is. But not constantly the way he used to. Now that he works full-time with Aber, he has made enough money to improve his radio set. He can reach radios overseas now."

"Dr. Weiss seemed to have set him on the right track. And so have you and Aber."

"Thank you, Fannie. Having Kayla and Jacob with me has been a blessing. It hasn't always been easy, but they bring purpose to my life. But what is Marek's problem with Adela?"

"He can't see why Adela can't be interested in a boy from the Temple. She's seeing a young man who's a dock worker."

"Fannie, are you talking about Lenny?"

"Yes! Do you know him?"

"I met Lenny. One afternoon, Adela brought him to the library to meet me. Yes, he certainly is a different sort than Marek, but he's a very sweet young man and I think he's crazy about Adela."

"I'm glad you say that. I had the same impression."

Fannie stops talking for a moment then turns to Rachel. There is a catch in her throat. "I don't understand Marek anymore. He's not the open-minded man I married." She cries, and Rachel puts her arm around her. Fannie sobs for a while then says, "Things seemed fine until the kids started having their own ideas, and Marek can only see them as strangers, because they don't think or act like he does. He worries Danny can't protect himself from the brutes in the world if he doesn't know how to fight. And he can't understand Adela choosing a man who's not like him. Marek looks sad all the time and frightened too. I think he's afraid of life. Adela is doing wonderfully. She loves Hunter. She has some great ideas for the store that will help us get through this depression."

"Fannie, when I met Lenny, he talked about wanting to improve working conditions for all dock workers. It seems that makes him more than just a dock worker. He may not be studious, but I think he's smart in his own way.

Fannie turns and looks at Rachel intensely. "I hadn't thought of it until you just said it, but that's like Mischa, helping the workers. I think I've told you about Mischa."

"Yes, you have. Wasn't it Mischa in Palestine who wrote to Daniel about Hannah?"

"Yes." Fannie pauses. She turns away from Rachel. She needs her private thoughts for a few moments. Then says, "Rachel, you never met Mischa. He wasn't really like Lenny. He played the violin and loved poetry, but the sweetness and wanting to help the workers is not so different from Lenny." Fannie sighs, "Rachel, sometimes when I get so angry and fed up with Marek, I think about Mischa and I feel like a bad wife, a bad person. Marek is a suffering man. He had some terrible experiences in Hungary and had to leave when he was around sixteen. He hasn't seen any of his family since he left. He may never see them again. He's upset about the kids. It's like Marek has a dybbuk, a tormenting spirit inside, and he can't let it out. Do you know the play, Rachel?"

"Oh yes I do, Fannie, and I think you're right." Rachel thinks, *He isn't the only one with a dybbuk. Aber has one too.*

Fannie goes on, "I love Marek, but he's changed. He's fallen apart since the kids became teenagers. I don't blame him for being out of his mind when Adela came home drunk. I was too. But he can't get past it. He hasn't been the same since."

"What you say doesn't surprise me, Fannie. I can see the change in Marek. He walks around now like he's carrying two big sacks of potatoes on his back. Of course, the depression doesn't help either."

"He worries about keeping the store going. But really, it's okay. We don't earn what we once did. But people still need clothes fixed and altered. So, we are in fact lucky for people with a business."

"How does he feel about Daniel's friendship with Luc?"

"He sees it as part of what makes Danny happy again. But I think it seems strange to him because as much as he agrees Luc is a fine kid, and he comes from a family who are like us wandering Jews, they are also different. He's scared of anything, and I mean anything, unfamiliar. He suffers. He loves us. I think I love him, but I must admit, I think he's become weak and close-minded." Fannie looks away, and weeps, then cries out, "And he seems to need me more than ever before. I must be strong all the time for him and for the kids. When we first married, he was the one taking care of me." She cries more. When she can stop, she turns toward Rachel and says, "It's so easy to talk to you. I feel lighter. But I hope I haven't put a burden on you."

"No, not a burden Fannie. We both need to talk."

"Tell me about you Rachel."

"I won't be surprised if you already sense what's going on with me. My problem is I'm deeply in love with your brother, and he can't let himself love me because of his dybbuk, maybe dybbuks, mostly from what he went through in the war, especially the brutal death of his fiancé."

"That death is unbearable, even to think about."

"These good men are so broken by what happened to them. Aber and I are the very closest of friends. We have similar interests. We want only the best for each other. Thank goodness Jacob and Kayla seem to be on their way to growing up, and since they arrived, we've raised them together. He loves Jacob and Kayla. He's been both a brother and a father to them. And in every way but one, he obviously loves me. But he claims he cannot love anymore. He's wrong. He forbids himself to know he loves me. I can see it and feel it, but he claims he can't. He says he can't love because he can't risk losing anyone again. He is sure if he did, he could never recover. He has shut a door on a part of himself." Rachel sighs deeply and looks out into the park. Turning to Fannie she says, "So, what do I do? Do I look for someone else? Aber and I have made a long history together. I can't pretend that's not true. Should I get a secret lover and stay with Aber?" Rachel pauses. She puts her face in her hands and shakes her head from side to side. "Fannie, I must unburden myself. I tried that. I started to spend time with a perfectly decent man. He's a professor at City College and an immigrant. He is truly a good person. We have a lot in common. We spent time together, then went away together for a couple of weekends. We made love—no we had sex. Maybe he made love. I could only feel I was betraying Aber, and I ended it. That poor decent man, a person perfectly suitable for me. I just said I must stop seeing you. Of course, I didn't explain it to him. I felt cruel. But I was also relieved. So here I am. I'm relieved I'm not betraying Aber. I don't think he would even feel I was betraying him. He probably would encourage it, because that is what he does. He encourages me in everything I do. So, we will be a tragic couple who take care of each other and who deeply love each other but one of us won't let himself know it. Until death do us part—I guess."

"Oh, Rachel, I wish I knew what to say to you. I have no words of comfort. I don't know that I could have guessed all you tell me. I can easily see how close you two are. I started to see what an interesting person Aber is when he wrote me letters during the war. They were full of his thoughts about the war and about our family. In so many ways you and he are a perfect match. I've always wondered why you haven't married. What you tell me is both very sad and not sad. I begin to think it's friendship that keeps us going. How many husbands and wives are good friends? I have no idea what the answer is." They reach out their arms to hug each other, then slowly and silently walk out of the park.

As they reach Rachel's building, they embrace again. Rachel suddenly turns at the doorway. "Oh Fannie! I forgot to tell you. Your friend Sadie wrote to Aber asking him to meet with her at the synagogue with the *rebbezin* (rabbi's wife). He doesn't know what it's about. He thinks it may be a carpentry job.

Fannie wonders, *Sadie meeting with Aber? What is that about? Hmmm...*

Fannie returns to her family and Rachel goes upstairs to Jacob and Kayla. Aber will join them later.

In His Own Way

It is the following Sunday. Lenny rings the Horvath's bell. This time Adela answers the door. Fannie gets up from her work alcove. Marek, who has been lying on the couch reading the Sunday paper, puts it down and gets up to greet Lenny. Adela has told Fannie and Marek that she and Lenny are going to see Jacob take part in some boxing matches at the gym. The four remain standing. Marek with obvious interest says, "Let me know how Jacob does. I've seen him train but have never seen him in a match. It's a great sport for a young man—builds strength and prepares him to protect himself and his family if he ever needs to. Do you box Lenny?"

"No, but I like to watch it. I'd like to box, but I don't have time to do the training."

Fannie says, "But you probably build plenty of strength from your work."

"Yeah, I guess so. If we didn't, we couldn't survive." Lenny looks back and forth between Marek and Adela. He looks searchingly at Adela for a moment. She sees this but is puzzled. Lenny takes the plunge. "Mr. Horvath, since you are so interested in boxing and since Jake is fighting today, would you like to come with us? And you too, Mrs. Horvath, of course."

Marek looks surprised, then pleased. "Uh yes. If it's okay. Fannie, how about you?"

"No, that's okay. Thank you, Lenny. I have work to do. All of you go."

Adela thinks, *Ohh! I'd rather be alone with Lenny.*

Marek goes to the coat closet and grabs his fedora, and the three leave to take the subway to midtown to the gym.

Fannie thinks *Rachel is right. Lenny is smart in his own way. I haven't seen such a light in Marek's eyes for a long time.* She sits at her worktable. The temperature has dropped, and she puts her blue shawl over her shoulders. As she sketches, she finds herself humming *Dayenu* (It would have been enough.) which they all sang at their recent Passover celebration.

The halls of the West Side YMCA gym at 63rd Street echo with the sounds of men shouting, balls hitting hard surfaces and the smell of sweat and chlorine. Lenny leads them to the boxing ring on the lower floor. Matches for the younger boys are already in progress. Mothers and fathers in metal chairs surround the ring screaming to their sons, "Come on Tommy, closer, closer, short jabs."

"Morris, keep those feet wide. You look like a toe dancer for God's sake!"

"Hit him in the chest, Pete, in the chest!"

"Ziggy, for God's sake, boxing is a contact sport. You fight like a girl!"

"Atta boy, Sy. Go, go, go!"

"Hit 'em Mo, harder, harder! Yeah!"

Adela resists the impulse to put her hands over her ears. She sees Marek waving wildly to someone standing in the back, on the opposite side of the ring. Adela and Lenny follow him. It's Aber. It's no surprise to see Aber at Jacob's match, but standing with Aber are Sadie, Fannie's old friend from the Lower East Side and her daughter Esther. The two are dressed in the long-sleeved dark dresses and black stockings of Orthodox Jewish women. Adela wonders, *What are Sadie and Esther doing here?*

Adela introduces Lenny to all three. Lenny shakes hands with Aber and then reaches out a hand to Sadie. She backs away and in a soft voice says, "Orthodox women must not touch men they are not married to. It is a sign of respect."

"Oh, I'm sorry, I'm so sorry!" apologizes Lenny, thrusting his hands behind his back. Esther gazes at the floor.

Aber explains how he and Sadie met this morning with the rebbetzin and a matchmaker. "They made a match between Jacob and Esther. So, this is the period of the *Tenaim*, (time period before a wedding) when Jacob and Esther will spend time together but will always be accompanied by a chaperone." Marek smiles broadly at Sadie and with gusto, calls out "Mazel tov!"

Adela thinks, *Ha! With Tateh along, they must wonder if this is my tenaim too.*

The boxing rounds for the younger boys are over. The crowd clears out. Adela, Marek, Aber, Sadie and Esther all follow Lenny, who leads them to ringside seats. Sadie requests the men to sit separately and leave a seat in between. Sadie counts seven seats into the row. Adela, Esther, and Sadie sit together in the last three seats. The fourth seat is left empty. Marek, Lenny, and Aber walk into the row and take the three outside seats. The empty seat is between Marek and Adela. Adela, clenching her teeth, thinks, *So THIS is my precious Sunday with Lenny!* She leans across Marek to look over at Lenny. He catches her eye, shrugs and makes a little low wave to her. She waves back the same way and sighs.

A bell rings. The matches, three rounds, three minutes long with a one-minute break between, begin. There are several matches before Jacob's. Marek is totally absorbed. His body follows the moves of the boxers, and he cheers loudly for each winner.

Jacob and his opponent come out. The opponent is a strapping blond youth. The two tap gloves and then each goes to his corner with his coach. Jacob has a full black beard and under his headgear, made of thick leather strips, he wears a yarmulke. His dark blue shorts are embroidered at one corner with a Star of David. He wears high-top black laced shoes. His face is distorted by his mouth guard. His gaze is focused on his opponent, who is equally focused on Jacob. Adela is taken aback when she sees him. *If I hadn't heard his name, I would never have known that was Jacob.*

The starting bell rings. The two boxers lead in with their left shoulders, keeping their chins covered with their left hands, and exchange light blows with their right, circling each other with quick light steps. Then Jacob steps in and delivers a punch to the chest. His opponent makes a quick cross punch with his left that lands hard on Jacob's right shoulder. Jacob responds with a fast double left jab to the chest. The opponent steps in close and pummels Jacob in the chest. The referee separates them. They spar around the ring with light punches and fast footwork when Jacob makes a powerful cross punch just below the breastbone. The opponent stumbles backwards, then recovers. Marek roars, "Atta boy, Jake!" and Lenny yells, "Go Jake!" The bell rings to end the round. The referee announces that Jacob won round one. Esther has turned around in her seat, facing away from the ring, her hands covering her ears. Adela covers her eyes. Aber applauds, and Sadie sits, silent and still.

The minute between rounds is up. The two boxers approach each other again. Jacob's opponent comes in fast, on the offense. With quick fast jabs to Jacob's torso, he backs him onto the ropes. The referee steps in and separates them. Jacob comes in quickly with an uppercut that lands on the chin but then backs away, letting his opponent again pummel him. Jacob's footwork is fast and skillful. He avoids and ducks the punches with skill but it's all defense. The bell for round two rings and the opponent is the winner of round two.

Marek yells, "Come on Jake. Now's your chance!" Jacob's coach is talking to him while rubbing down the shoulder that took a hit in the first round. Jacob is nodding while his gaze stays on his opponent across the ring. The bell rings and Jacob springs off his stool. With lightning-fast footwork he forces his opponent to move backwards around the ring. The opponent tries to land a punch, but Jacob keeps enough distance so the punches don't land, and when they could land, Jacob ducks as they come. It is brilliant footwork and fine offense. Marek yells, "You got em now, Jake. Keep it up-go, go, go!" Lenny yells louder than Marek. "Jake, Jake, Jake!" Adela opens her eyes and looks over at Lenny, who now is only thinking of the fight. She watches him, this excitable, exuberant young man, as if seeing him for the first time from a distance. *So, this is Lenny. My Lenny.* The crowd roars, and when she looks back at the ring, she sees that Jacob's opponent is on the ground. The referee yells, "Four, five, six, seven" The opponent gets up. He comes back at Jacob with a cross punch that lands again on Jacob's right shoulder. Jacob winces and the bell rings. The match is over. The referee calls out, "The winner is—Jacob Liebermann, two to one."

Marek grabs Lenny's hand and raises their two arms in a cheering victory salute. Aber stands cheering and clapping. Sadie and Esther sit quietly.

When Jacob comes out dressed in a white shirt and black pants with his *Talit* fringes hanging out of his shirt, Aber, Marek, and Lenny rush over to him. They all pat him on the back and yell praises. Marek introduces Lenny to Jacob. Sadie and Esther get up to stand next to Aber. He and Jacob will escort Sadie and Esther on the subway back to the Lower East Side before returning uptown. Lenny and Marek shake Aber's hand while Adela leans over to hug Sadie and Esther saying, "Mazel tov for the tenaim."

As Adela, Marek and Lenny walk to the uptown subway, Lenny and Marek keep talking about the fight and how Jacob skillfully turned his defensive moves offensive in the third round. "His footwork is excellent," says Marek, "but he could improve the power of his punches." Marek goes on again about how important it is for a young man to be strong enough to protect himself and his family. Lenny agrees. He stands to get off the subway at the next stop. He smiles sheepishly at Adela, saying he will come by to pick her up next Sunday. She, a little cooly, says, "Okay, see you then."

Marek and Adela get off at the next stop. As they walk to their building, Marek says, "Jacob and Esther! It never occurred to me that they would become a match. I can't wait to tell your mother. Boxing has done Jacob nothing but good. It's made him into a man."

With irritation, Adela says, "Tateh, there are plenty of ways a boy can grow up. It's not only by boxing. Look how much Danny has grown up since he's been acting."

Marek mutters, "Acting! How can a person be serious about acting?" They walk on in silence for a while when Marek says, "That was good of Lenny to invite me to come along."

"Yeah, I guess it was," murmurs Adela, turning away and rolling her eyes. *I only hope this is the end of my tenaim. But I have to say, I haven't seen Tateh look so happy in years. He actually grabbed Lenny's hand to cheer Jacob at the end. I couldn't have imagined it.*

More silence, then Marek says,

"I think Lenny is a fine young man, Adela. He understands how important it is for a man to be strong. He said he'd like to box but has no time now. But he does the kind of work that makes him strong, and he must be fast on his feet too.

Wow! thinks Adela. *I think Lenny may have won him over.*

Growing Up

1⁹³²Marek and Fannie are having their evening tea when Daniel rushes in from outside. He has been working as an understudy at the Yiddish Theater and is now at the theater most nights. He is breathless from running up the stairs, sure he could reach the apartment sooner than the old elevator could.

"Mama, Tateh, I have great news. I have a part in the next play 'The Girl from Yesterday', with Molly Picone playing the lead. Molly Picone!! She's a great star. It means that this play should go on for a long time. No matter if the play is good or bad, people will come to see Molly Picone. So now, Luc and I are both working actors. I can't believe it. It's really happening. We are both WORKING! He is in "Black Souls" at the Provence Town Playhouse on MacDougal Street and I'm downtown on Second Avenue. We're not even far apart. Mama, Tateh, we can afford rent now. We want to move into an apartment in Greenwich Village. It's a dream come true. We're both working actors, and we can afford to live in an apartment near where each of us is working. This is what I've always wanted. I can't believe it's really happening."

"Danny, Danny, stop! I can't take all of this in at once." Fannie has been hit by a tornado. *Oy vey iz mir! He wants to move out. He's only twenty. Oy, at twenty I was already married. I was a mother, his mother, and Adela's mother too!!* "Danny, okay, so what is this part you got?"

"It's not a huge part, but it's Molly Piccone's brother, so it is an important part—a great part for my first professional debut. It's a comedy. Mama, maybe you'll be doing costumes for it. Rehearsals start next week. The director wants it to go up in September."

Marek, stone-faced, says, "And what about your work in the store?"

"Oh, Tateh, of course I'll do the deliveries. I'll be working mostly at night. Rehearsals start at seven in the evening, and then of course the play is at night. Oh, yeah, except for Wednesday matinees. Maybe I can do deliveries on Sundays."

"And what is this about moving out, all the way downtown no less?"

"It's only a subway ride away Tateh, a half hour, only a half hour."

"Yes, that's on the express. You can't always get on the express. And you know Danny, most children live with their parents until they get married. You don't seem to be anywhere near getting married."

"Tateh, I'm an actor; it's not the usual kind of work for family life. I'm out at night, maybe even going on tour. Right now, I intend to be an actor. I have a chance now, in a play with Molly Piccone. Very few new actors get a chance like this. Tatch please, it's what I dreamed of since I was a kid and went with Mama to dress rehearsals. Remember, my first mama was an actress. I think it's in my blood."

"What do you mean in your blood?"

"You know, inherited. And also, Mama took me to the theater with her."

Marek swivels a look at Fannie who shrugs her shoulders and looks to the heavens.

"Marek asks, "We're still in a depression. Do you think people are going to spend money to go to plays?"

"They do," says Daniel, "especially for comedies. People want to laugh. Tateh, this is what makes me happy. This is what makes me proud to be me."

Marek is shaking his head, trying to take it all in. "Okay, okay," says Marek, shrugging and turning his palms up. "But why does this have to mean moving out?"

"Because Luc and I are best friends. We help each other to learn lines. We each understand what it means to be an actor. No, you're right, I'm nowhere near getting married; that's true. But I will be working. I am about to be a professional actor. I've worked hard to get here."

"That tells me nothing, about why you think you have to live together, spending money on rent, not helping with the store."

"Tateh", Daniel pulls up a chair next to Marek, "Tateh, try to understand. I'm growing up. You were on your own at eighteen and working for a tailor. I'm already twenty. You learned your craft. You spent time with the other tailors where you worked. I want to spend time with other actors. We learn from each other. Luc and I learn from each other. And Tateh, I'm happy when I'm with Luc."

Marek takes a deep breath. He raises his hands in a gesture of helplessness. "I can't make you stay Danny. I can't make you do work you don't want to do. I can't make you unhappy." Marek sighs deeply. His voice breaks, and he tenderly places his hand on the back of Danny's head. "I love you, Danny. You are my eldest son. When I first met your mother, you were hardly more than a baby. I loved your mama the first time we met. I met you at the same time and I loved you right away as my son. I don't want you to get hurt. I want you to be happy and well. I want you to be respected. I want only good for you, Danny."

Daniel is crying now, and so is Fannie. "Tateh, Mama, I know you both love me, and I love both of you, but I must be who I am, and I'm still learning that. I know I can be an actor. And Luc is the first friend I've ever known who is as important to me as my family. Kids grow up. They can still love their family AND move away. I'll come home for

Shabbos every week. There's no performance on Friday nights." This seems to calm Marek.

Fannie asks, "When are you and Luc thinking of moving?"

"I don't know exactly, but when we've talked about it, we figured as soon as we were both getting a regular paycheck. He's getting paid now. And I'll get paid as soon as we start rehearsals. That's next week." Daniel breathes deeply, then yawns, saying, "I think I'll go to bed now." He hugs Marek and Fannie and says goodnight.

Marek and Fannie reach for each other across the kitchen table and clasp hands. Fannie sighing, says, "And soon it will be Adela too. She's been with Lenny for a year now." They stand. Fannie starts gathering the teacups. Marek takes them out of her hands and comes around the table to embrace her. They both weep.

Marek, his voice breaking says, "It's a different world Fannie." She nods and they continue to embrace.

Another Talk in the Park

Rachel and Fannie plan to meet again at their bench in Fort Tryon Park. Rachel arrives first. She carries a copy of The New York World-Telegram under her arm. She sits on the bench, opens the paper and reads, becoming so absorbed she only looks up when she hears Fannie say, "So Rachel, what's in the news?"

She puts the paper down and stands up to hug Fannie. As they sit Rachel says, "The news is both hopeful and very grim at the same time. The good news is that Roosevelt looks like he might win with his New Deal and the promise to get the country back on its feet. But in Germany there is chaos. The Nazi party is growing every minute with Nazi thugs on the streets beating up Jews. And most worrisome of all is that Hitler has become a German citizen because he plans to get elected as chancellor. Can you imagine? Fannie, it's really happening. And there are your brothers in Vienna. Aber keeps writing them."

"I know he does, and so do I. I'm worried because usually when I send a letter within three or four weeks, I get a letter back. It's been two months now and no word. Has Aber heard anything?"

"No, not a word back. Aber is furious they are so gullible to believe they were safe."

"How are you and Aber doing?"

Sighing, Rachel says, "No different. It is what it is. I can't say I'm resigned. But I can say I can't imagine being with anyone else. I love him and can't pretend I don't. So, I take him as he is." She shifts the topic.

"I think it's wonderful that Jacob and Esther are going to marry. I think it works for them. Esther is very shy, and so is Jacob. He's found his way at the synagogue and with boxing. He seems happy and so much more confident. Sadie is thrilled. So soon we'll have a wedding."

"How will it be for Kayla when Jacob moves out."

"I think Kayla will be alright. She loves Hunter. She wants to be an elementary school teacher. She'll have to lose her accent for that. Also, as you know, Adela took Kayla under her wing at Hunter, and Kayla has made her own friends now, as well as Adela's."

"Rachel, I know you know about Danny being a part of the Yiddish Theater now. Did you know he and Luc are planning to move together to an apartment in Greenwich Village?"

Rachel's eyes open wide. "No! I didn't know. I'm surprised." She pauses and looks away, staring out at the trees and river. Then, looking back at Fannie says, "But maybe not so surprised."

"What do you mean?" asks Fannie. "What do you mean, 'not so surprised'?"

"They bring out the best in each other."

"Yes, but..."

"It means Daniel has the courage to be who he is; and Luc has helped him do that." There is a long pause. Fannie looks down, then meets Rachel's eyes.

"You mean...?"

"Yes."

"Oh, Rachel, I don't want him to be hurt!"

"Fannie, he's an actor, and a very talented actor. He and Luc will be among friends living in the Village. They will all support each other."

"But acting is such a risky profession."

"But look at how well they're doing already. And there are rumors that if Roosevelt gets in, he'll create jobs for a lot of people including actors. He thinks about setting up federally supported theaters all over the country."

"Right now, we're still in a depression."

"You and Marek have figured it out. You're managing. I think Daniel and Luc will figure it out too."

"I have to say, Danny is happy. Fannie looks down at her hands and then back at Rachel. "Rachel, you said, Danny 'has the courage to be who he is.' I hadn't thought of it that way. It fits our Danny. When he searched for his father, he said he needed to know the truth of his beginnings, even if it was bad."

"Remember, Fannie, he found out his father changed for the better at the end of his life when he could love someone."

"Yes, I guess without searching, he would never know that. Did you know he didn't tell us what he learned about Mendl until, maybe a year ago? He held it in for a long time."

"I often think about his back story of Iago," says Rachel. "I suspect, because of his search, Daniel was able to see Iago as not only a villain but also a tortured soul."

"Marek worries about him. He's convinced Daniel's not prepared for our harsh world."

"Were any of us prepared?"

"Hmmm, I certainly wasn't!" *I was sold into prostitution by my uncle! And here I am. I survived even that!*

"How is Marek dealing with Daniel moving out and living with Luc?"

"Maybe resigned? No, not resigned. I think it's more like defeated. He always goes back to Danny isn't physically strong enough to protect himself, and acting is no career. But he also knows he can't stop Danny. If he tried, he'd lose him for sure."

Both pause when they hear birdsong nearby. Rachel excitedly says, "That's a cardinal calling for a mate! The cardinals are singing, and Jews are being beaten in Europe. What a world we live in!" She turns to face Fannie again and asks, "How is Adela doing?"

"I think Adela and Lenny are really in love. They've been together more than a year now. Marek still wishes she were with a Jewish boy, one of the boys from the Temple youth group. But clever Lenny has won him over. Marek sees Lenny as physically strong and devoted. He's devoted to Marek as well as to Adela. He and Marek go to boxing matches together and analyze what happens in each match. He sees Lenny as someone who can protect both Adela and himself. But Rachel, he will never see anyone as good enough for Adela. Well maybe if it was someone just like him. Speaking of tortured souls, I think Marek is a tortured soul. He's haunted by his past. I'm so lucky to have some of my family here. No one in his family came. I love Marek. He is very good to us, takes care of us, and is completely trustworthy and devoted. I guess I hoped for more poetry, more excitement. But I have safety with Marek. I needed safety when we married. I probably still need it."

"We have two good men Fannie. But they have their ghosts."

"And we have ours."

Both women are quiet for a time. Fannie turns to Rachel and says, "Oh Rachel, you are so wise. Thank you." They leave the park.

Another family

ear Mr. and Mrs. Horvath,
My husband Enzo and I will be very happy if you and your family
come to our apartment for dinner next Friday. We have met your lovely
daughter Adela and are so pleased she and our son have become such
good company for each other. We hope for the chance to meet you and
your family. We live at 145 East 125th Street. We are in apartment
number 5.

Regards,
Isabela Russo

Dear Mrs. Russo,
Thank you for your invitation. My husband, Marek, our children
and I look forward to meeting you and your family next Friday.
We too have met your fine son and see how much our Adela and
your Lenny enjoy their friendship.

Regards,
Fannie Horvath

On the following Friday, five members of the Horvath family take the
subway to 125th Street and then another subway to go east to Lexington
Avenue. Daniel can't join them because he is accompanying Luc and

his family to an opening at the Met Opera, an opera for which Bertrand created the scenery.

The Russo's apartment building is a five-story brownstone. There is a business of some kind on the first floor. To her surprise, Fannie notices some gold Hebrew lettering on the window, but the words are unfamiliar to her. She points them out to Marek. He is puzzled too. He says out loud what each letter is but doesn't know what they mean. They climb the stairs to the top landing where there is only one door and ring the bell. Enzo opens the door, and Isabela and Lenny are beside him. Enzo is an older version of Lenny, also a strongly built man of short stature with broad shoulders. He has a strong Roman nose and full lips. He wears a starched white shirt and a vest. He shakes hands vigorously with Marek, who notices his dry, calloused but fleshy palm and strong grip. Isabela too is short and full-figured, with a fine-boned face and large dark eyes. Her gray-streaked, dark hair is held back in a low bun. She wears a black shirtwaist and a tweed skirt. She has a radiant smile and offers both hands to Fannie, who takes them into her own. With exuberance and strongly accented English, Isabela says,

"Please call me Isabela. I am so happy to meet you finally." Fannie introduces Marek to Isabela. Marek gives Isabela a slight bow and Isabela introduces Fannie to Enzo who smiles broadly saying,

"Welcome to our home."

As Adela enters, Isabela puts out her arms to hug her and says, "Adela, we're so happy to meet your family."

Each of the Horvath children is introduced. Isabela explains that their eldest, a daughter, Cecilia, is with her in-laws tonight. Enzo calls into another room.

"Elio, Marco, Arone, come, say hello to Adela's family." One teenager and two younger boys rush in. They too are all wearing gleaming white starched shirts. Each shakes hands with Marek and Simon and, like their father, gives a little bow to Fannie and to Miriam. The youngest, Arone, however, grabs Adela's hand saying,

"Come see the game we're playing, Adela. Come play with us." Adela, looking back at the family, lets Arone bring her into one of the back rooms. Isabela calls to Arone, explaining he can show Adela the game and maybe play later, but soon we will eat dinner.

The Russo apartment takes up the whole 5th floor; however, it is still small. To accommodate eleven people for dinner, the Russos pushed the modest but well-kept furnishings against the wall of the living room. The table has been extended with two card tables at each end, so its length reaches from the dining alcove far into the living room. The elongated table is covered with a white damask cloth and set for eleven with wine glasses for all except the younger children. A vase of yellow and orange flowers is at the center. Isabela, with a laugh, points out that tonight there is no other place to sit except at the table, so she invites everyone to take a seat. Enzo stands at the table end in the dining alcove and invites Marek to take the seat at the other end. Next to Enzo is a small chest. On the chest are two unlit candles in ornate silver candle holders. Once everyone is seated and quiet, Isabela asks Fannie, "Fannie, will you light the candles with me?" Marek and Fannie quickly exchange surprised looks then Fannie says,

"I am honored to Isabela." She leaves her seat next to Marek to stand beside Isabela who lights the candles. The two women say the blessing over the candles together. Fannie, tears in her eyes, thinks, *I hope it will help Marek to know this is a Jewish family.* When the prayer ends, Fannie and Isabela embrace. Lenny who is next to Adela grabs her hand under the table. The two smile broadly at each other.

Enzo blesses the wine and the challah, which instead of the usual long braided shape, is also braided but in the shape of a large muffin, like a panettone.

After the blessings, Isabela turns to Lenny, "Leonardo..." then says something in a language that Fannie feels she has heard before, perhaps in the past, but cannot place. Lenny gets up and says, "Si Mama." He goes into the kitchen and returns carrying a large tureen of soup. He sets it down next to his father.

"Isabela," Fannie asks, following her into the kitchen, "What language are you speaking?"

"Oh, yes, sorry, that's Ladino. I was born in Spain, then my family moved to Ferarra, where Ladino was also spoken by some of the Jews."

Fannie asks, "Does Enzo speak Ladino too?"

"Yes, Enzo and I met in Ferrara, where he had a furlough during the War. His grandparents came to Italy from Turkey. Speaking Ladino was the first thing that drew us to each other."

"Oh, Ladino, of course! Now I remember," says Fannie. I heard some of the Italian girls I worked with at the factory speak it. I think they were from Ferrara. It took a while before I realized they were also Jewish. And they didn't realize when they heard Yiddish that we were Jewish. When did you leave Ferrara?"

"As soon as the war ended. Enzo came back to find me, and soon we married. So, I moved to his town, Livorno. There's a big port there. He worked at the docks, like his father before him"

Fannie and Isabela return to the table with soup bowls and serving utensils. Enzo dishes out the soup. It is familiar chicken soup but has a vivid red color from tomatoes and is flavored with escarole.

Again, Lenny is asked to bring out a heavy platter for the main course. This time it is a dish totally unknown to the Horvath family. Isabela explains it is lamb cooked with artichokes and fava beans, a large flat bean like a big lima bean, and fragrantly flavored with garlic and fresh oregano. Marek and Fannie find it delicious and like nothing they have ever tasted. Along with the lamb is spinach cooked with raisins and pine nuts. There are also plum tomatoes, roasted and stuffed with rice. Everyone eats heartily. Marek, Lenny, Enzo, and Elio all pass their plates for seconds. Elio looks to be around fifteen. Marek thinks, *I wonder if he would like a job doing deliveries.*

During the meal Marek asks about the business downstairs. Enzo explains that his brother-in-law, who lives with his family on the second floor, owns that business. "It's a funeral home, the only Ladino funeral home in Italian Harlem."

"And the Hebrew letters?" asks Marek.

"Yes, like your Yiddish, Ladino is written using Hebrew letters."

After the main course, the younger children become restless. Enzo says to Elio, "Take your brothers and Miriam and Simon into the other room and play a game with them."

Arone calls out to Adela, "You come too Adela, please, please."

Adela gets up and hugs Arone, saying, "You go with Elio now, and later I'll come in and kiss you good night." Arone pouts and, stamping his feet on the floor, follows Elio and the others.

Lenny and Adela stay at the table but remain quiet, listening to their parents talk about their immigrations. Isabela serves almond cake and tea.

Isabela asks Fannie why she left Austria. Fannie describes how her father, a paymaster in a salt mine was beaten, then fell ill and died. She was sent first to Budapest and then to New York to work and send money home. As she speaks, she thinks, *I must leave so much out of this story.* Then Marek, realizing that he in no way wants to tell the real story of why he left Budapest, quickly turns to Enzo and jumps in to ask about why they left Livorno.

Enzo talks at some length about the rise of Fascism in Italy in the 1920s. As a dock worker, he was working to improve the dangerous working conditions and was accused of being a communist. "The fascists assume all Jews are communists. Italy is impossible now because

Mussolini is really tightening the noose around anyone he thinks is disloyal to fascism.

Here in America, more unions are getting controlled by criminals. Lenny is speaking up for the workers. We are very proud of him, but we worry. Also, like in Italy, any Jew is assumed to be a communist."

Adela senses Marek's nervousness. She turns to Lenny and nods. Lenny rises from his seat. All fall silent. Lenny, his hands clasped at chest level, his voice shaky, turns to face Marek. "Mr. Horvath, I must tell you, I love your wonderful daughter with all my heart and all my soul. I want to protect her and be with her for the rest of my life. I ask you Mr. Horvath, if you will please give me your permission and your blessing to marry your beautiful Adela."

Fannie puts her hand to her mouth as she takes a sharp intake of breath. Marek gets up, comes around to Lenny and embraces him. Lenny starts to cry as he says, his voice cracking, "Thank you, thank you, Mr. Horvath." Marek, with great emotion, says to Lenny,

"You will be a son to me Lenny. From now on, call me Tateh."

Fannie rises and comes over to embrace Adela and Lenny. She tells Lenny, "Please Lenny, call me Mama."

Enzo and Isabela knew before that Lenny was going to ask Marek for Adela's hand. Enzo reaches into his pocket, takes out a small velvet box and hands it to Lenny, who takes Adela's hand and places the small box onto it. This is a big surprise to Adela, who opens it to find a ring with a tiny diamond.

"Lenny, she exclaims, how can you do this?"

"It was my mother's. Her grandmother gave it to her, and my mother wants you to have it." Adela runs over to embrace Isabela.

Marek asks, "When do you plan to get married?"

Lenny answers, "When Adela graduates from college, so in about a year."

Fannie thinks, *This is a fine young man Adela chose. He's her first love.* She shakes her head as though trying to shake something away. *What's wrong with me? Why am I thinking of Mischa? Lenny and Mischa are not alike, except for their labor organizing. Dear God, please let Lenny be safe! Maybe it's about first love. Mischa gave me a ring too. Yes! And I still have it. STOP thinking of Mischa!*

The Horvath family slowly gets ready to leave. Marek and Enzo shake hands, laugh and pat each other on the back. Fannie is busy talking to Isabela and planning for when they will come to the Horvath's for Shabbos or Shabbat in Ladino.

Lenny and Adela stand at the door holding hands. Lenny lifts her hand with the ring to his lips. The Horvaths gather up Miriam and Simon, who had a good time playing cards with the Russo boys. Adela lifts Arone into her arms, hugs and kisses him and tells him they will play a long game together the next time she visits. The parents are saying goodbye. Lenny says to Adela, "I'll pick you up at Tateh's store after work."

On the way home on the train, Marek picks up a newspaper that was left on the seat. Miriam and Simon are tired and quiet. Fannie, sitting next to Adela, asks, "When did you realize Lenny is Jewish?"

"He knew I was Jewish when he first saw the *mezuzah* (small parchment scroll) on our door frame. That's when he told me he was Jewish. He asked me not to tell you and Tateh because he wanted to make sure Tateh liked him, no matter what his religion, and that he was okay with his being Italian. He didn't worry about you, just Tateh."

"Hmmm!" says Fannie "He figured that one out."

"Yes, he did. But he also likes Tateh a lot and enjoys being with him. They are both intense sports fans, especially boxing"

1933

Six months later, Adela is alone in the tailor shop. Marek is out buying supplies. At Shabbos dinner the night before, she asked Daniel to meet her there the following day at noon. She said it was urgent. When Daniel arrives at the shop, Adela puts out a sign saying, "Back at 1:00 PM." She motions to Daniel to come into the back. She is wringing her hands and is as breathless as if she had been running. "Adela, what's the matter?"

"Danny, I need your help. Lenny and I need your help. The thugs are after Lenny. The unions are controlled by criminals, and they send hitmen after anyone who challenges them. They're after Lenny. But it's worse than that. They're threatening to come after his family, all of them, even his little brothers, unless he stops organizing the dock workers. Danny, we're desperate! We must leave the country now! Can you write to Mischa in Palestine right away and tell him we want to come to his kibbutz?"

Daniel, his mind whirling from what he is hearing, focuses his eyes on Adela. He nods as he tries to take it all in. *Mischa! I don't know Mischa except for a couple of letters we exchanged.* "Oh my God Adela! Yes of course I will. But what will you do right now?"

"Lenny's dock supervisor is helping. There's a ship leaving in three days for Marseille. Once we get there, we'll find a way to get to Jaffa. In the meantime, Lenny is not going to work. He hopes they think he's already left. He sleeps here at night. Oh Danny, I'm so scared!"

Daniel asks, "Does Lenny's family know what's happening?"

"Yes, they're terrified. They left Italy when his father was threatened in the same way."

Adela is sobbing. Daniel puts his arms around her saying, "We'll figure this out, Dela. Of course, I'll write to Mischa right away. Do you need money? I have some. I'm getting paid now."

"No," she says, "We have enough for the trip."

"You'll need more. Here I just got paid" He takes twenty dollars from his wallet and gives it to her. "Do Mama and Tateh know?" asks Daniel.

"Not yet, I'm going to tell them later today."

"Mischa won't get the letter until, at the earliest, when you're in Marseille."

"We'll send him a telegram when we get there."

"And Danny..." Adela cries more intensely. "I'm expecting!" She sobs so forcefully she loses her breath. "I'm scared. I'm so scared I'll die, or the baby will die, like my first mama, or something will be wrong with the baby, like that baby you found in the street. I'm so scared, Danny." She cries onto Daniel's shirt while he holds her. When she can speak again, she says, "I'm NOT telling Mama and Tateh about the baby. They'll only try to make me stay. I must leave with Lenny. Oh, I almost forgot; we got married a few days ago at City Hall."

Daniel concentrates to stay calm. "Dela, we'll take care of this. We'll get you and Lenny to safety. Do you want me to be with you when you tell Tateh and Mama?"

"Yes, oh yes."

"And where's Lenny now?"

"He's with Rachel at the library. He's staying there all day and then coming here at night after dark, then leaving early before Tateh comes in. He's afraid if he goes home, they'll come and get him and hurt the family. If they show up, his father will tell them he's left the country."

That evening, Marek and Fannie are surprised when Daniel shows up. Adela comes out of the bedroom when she hears him enter. The twins are already in bed. Fannie, seeing how upset Adela looks, urgently asks, "Adela, darling, what's the matter?"

"Mama, Tateh," Adela stammers, bursting into tears.

"Adela, my dearest Adela," cries out Marek, "are you alright? What's the matter? Tell me!"

"Mama, Tatah, Lenny, and his family are being threatened because of his union work. We have to leave the country. We're going to Palestine, where Mischa lives."

"Oy vey iz mir! Oh, Adela, Adela!" Fannie rushes over to her.

Marek, desperately, "Lenny of course has to leave but not YOU Adela."

"Oh yes, Tateh, I must go with him. We got married. When we knew what was happening, we got married. Sobbing and gasping she says "—at City Hall. I'm sorry Tateh, so sorry we didn't tell you or his parents. We have no time. Lenny is fighting for the safety of his family and for himself."

Marek turns white. He can't catch his breath. He staggers to the couch. Fannie rushes to help him and loosens his collar. Daniel races to the kitchen and comes back with a glass of water. Adela slumps into a chair and sobs. As Daniel helps his father take a drink of water, Fannie goes to the bathroom cabinet and takes out a bottle of smelling salts. She opens it and puts under Marek's nose. This revives him. He is composed for a moment and then puts his face in his hands and moans. The others wait until his moaning stops. Fannie asks where Lenny is staying. Daniel answers for Adela, explaining about his hiding in the library and tailor shop. Fannie asks more about their plans for leaving. Adela tells her about the ship that will sail to Marseille, where they will get another ship to Jaffa. Daniel tells of his plan to write to Mischa right away, and he should have the letter by the time they arrive in Marseille.

Fannie thinks she too is about to faint and feels for the smelling salts in her pocket. What she has just heard takes a moment to sink in. "Adela! you're a married woman!"

"Yes, I am Mama."

Adela rushes over to Fannie, who takes her into her arms, saying, "It's hard to believe, even though you and Lenny were engaged." Fannie is quiet for a moment, then says, "Adela, I have an idea. If I can get the rabbi to do it, would you agree to have a little Jewish wedding, with the two families, in the back of the store tonight? We could send a taxi to pick up the Russos."

"Okay, Mama, okay, if it will help Tateh. I'll go to Lenny now."

Daniel and Adela leave. Fannie goes to Marek and says, "Come, my darling, let's lie down together. Marek gets up. Fannie puts her arm around his waist, and he puts his arm around her shoulder. They go to their bedroom and lie together on their bed, both looking at the ceiling. Soon Marek turns on his side towards Fannie. He says, his voice hoarse, and cracking, "I will never see my mother and sisters again, and now I will never see my darling Adela again."

"No, Marek, that's not true. We'll visit or they'll visit here when it's safe again. And maybe when we are old and don't work anymore, maybe we'll move to Palestine."

He wraps an arm around Fannie's waist and then folds his legs and other arm into a fetal position. He moans quietly until he sleeps.

Fannie thinks, *Oy vey, history is repeating itself. First Mischa escapes to Palestine, then Hannah and now Adela and Lenny. How can this be? Who is next?*

Under the Chuppah (Wedding Canopy)

It is eleven o'clock the same evening. Adela and Lenny, Marek and Fannie, Daniel and Luc, Rachel and Aber, Enzo and Isabela, Cecilia, Elio, and the Rabbi all crowd into the back room of the tailor shop. The shades in the front room are lowered, and the back is lit only by two small table lamps. All the adults appear tense and move stiffly in the crowded room, but greetings, handshakes and embraces are exchanged. Each family has brought a bottle of wine and glasses. The rabbi from Temple Emanu-El greets and welcomes everyone. He asks if everyone is ready to begin. Fannie asks for a moment of time. She reaches into a bag she brought and pulls out the blue and white tablecloth Adela used for the childhood game she played with Marek, and called, "Tateh, make me the sky." Fannie quickly explains this to the Russos, also telling them it was used as the chuppah for Marek's and her wedding. Fannie asks Daniel and Elio, Lenny's eldest of his younger brothers, to hold it over the couple. This immediately seems to lower everyone's tension, and even Marek smiles when he sees the blue and white tablecloth making the sky for his beloved daughter and Lenny. Lenny has been holding the rings used at the City Hall ceremony in his pocket. He hands them to his sister Cecilia and asks her to hand each ring to him and Adela when the rabbi asks for them. The ceremony is performed. Lenny breaks the wineglass with one sharp crack of his heel, and the couple are married

235

by both the state of New York and in the Jewish tradition. Many hugs and kisses are exchanged. Despite the terrifying circumstances, there is a celebration. Toasts are offered to the couple and to the families. Then Marek lifts his glass and toasts Fannie, "To my beautiful wife of many years, I will always love you and don't know how I would ever survive without you."

Three days later, again after dark, the families gather again at the back of the store to say goodbye to Lenny and Adela. Marek takes Lenny aside and gives him one hundred dollars. They embrace, and Marek whispers to Lenny, "Lenny, please take good care of Adela."

"Believe me Tateh, I will. Your wonderful daughter is my heart and soul."

The couple takes a taxi to the port. It is too dangerous for the families to see them off at the dock. Lenny's supervisor gets them onto the ship as soon as they arrive and they quickly go to their sleeping quarters. The ship will sail in the morning.

Meanwhile, Aber hails a taxi for the Russo family. Daniel and Luc take the subway downtown. Although it is early February, it is not very cold. Fannie, Marek and Rachel will walk home to their neighborhood. Aber accompanies them. After Fannie and Marek enter their building Aber brings Rachel to her door. Rachel asks Aber, "Do you think they'll be safe in Palestine?"

"There are big Arab uprisings in Palestine now. But with Lenny targeted here, they will be safer there, at least for now."

"What do you mean, Aber, 'for now'?"

"Hitler got elected chancellor in Germany. He was elected! This was no Beer Hall Putsch like in 1923. He now has the support of most of the German people and many others throughout Europe and elsewhere. He has already set up a prison in Dachau, where he's sending any citizen who openly disagrees with him. There will be no stopping him. No place is safe. I think my brothers are doomed. We all may be doomed." Rachel reaches out to Aber. They embrace, clinging to each other for longer than usual. As they part, Aber says, "I'll meet Jacob here in the morning. We have a job in the Bronx." He leaves to take the subway to the men's Y.

Dear Uncle Mischa,

Once again, I am writing to ask for your help. My sister Adela and her new husband Leonardo (Lenny) Russo are on their way to Marseille where they will send you a telegram as soon as they find a boat to Jaffa. Like you once did for the garment workers, Lenny has been organizing the dock workers and, again like you, he was threatened with harm to himself and his family for his union activities. I hope Lenny and Adela can be welcomed at your kibbutz.

Also, Uncle Mischa, I want you to know how helpful it was to me to receive your letter with your pictures and memories of my mother, Hannah, and of me too. Perhaps it might be of interest to you to know that, like my first mother Hannah, I too am an actor and now am part of the repertory company of the Yiddish Theater on Second Avenue.

I hope we might meet someday when my family and I come to visit Adela and Lenny in Palestine.

Yours Sincerely,
Daniel Moshe Horvath

Dear Daniel,
Rest assured, I will gladly meet your sister and brother-in-law in Jaffa. They will be welcomed into our kibbutz.

Congratulations on becoming an actor. Your first mother would be thrilled to hear that, and I have no doubt that your mother, Fannie, and father are also very proud of such a fine accomplishment as being a part of the great Yiddish theater of Second Avenue.

Please give your mother, Fannie, my regards. You and all your family are always welcome at Kibbutz Degania for either a visit or to live here.

Warmest wishes to you and to yours,
Uncle Mischa Ben Natan

Dear Mama and Tateh,
I know you received our telegram when Lenny and I arrived safely in Jaffa. Mischa met us at the boat in his truck to take us to Kibbutz Degania.

Mischa has been kind to us in every way. He and Lenny immediately talked about their shared experiences as labor organizers. Mischa's wife, Aviva, is lovely and welcoming. We spend a lot of time with the family. They have three children.

As a married couple, Lenny and I don't live in the dormitory. We have a little wooden house with two rooms.

The land around us is beautiful, full of date palm trees. I am sure you never saw date palm trees. They are like no other tree. We are right near the Sea of Galilee, where we swim every day.

We will both work on the kibbutz. Lenny has his dream of becoming a farmer. I will sew and design costumes for the kibbutz theater group. While there are many Yiddish speakers here and some Ladino speakers, we will learn modern Hebrew.

I have important news. I am expecting a baby four months from now. Lenny is thrilled. But Mama and Tateh, I am so scared because of what happened to my first mother and to the baby. I want more than *anything in the world for you both to be here when the baby comes. Tateh, I know you cannot leave the store. So, Mama, can you please come and be with me and pray with me that the baby and I both survive and are healthy? I am so scared. I love you both so much.*

Your Adela

As she reads the end of the letter, Fannie exclaims, "Oy vey! She's afraid she's going to die!" Shaking, she shows the letter to Marek.

"Fannie, you must go and be with her. And NO midwives! She must have a doctor! Oh, my darling Adela! I don't know what I'd do if something happened to her. Parents must die before their children. They must, they must!"

"Of course I'll go." says Fannie. As she says this, her shakiness subsides, and she begins to plan. *Let's see. Four months from now, I should have all the designs in for the next two plays. Yes, I just need someone to supervise the sewing and do the fitting. Maybe Sadie can do that. She's a very good seamstress. And she can do the fitting too. I think she'd like that.* "Marek, do you know when Jacob and Esther are getting married?"

"No Fannie, I don't?"

I must find out. "Yes, yes, Marek, of course I'll go to Palestine. I'll see to it that a doctor delivers the baby. Lenny and I will do everything to keep Adela safe. I'll write to Adela and tell her I'm coming." *Maybe Lenny can pick me up in Jaffa. I'll write to them right away."* She looks at the clock. "Marek, I must go now. I'm meeting with the twins' teachers. Don't worry, dearest, Adela will get the best care. I should be home in an hour. Here's the Forverts. I'll be home before you finish reading it and we'll plan my trip together.

Fannie rushes out the door. As she walks, she thinks, *Oh my God, I'm going to Palestine! I'm going to see Mischa. I can't get that out of my head. That old rucksack with my diary and the letter from Mischa. It's still in the back of the closet, on the upper shelf. What if the boat sinks, I die, and Marek finds it! Why do I keep it after all these years? I meant to ask Rachel to keep it a long time ago, but then I forgot. I must look for it in the morning. All those pages are all about Mischa and how much I loved him. Marek knows about Mischa. I told him before we married. But he'd wonder why I kept it. The poetry from Mischa is in it too. And oh yes, the ring! Marek would wonder why I needed to hide it. I must get rid of all of it right away and not wait until I go. I'll burn it all in the sink after everyone leaves tomorrow. But what about the ring? I can't think about that now.* She opens the heavy door of Miriam and Simon's school.

The next morning after Marek and the twins leave, Fannie pulls down the old canvas rucksack from the top shelf of her bedroom closet. The canvas is stiff with age. She pulls open the snaps and sees notebooks and some rolled-up pages of the Forverts. She tries to pick up the old newsprint, but the brittle yellow pages crumble in her hand. *What's this!* She remembers that before she had the three cents to buy the small notebooks, she used discarded pages of the Forverts to write her diary, right over the printed words. She crushes the newsprint right into the rucksack until it is dust. She takes out the notebooks, also yellowed and brittle, then finds a velvet bag and inside is the ring, a heavy gold wedding band. There is also a long, narrow red ribbon and a small bit of paper rolled like a tiny scroll tucked into the center of the ring. Fannie unfurls it. She sees two lines from <u>The Song of Songs.</u> "I sought and found whom my soul loves." and the other, "You are beautiful, my love, as lovely as Jerusalem." Fannie looks at the clock. It is 9:15. She thinks, *I have until 11:30 when I must help Marek in the store. What did I write?* She settles onto the floor and puts the collection of notebooks next to her. They are dated. She puts them in order. The oldest one is so faded she cannot read it. But the second one is clearer.

Nov. 1910

When I visit Mischa, his father always greets me warmly. He calls me "Fannie," but sometimes calls me *shaina maidel* (pretty girl).

I was so young, fifteen, maybe sixteen. I was Adela's age at the time she came home drunk! She picks up another notebook.

March 24, 1911

Mischa tells me he loves me, and I tell him I love him. I always say it after he does. Why do I always wait for him to say it first?

Here is something about the Triangle Shirtwaist Factory fire. Mischa supervised all the seamstresses on our floor. He saved me in that fire and saved a lot of other girls too.

March 26, 1911

He made many trips up and down with the elevator, bringing people out of the 8th floor. He couldn't go higher because flames started coming down the elevator shaft. He was covered with sweat and soot. His hands were burned, and he coughed from the smoke. That elevator I hate and Mischa, who I love, saved many lives.

I'll never forget the sound of bodies hitting the pavement. I'll never forget the blood and the tangle of limbs. I'll never forget the smell of burning flesh. I'll never forget the sirens and the screams. I'll never forget my fear as I waited in the crowd, searching the doorways for Mischa and Hannah to come out. Hannah came out first, not from the building, but from around the corner. It was a miracle.

I haven't thought about that for so long; not since Dr. Weiss asked me about it. I wonder if Mama heard about it in Bolekhiv. She must have been so scared until she got my letter that I was all right.

And here I write about Mischa's father being beaten in the street because Mischa was organizing the factory workers. It's just like right now. This is when

Mischa and his father fled to Palestine. He begged me to go with them. Here I write about why I think I can't go.

May 2, 1911

Esther died. My tateh is dying, Mama is despondent, and my family is struggling and depends on the money I send them. I may never see any of them ever again. Maybe Mischa can eventually bring his family to Palestine, but he can't bring all of mine, too. If I go with Mischa, I abandon my family in Bolekhiv. If Mischa doesn't go, he abandons his tateh. Suddenly, I know in a way I haven't let myself know, Mischa is the center of my life, my safe harbor, my anchor. Because of him, I go on even after losing my Esther and probably soon losing my Tateh. Mischa loves me, and I love him. My love for him is new but also feels like family love, especially when we are together with his Tateh. If I don't go to Palestine with Mischa, I abandon him, he abandons me, and I'm alone. If I go to Palestine, I abandon all my family in Bolekhiv. I will never have the money to bring them to America or Palestine. I never imagined how hard all this could be. My heart is more than broken; it is torn apart.

I remember writing a letter to Bintle Brief, the advice column in the Forverts newspaper. Here is the letter Bintle Brief sent back to me.

Dear Young Woman with a very wounded heart,
You are forced to make this very painful decision so quickly because of the cruelty that sadly exists in the world. There is no correct answer except the one you think you can live with right now. Inevitably, you will have times when you regret the decision you make. Life will be a harsh desert for a while. I hope before too long, you find some oasis, some soothing spring, some peace.

Bintle Brief

I can't read these next entries. They are too faded. I remember telling Mischa all the reasons I couldn't go with him. We were sitting on his apartment stoop.

He would not look at me. I tried to put my hand on his back, but he jerked it away. He said something like. "You've given me wounds all over my body." Then he cried so hard, with such pain and such moans, I thought he was going to fly apart. Eventually we went up to his apartment, and his tateh could tell right away I wasn't going with them. His tateh was kind. He blessed me. And then, Mischa begged me to come to the pier when the boat was leaving. I dreaded it but went.

Fannie turns several pages of the diary and finds the entry where she goes to the pier.

> I arrived at the pier early as passengers slowly boarded. Finally, I saw Mischa and his tateh on the first deck. They signaled that they also saw me. People on the ship threw streamers to people on the pier, who grabbed them. Mischa motioned, he was going to throw a streamer to me, but it looked different from the paper streamers everyone else was throwing. He aimed it, and it came right to my hand. I grabbed it. It was a narrow red ribbon tied around some paper and something heavy that weighted the end of the ribbon. I opened the paper. It was a message and wrapped inside was a heavy gold ring. The message read, "I sought and found whom my soul loves." and then, "You are beautiful, my love, as lovely as Jerusalem."
>
> The ship's whistle blew. Mischa let go of his end of the ribbon. I gathered it in and held it to my heart. Smoke rose from the stack. Four tugboats slowly hauled the ship from the dock. The ship sailed.

What did I think? Did I think it meant he was going to come back and be with me, leaving his father in Palestine? Did he think I was going to change my mind and join him? Was he telling me to wait for him?

This next must have happened right after. When I went back to Sadie's apartment on Pike Street.

I curled up on the sofa, and although the weather was hot, I wrapped myself in Esther's shawl and Sadie's quilt.

This must be the dream I had.

The door to the apartment flies open. Mischa stands in the doorframe. "Mischa, you're back!"

"Of course, I'm back. Tateh is on his way to Palestine. I'm here for you." We embrace. I snapped awake. My arms embraced only Sadie's quilt, and Mischa left again. This is cruel. Will Mischa keep haunting my dreams only to disappear again across the sea?

Oh yes, here it is. I remember this too well.

August 1911

...almost three months—there is no word from Mischa, and I'm shocked to find myself angry. The ring and ribbon are a burden. Why is he tying me to him when we are unlikely ever to find our way to each other? He is clever and sweet, but it is always his way. He decided when the women at the factory were ready to use the machines. He chose to spend Sundays organizing the workers, and he decided to go to Palestine. Is this what Sadie understood and was trying to warn me about? Am I a puppet dancing to his tune, held up by a red ribbon? He threw the ribbon and ring, hooking me like a fish. But he let go. Mama let me go. Why? Did she want to get rid of me, ...

I can't make out the rest. I was so angry. I didn't know then how angry I could be.

Here is a letter from Rivka. It's on that thin blue paper and very hard to see. Mama was dying and she confessed to Rivka about her affair and her pregnancy with Esther and me. I wonder if her lover was Piotr. There it is! That sentence! "The twins are my biggest joy and my biggest shame." Was I a constant reminder of her shame? Is that why she decided I should be the one sent away? I know

Esther was too sick to go, but why not one of the boys, or at least one of the boys with me?

Here's a letter from Mischa, finally. But it came only after I wrote to him asking him to help Hannah. Danny was already six months old. Mischa left in the spring of 1911, and Danny was born in February 1912. So, it had been more than a year since he left, and I hadn't heard from him.

Dear Fannie,

First, of course, we will welcome Hannah into our kibbutz. She has had a hard time. Here at the kibbutz, we accept people as they are. We don't ask what they had to do to survive.

Fannie, I'll try to be honest with you and tell you why you haven't heard from me. This is painful for both of us, but you deserve better than my hiding from you. I realize hiding is exactly what I've been doing. In your earlier letter, you called me heroic, or I try to be heroic. The last is true. I try to be heroic because, deep down, I know I'm a coward. I've been cowardly many times in my life. The first time I was cowardly with you was when I was too afraid to ask you to dance with me, and I asked Hannah instead. I know I hurt you then, and Fannie, I have now hurt you again and much worse. I should have found some way to send Tateh to Palestine and stay with you in America. I was desperate to protect him and responsible for what happened to him. Then I wondered whether I should leave Tateh here and come back to you. But here is the truth. Like Hannah, I've gotten myself into a complicated situation. Hannah was a victim. I was stupid and weak.

Every night I keep dreaming of you and my poor dead Mama. When I wake up, I'm unsure who died, you or her. You and she melt together in my dreams. Poor Tateh doesn't know what to make of my sobbing.

The days are full of hard work, the evenings are social, or I have guard duty. Even so, I have never been so lonely. And here is the most troubling part to tell. I found comfort from a young woman in the kibbutz who reached out to me. As I write this, I ask myself, was it comfort or distraction from my pain? Maybe both. She is a perfectly fine woman. I respect her, but I don't love her. When she invited me to be intimate with her, I accepted, and she became pregnant. Despite the spirit of freethinking here, the woman's family and the elders of the kibbutz pressed me to do the honorable thing and marry her. Your cowardly Mischa consented. I married her. We do have a lovely child, a girl we named Shira. I hold the secret that the name Shira was the Hebrew name I thought was right for you.

Fannie, Fannie, I wish I understood myself. I'm so sorry for what I have done, so sorry for what I have gotten myself into, sorry to lose you, and sorry for hiding from you. I don't expect you to forgive me. But Fannie, please know I loved you, and I love you. I feel unbearable shame for my cowardliness and unbearable sadness for what I allowed myself to lose in abandoning you. I grow physically stronger every day, but I know I am weak in will. I wish I had the strength to leave and come back to you. What is it with us? We are so bound to our parents, so bound to our tradition, so bound to what we are told is the right thing to do. And yet I try to be a freethinker. I am no freethinker. I am a pitiful child and a fool.

You should also know my tateh is very disappointed in me and wishes you and I were together. He loves you as his own daughter. The only thing that comforts me is that I experienced great love for you. I hope that can also comfort you. I will never forget you.

Mischa

I remember I couldn't write him back right away. I was so angry.

Diary, I have never been so furious. Yes, Mischa, you are a coward! I will not be your puppet on a red ribbon! Pine for me all your life if that's what you need to do. Beat your breast in shame and remorse. The fact is, you're choosing your loveless life because other people say it's honorable. So much for your "Song of Songs" that sanctifies love between two people. So much for "Leave your father and mother and cleave to your wife." You are in love with other people's big ideas and ignore the truth of your heart and what we brought to each other. Yes, the desert is where you belong. Your heart is a desert.

Diary, right after I wrote this, I went to sit on the stoop. I sobbed, wailed, and shook like Mischa did when I told him I couldn't go with him. I was flying apart. I let myself go. I must have been very loud because soon, I felt Sadie's arms around me, trying to hold me together. Every part of me ached, and I knew I could never erase the love I felt for Mischa anymore than I could erase the love I still feel for my Esther and my tateh.

After reading this, Fannie feels her breath come fast. She puts her face in her hands and rubs her eyes. She sighs deeply and goes on reading.

Diary, I keep thinking about Mischa being intimate with the kibbutz woman. He wanted us to be fully sexual. I pretended I was a virgin, telling him I wanted to save our ultimate intimacy for marriage. That was a lie. The truth is I feared if he entered me, I'd panic with memories of the brothel. If I told him about the brothel, I feared he'd find me disgusting and get rid of me.

Why am I so ashamed of being a victim?

I go on here about stealing some dress. What was that about? I don't remember stealing a dress–but I guess I must have. When could I have stolen a dress? Oh yes, a filthy old thing, out of disgusting Fester (uncle) Oscar's cart–not even a cart, but a stinking old baby carriage. I was living with him and his wife when I first came and worked for him. He tried to molest me. I ran away but first stole a dress out of his cart, for no reason. I can't remember what I did with that dirty rag.

Here I write something about "betraying Sadie." Oh yes, that's when Sadie needed a wet nurse for her baby Little Esther. Little Esther who is soon to be married! Sadie had to go back to work. Secretly, I brought the baby to Hannah who was nursing Daniel at the same time. It was when Hannah was trying to survive by being a prostitute. I did it because I was so lonely and it was the only way I could spend a little time with Hannah. Sadie was furious when she found out.

Fannie lays the diary face down on her lap. She sighs and feels her eyelids grow heavy. She wants to sleep but is slapped awake by the memory of being forced to dance naked by her Hungarian uncle when he sold her into the brothel. *I was four or five years younger than Adela is now! I was kidnapped into that brothel, and I escaped. Why do I still feel so dirty when I think of it? Marek accepted me before we were married, even when he heard about that. But I was afraid to tell Mischa, and I lied to him, or at least let him think I was a virgin. I didn't love Marek yet when I told him. I already loved Mischa. Loving him made me a coward. Or was it needing him too much?*

Fannie is fully alert again and she turns the page and reads.

If I had been fully intimate with Mischa and maybe gotten pregnant, would we be together now? Would he have stayed in America and maybe sent his tateh alone to Palestine so I could still help my family? Or would I feel trapped into going to Palestine and abandoning my family? I don't know.

There was a time I was sure it was bashert (destiny) that Mischa and I were together. Now I see there was so much keeping us apart, our own weaknesses, the hard life in America, the fates of our families, the fire, and all that followed it. We are two cowards who love each other.

I'm weighed down by what I've become in America. I'm ashamed of being a whore, a thief, and a liar. I betrayed Sadie. I'm selfish and weak. These are all true since I left home. Is this the cost of survival? In Budapest, I was held hostage, but in America, I seemed to lose my sense of right and wrong. Is this what loneliness and fear do to people?

Several pages are faded. She turns each page and comes to one that is clear again.

I realize, even while trying to survive, I found a powerful loving friendship with Hannah and deep soulmate love with Mischa. Loving them saves my soul. And while Hannah and Mischa are new in my life, I am sure that loving them comes from loving Esther and my family. So, whatever I have done, by bad circumstances or bad judgement, I'm capable of deep love and hope to love again.

Diary, I stopped short after writing the last sentence. "I'm capable of deep love and hope to love again." I must write to Mischa.

Here is my letter to Mischa. I must have written it right away and then copied it into the diary.

Dear Mischa,

Thank you for helping and welcoming Hannah. She feels lost right now, but I believe she well might make a meaningful life for herself and her child at your kibbutz.

Mischa, I feel compelled to respond to your last letter. This is not a letter of forgiveness. You have done nothing that needs forgiving.

We left our homes and came to America to save our families. Life here turned out to be rough and mean. Despite that, you and I found deep love and wanted more than anything to make a life together. When your tateh was assaulted, you could not forsake him. My family survives because of the money I send them. We did what we believed we had to do at the time.

Recently, I feared that while my body might survive, my soul would not, and this has prompted me to write this letter to you. I cannot allow my soul to die. Even as I write now, I relive our shared tenderness and desire. I wish I had allowed us to fully consecrate and consummate our love. Isn't it what "The Song of Songs" teaches us as holy? My reluctance to allow us that holiness comes from a part of myself and my history I failed to share with you. I feared if you knew my secrets you would no longer want me. It is my cowardice. I wish I had dared to be fully honest with you, to trust you would still love me, and to have allowed myself to love you with every bit of my body and soul.

Mischa, I will never forget what we had together. It lives in my memory, in my heart, in the marrow of my bones. May the memory of our love for one another be for a blessing.

Go, Mischa, live and love your life. I will try to do the same. Mazel tov on the birth of your daughter Shira.

Fannie

Diary, I copied this letter onto your pages. I know in sad times, I will need to remind myself of what I felt and wrote.

Here is Mischa's answer.

Dear Fannie,

Thank you, thank you many times for your loving letter. We fell in love in America, the supposed land of freedom, but only now are we slowly learning the true meaning of freedom, to dare to be entirely who we are, with our strengths and frailties, and to trust in our love for one another, whatever is past, present, or future.

When I first saw you at the shirtwaist factory and again when you sang and danced at the settlement house, I saw your inner beauty rise like the sun. Yes, the memory of our love will always be for a blessing, whether we ever meet again or not.

Always,
Your Mischa

Fannie again feels an urge to sleep. But sleep will not come. She is swept into an undertow of sorrow and pain. Moans, low and deep, then percussive, racking sobs, again and again—exhaustion—weeping—washed ashore. She shudders, gasps. Finally, breath returns, long and slow. A culmination—the painful pleasure of shimmers of light after blackness—a birth—a letting go, the release of a dybbuk, the retreat of a ghost. She waits for breath to come evenly, easily.

Gathering up the notebooks, the words from <u>The Song of Songs</u>, the ring, and the ribbon. She puts them back into the rucksack. She will ask Rachel to keep it all until she goes to Palestine, when she will take it with her. She repeats to herself, *May the memory of our love be for a blessing. I am going to Palestine.*

Dear Diary

June 1933
Dear Diary,
It has been almost four months since Adela and Lenny left for Palestine. This is the first day on board the ship going to Marseille. It is an understatement to say it is a different experience than my first sea voyage in 1910 in steerage class. I am traveling third class. I have a small but comfortable stateroom. There is an upholstered seat that opens into a comfortable bed with fresh sheets, a lamp, and a sink. A toilet is just down the hall. I go to a large dining room for meals where the food is quite good. I can go up to the deck where I can walk or recline on deck-chairs and read or doze while I watch the movement of the sea. I also have a ticket for a boat to Jaffa that leaves Marseille two days after I arrive there. I hope to see something of Marseille. I've never been there, but it has been so long since I have been in a European city, I would love to see it. Maybe there will be a tour bus.

Aber tells me not to travel anywhere in Palestine now because of the Arab uprisings against both the Jews and the British. He pleaded with me to go directly from Jaffa to the kibbutz and to stay near the kibbutz all the time I am there. I would love to see Jerusalem. At least I will get to see the Sea of Galilee where the kibbutz is located. Anyway, I am going because Adela needs me when she delivers her baby. Hopefully I'll get to see Jerusalem someday. I can't believe it. I'm going to be a bubbe!

Day Two

I have now spent twenty-four hours alone. I can't remember the last time I was alone that long, maybe in 1910 when I ran away from Fester Oscar's apartment. I certainly was never alone on that first ship. I will have ten days of being alone and more on the ship to Jaffa. Diary, you will be my companion.

Our whole family, including Luc, Aber and Rachel, came to see me off. And all the Russos came too. They have had no harassment since Lenny left. Only once, someone came to the apartment looking for Lenny. Enzo told them Lenny is no longer a dock worker and that he left the country. Thank goodness they believed Enzo and no one has come since.

We all miss Adela and Lenny more than we can say, but they seem safe, and Adela, so far, has had a perfect pregnancy. There is a doctor living on the kibbutz that has set up a maternity practice. She delivered all of Misha's children and most of the babies born on the kibbutz.

Marek continues to be despondent about Adela's leaving. But there is no doubt in my mind she did the right thing to go with Lenny. Unlike my situation when Mischa left, our family does not depend on Adela for survival like mine did on me. Adela had so many good ideas for the store, like patterns and slipcovers. It keeps the store going even in the depression.

I told Marek, after the baby is born and I return, I will take over the store for a month and he can go to Palestine for a visit. I wonder if there is a way Danny can go with him. I'm sure Danny would love to make a return trip to Palestine, even if he has no memory of living there.

Oh Diary, this hurts to remember. Right before we left for the pier, Marek whispered to me, "Fannie, you will come back to me, won't you?" I was startled to hear him say it. I am quite sure he never saw my diary or looked in the rucksack, but he must have sensed something. Or maybe it is just his unrelenting sadness. I'm sure he misses Lenny. I often saw sparks of his old self when he was with him.

What will it be like to see Mischa again? I guess he was about nineteen when he left, and I was around seventeen. Now I'm around thirty-seven or thirty-eight and he is around forty! We never knew our exact birthdays. My kid's birthdays are so clear to me. So much has happened. We have lived such different lives since we knew each other. I suspect his father must have passed away by now. He was such a kind man and so loving toward me. I remember how we used to sing together at Shabbos and Mischa played his violin.

I have the rucksack. I brought it to Rachel soon after I opened it, then packed it in the valise I borrowed from her.

Palestine

Fannie sends a telegram to Marek: "Arrived safely at Kibbutz Degania. Lenny picked me up in Jaffa. Adela is strong and healthy. I'll send a telegram when Adela is in labor. Love to you and the kids, Fannie"

Dear Diary,

I cannot stop feeling this is all a dream. Lenny arrived at the dock in Jaffa in a truck, and we drove right to the kibbutz. I had no time to spend in Jaffa, except to see that it is a bustling city port. I could imagine Lenny hard at work here, but he says he is so happy to be a farmer.

Driving from Jaffa to the kibbutz, inland from the Mediterranean, I saw wide expanses of land like I have not seen since leaving Bolekhiv. I imagined Mischa in a desert, but where he lives is not a desert. The land is full of trees and flowers, hills, and valleys. Date palm trees are the skyscrapers here. They are giants with thick masses of wild hair. I love the olive trees. As they grow old, they become gnarled and twisted. A grove of old olive trees looks like a bunch of grandmothers bent toward each other gossiping.

We drove through rolling hills and twisty roads and suddenly came upon the Sea of Galilee. Across Galilee is the rocky plateau of the Golan Heights.

Kibbutz Degania, surrounded by hills, is where the Jordan River meets the Sea of Galilee. I have never seen such beautiful land.

Degania overflows with orchards and vineyards and rows of growing vegetables and herbs. Flowers are everywhere. It is a Garden of Eden. However, day and night, standing on the high ground is the Hashomer, a self-defense group who guard against Arab uprisings in the Jewish settlements. All the men who live on the kibbutz also take guard duty. It is a chilling reminder of what Aber never forgets. There is no safe place.

How can I describe seeing Mischa for the first time in so many years? It was a generation ago. He came out of his house as soon as the truck drove up. He is still handsome Mischa, but not the boy I remember. We were both awkward at our first meeting, strangers yet not. The boy I knew and the man I met today kept shifting images that didn't quite match, yet did.

His curly black hair is streaked with gray. He is darkly tanned, like everyone here. Also, he is a broader, bigger person than I remembered. I must keep in mind we were both younger than Adela the last time we saw each other, barely out of our childhoods. Sadly, his father died five years ago but enjoyed his last years in the kibbutz.

Mischa's wife Aviva is just as Adela described. She is warm, lively, and talkative. She is Sephardic and a Sabra, born and raised in Palestine. Her family came from Turkey. Her first language, like Lenny's family, is Ladino.

Soon Aviva and Mischa's sons Omri and Yoram came in. They are one and two years older than Miriam and Simon. In Omri, the older, I could see the boy Mischa. Shira, the oldest, is a beautiful young woman, a little younger than Danny. She is a dancer and wants to go abroad to study. When I met Shira, I couldn't take my eyes off her. I felt so curious about her, then realized the conception of Shira is what sealed the reality that Mischa and I would never be together.

As soon as we arrived, Lenny went to get Adela and brought her to Mischa's house. Adela is very pregnant and looks well, in fact, radiantly beautiful, but is still frightened for the day the baby comes. It was so good to hug her. I could feel her body relax a little. Tomorrow, Adela and I will go to see her maternity doctor. She is an older woman who did her medical training in Vienna, like Dr. Weiss.

We all had dinner together at Mischa and Aviva's house, a light supper of salads. Everyone usually eats lunch and dinner in the big dining hall. But tonight, Aviva planned to make our meal at home.

I still feel I will wake up from this dream. I can't believe I am really in Palestine.

The next morning, Aviva went off to teach school. Shira went to her rehearsal for a folk-dance festival. Mischa and I sat over coffee.

He put his cup down, looked at me and said, "Fannie, Fannie, Fannie, is it really you?" Then he asked, "Do you feel like you're dreaming this?"

I answered, "I do, ever since I got on the boat, and now that I'm here, even more." He suddenly looked sad and said,

"For a few years after my father and I arrived, I had the same dream over and over. You suddenly arrived here. But then I woke, and you were gone."

Diary, we had the same dream!

Mischa seemed to be studying my hands holding the coffee mug. Then he said, "I remember teaching you how to use the sewing machine at the factory. I put my hands on yours to guide you. At that moment I knew I loved you. And do you remember how we washed the dishes at my house, my father sitting close by and dozing off? I took your hands under the suds, and we played with each other's hands and fingers. Do you remember Fannie?"

Diary, a ripple of warmth shot through me. It felt wonderful and scary at the same time. "Yes," I said to Mischa, "I remember. I always wondered if your father was really asleep." I gathered myself together and said, "Mischa, I would like to visit Hannah's grave and maybe look around the kibbutz. Then I need to be with Adela."

I sprang out of my seat. I was afraid of what my body wanted. We walked first to the cemetery. The path was deserted. All the way I wrestled against a force stronger than me. But when I came upon Hannah's grave, it all subsided. I was alone with Hannah, my dear, beloved Hannah. I could not have survived those first years in New York without her. She was my sister-mother-friend. Her stone reads, "Hannah Weitzner 1895 to 1914" and below it says, "She brought spirit and beauty to Kibbutz Degania."

I picked up a small stone and placed it on her grave. I picked up another stone and put it on her grave and then into my pocket to bring to Danny.

Mischa and I walked around the kibbutz. He made a special point of showing me where Hannah and Daniel slept, the nursery where Daniel was cared for during the day, and the little theater where Hannah directed plays and acted. "We miss Hannah," he said. "She brought so much joy to our kibbutz life. If Daniel ever wants to move here, I'm sure he could practice his art and make a meaningful life. He was a wonderful young child, always cheerful until Hannah fell ill. I enjoy his letters. He sounds like an admirable young man and very thoughtful."

"He is all you say, Mischa."

"Has he fallen in love, Fannie? He is the right age to fall in love."

"Yes, I think he has. Has Shira?"

"Not yet, that I know of. She is very serious about being a professional dancer. It is such a demanding discipline; it takes all her focus and energy now. I hope she will also allow herself a life besides dance. That reminds me, there is folk dancing tomorrow night. Would you enjoy going, Fannie?"

"I think I would, depending on how Adela is feeling. I still do the traditional Jewish dances at weddings and bar mitzvahs. Adela has taught me some of the new social dances, like the foxtrot, the jitterbug, and the Charleston. She will probably get people to do those dances here."

"I remember when I played my violin, and you danced. We were working at the Shirtwaist factory then."

Diary, of course, I remember. So much happened when I left Bolekhiv. It all happened so fast, one thing after another. I left my family to work and send them money. First, I went to Budapest. I escaped from a brothel in Budapest, then went to New York, to the Lower East Side. Then I had to escape from Fester Oscar. I had no place to live, so I slept on Hannah's fire escape. Esther, my twin, died, and soon Tateh died. I met Mischa, then the fire. How can I ever forget the fire? Mischa's father was beaten in the street; they escaped to Palestine. I was so alone. But I knew by then I was a good seamstress and could work. Then Hannah, when she was dying, sent Danny to me. Then I met Marek with Adela. All this happened in a short time. I am breathless writing this. How did I do it? And in the middle of it all I was crazy in love with Mischa. Maybe that's how I did it! And then Mischa left. Diary, I have never put all this history together before. What a blessing to have loved Mischa and Hannah. Without them, I would have perished.

Adela and I went to see her maternity doctor, *Dr. Froelich* (happy). I hope her name bodes well for Adela. She was reassuring and talked about Adela's good health throughout her pregnancy. After examining her, she said the baby was in the right position and the delivery could be any day now. She did not expect any problems.

However, after we left, Adela burst into tears. She continues to be terrified that she, or the baby or both will die. Beyond quoting the doctor, there was nothing I could say to guarantee it wouldn't happen. Her fear was contagious, and all I could imagine was the horror of losing Adela and then having to tell Marek that Adela had died. I don't think he would survive it. I could not let her see my fear. So, I just held her until she cried herself out. She pleaded with the doctor for Lenny and me to be with her when she delivers. We will of course be with her, one on either side of her. I hope Lenny can take the screams and the blood. I think he can. He told me on the trip to the kibbutz that he helps to deliver the calves, so he knows a little about what to expect. But it's different when it's your wife.

When I got back to the house, I asked Aviva to bring me to the place where I could send Marek a telegram to let him know the doctor's reassuring words.

The next night, I joined Mischa and his family at folk dancing. There were the usual circle dances and some exquisite partner dances Shira choreographed to music written by one of the kibbutz musicians. There were singers in the group too. The words are in modern Hebrew, from <u>The Song of Songs</u>. First, Shira spent time teaching the new dances to the group. When it was time to dance, people chose partners. Mischa and Aviva were together. I expected to watch and moved to a seat on the side when young Omri came up to me and invited me to dance. He is a little older than Simon. He did very well, and when I complimented him, he said Shira had given him a private lesson earlier in the day.

For the next dance, Shira asked people to change partners. Aviva came by and asked Omri to dance with her. And there was Mischa by my side. The words of the song were again from <u>The Song of Songs</u>, "I am my beloved's, and his desire is toward me." The movements were first slow and languorous, then quickened to the rhythm of an accelerating heartbeat, a gradual return to the first slower rhythm, and again, a quickening.

Diary, while dancing with Mischa, I struggled at first to concentrate on the precision of the steps and the timing and to be aware of others dancing near us. But the movement, the music, the words and the intoxicating spell of Mischa's presence, I surrendered to the dominion of my body, the magnetic force of my partner, my twin, my shadow, my pulsing blood.

When the music and dance ended, I could not tell how long it had lasted. Shira announced the next dance and asked us to change partners.

I bolted from the hall. When I breathed in the cool night air, I felt something inside me crack open. I cried like I cried when my sister died and when Mischa left for Palestine. I cried for the joys I lost and the joys I have, for the cruelties I endured and for loving, for friendship, for memory, for freedom, for restraint, and for how it all will be lost, perhaps in a moment, or with some time to hold it precious. Adela can die, the baby can die, or they can be given life to savor and endure.

When the music stopped, Mischa came looking for me. We sat side by side in silence, looking into the night. Then I turned to him and said, "May the memory of our young love be for a blessing." He took a deep breath and said,

"Fannie, my dearest young love. It will always be for a blessing."

Reaching into my skirt pocket, I took out his gold ring, kissed it, took his hand and placed it in his palm. He then kissed the ring and slowly, with care, placed it in the breast pocket of his shirt.

We sat quietly for a few more moments. He returned to the dance. I walked to the house to get the rucksack.

Diary, I am writing you my last entry. I will walk to the Sea of Galilee and ask its waters to accept my rucksack with all it holds.

Fannie returns to the house. Later, Mischa and his family come in. They all go to bed. In the middle of the night, Aviva wakes Fannie to say someone came with a message. Adela is in labor.

* * *

In New York, Jacob shouts out his call sign over his ham radio, CQW2ABOX. Then he shouts ZC6, the call sign for Palestine. He turns the dial looking for the frequency band that will connect him to Jafa.

Marek, Aber, Rachel, Daniel, and Luc are all crowded into Jacob's bedroom waiting to hear the news about Adela and the baby. Jacob makes several tries to get through. There is a lot of static when finally, a man's voice with a distinctly British inflection comes on.

"This is Zulu, Charlie, 6 Echo,4, Bravo."

"Hello Echo, 4, Bravo," says Jacob. What is your *QTH* (location)?"

"I'm in Jafa in British Palestine. *QRZ* (Who is calling?)?"

Jacob repeats his call sign then says, "I'm QTH New York, U.S.A. Can I get a call sign for Kibbutz Degania?"

"Yes, we have regular contact with Kibbutz Degania. My *XYL* (wife) is from there. The call sign is Echo, 4, Bravo, Sierra, Alpha, Bravo, Romeo, Alpha.

"Copy. Thank you," says Jacob. "What time is it where you are?"

"Eight pm. And where you are?"

"1:00 pm."

"Good luck with your call."

"Thank you and *73* (Best regards)."

"You are welcome. jumping off."

Jacob brings up the call sign for Kibbutz Degania. A woman answers in English with the familiar accent of someone whose first language is Yiddish. Marek punches the air and yells "Mazel tov Jake!" Rachel gasps, putting her hand to her mouth and under her breath whispers, "Amazing! We're connected to the kibbutz!" Call signs are exchanged. Jacob asks if Fannie Horvath, who is staying at the home of Mischa Ben Natan, can come to the phone.

"Yes, certainly. I will get her. She's been expecting your radio call. Please hold on. I'll get her."

Aber comes over to Jacob and puts his hand firmly on his shoulder. "Great work Jake!"

Lenny reaches the Kibbitz phone first. "Hello" he says into the receiver.

Marek jumps up and shouts into the receiver over Jacob's shoulder, "Lenny, is Adela all right?"

"Yes, yes, she's fine, a little tired but in good health. She's very strong. She had a perfect delivery."

Marek takes a deep breath and, with a long exhalation thanks God. "*Barukh Hashem Adonai*" (Blessed be The Name of the Lord). He hears a sound, a loud rhythmic sound; *Whaa, whaa, whaa!*

"What's that? What am I hearing? Is everything all right?"

Fannie's voice comes on, calm and soothing. "What you hear my dearest Marek, is the strong cry of our healthy first grandson, Gabor Avram Russo."

"Gabor Avram!" Marek wipes his eyes, his voice breaking, "Adela, Lenny, you named him for my father and my brother! Now in tears, bowing his head Marek prays in Yiddish and Hebrew. "A dank Hashem. Barukh Hashem Adonai." The baby's cries grow louder and stronger.

The End And Beginning